The Unexpected Visitor

Order this book online at www.trafford.com
or email orders@trafford.com

Most Trafford titles are also available at major online book retailers.

Printed in the United States of America.

ISBN: 978-1-4269-0266-6 (sc)
ISBN: 978-1-4269-1125-5 (e)

www.trafford.com

North America & international
toll-free: 1 888 232 4444 (USA & Canada)
fax: 812 355 4082

"King Harald Hårfagre of Norway was theatrical, why else did he in the year 865AD declare to not cut or comb his hair until he defeated all the regional chieftains.

Europe must have gotten a bit uneasy whenever the fair headed King called out for his barber, bad enough for the countries dealing with the ferociousness of the tribes, let alone a united Viking Kingdom. His hair grew for years until he won the final battle and crowned himself the true King.

In today's standards, the king was a marketing genius creating a fearsome image out of his appearance. Then we have the masterminds of Norwegian intrigue who promoted their infamous trademark, the Vikings.

Imagine a frightening totem carved into the stem of an odd shaped ship silently moving through the water towards the village and a child screams out, "Vikings!" the entire village scatters leaving behind their possessions, an easy heist"

Sharon Hoffman

"Odin, the Norse god of death, hung himself from Yggdrasill, the ash-tree of knowledge, to obtain magical powers. He became a celebrant of violent death, at times taking the form of a wolf to linger near the victim. The Vikings understood their god and when the lone wolf appeared, they knew death was imminent and that Odin would greet them at the entry of Valhalla."

Norse Mythology

Contents

Acknowledgements.

I would like to dedicate *The Unexpected Visitor* to the Peasants of the mountain farms who are still alive and to the souls of those who have passed away. I will also like to recognize Sakarias Ansok for his remarkable documentary books and Magne Flem for his excellent photos about the life of these people. Honor also to the non-profit organization, Storfjordens Venner for the work to restore the ramshackle buildings, to my mother Astrid for her good sense of humor and to Jan-Olav Dimmen for his life-long voluntarily work with local history. A thank you note to my Canadian editor Kathleen Burgess for her excellent suggestions Thank you; you have all contributed to make this book possible. And last, but not least a sincere thank you and blessing to my American co-writer, needless to say; without you, I wouldn't have even started.

Introduction

The story of *The Unexpected Visitor* or Jenny as the original title was began almost fifteen years ago in Wichita, Kansas when I worked at the corporate headquarters in a major US company. At the office, I met a wonderful woman that inspired me to begin writing about what she thought of as a fascinating life of my ancestors. Although The Unexpected Visitor is a fiction, it is based on true stories unfolding on mountain shelves seemingly carved into the precipitous mountains above the legendary Geiranger Fjord. The chapter Midwife for example, is not only a dramatized story about the ageing Jensine Gronningseter's unbelievable journey across these hostile mountains to bring a new baby into the world; it also reveals that even getting the message out to the Midwife could be a challenge by itself. With the chapters: The Midsummer Visit, The Wedding, and The Christmas Present, I have attempted to reveal common customs and local humor based on hours and hours of research and interviews.

As it hopefully will be clear for the reader, the area had so much more than natural disasters, hardships and dangerous ravines. The extraordinary warmth and light those Peasants emitted baffled every visitor, wondering how people living literally on the edge could be so friendly and compassionate. One would never leave an encounter with them unchanged. I certainly do believe that we all have a lot to learn from a lifestyle that focuses on getting what we need by helping each other rather then an endless struggle of competition to accumulate more and more of things we could easy do without; so it is my desire that the love, compassion and helpfulness they demonstrated toward other people and their harmonious work with nature may inspire present and future generations.

So why concealing the name of my creative co-writer, source of inspiration, coach, mentor and loving friend? After patiently been waiting for many years for you my dear to submit your corrections, I realized that this had turned into a matter of have, or have not. I could continue to do nothing and let the story remains unpublished indefinitely or I could do something about it, take the ball and run with it and make a potential unpopular decision. I have chosen the latter and since you didn't agree to publish this version, I assume that you didn't want to be associated with it either; therefore I am concealing your name, but by no means discrediting you.

Regardless of your reaction however, I will be eternally thankful for everything that you have taught me and the spiritual path you led me on. That alone outweighs hundred folds everything else. Please know that at any time as you may wish, I will unhide your name, consider your suggestions and issue a new version or perhaps you will continue where this story ends, who knows the door of opportunities is always open.

So why now, why not let it be, why not let the story remain in a computer memory and continue to wait for the Magical Wand to take it to the press? First of all I believe that the Magical Wand now needs a hand to hold and guide it; second, the characters trapped in the computer yearn to get out, they are tired of waiting, "*it's just a simple story, and it doesn't need to be perfect.*" I can hear they are saying. And third, during the last few months there have been certain events in my life that have made me push for this release, not at least the recent passing away of a dear friend that had patiently been waiting a decade for the opportunity of reading it. I apologize that you didn't get a chance to read the story about the Mountain People you admired so much while you were among us. Life is indeed passing by very quickly, isn't? When I realized that I could easy be following in your footsteps, the decision to publish this version wasn't that difficult after all.

Although any landscape is best projected on a picture, I have done my best to portray some of this incredible scenery by words, leaving the rest to the reader's imagination.

Bjorn S. Dimmen
April 2009

The Mountain Farm

"Where there is room in the heart, there is room in the house" Norwegian Proverb

"The executioner decapitated her and staked the head to a pole as a warning for other young women with similar deeds in mind." The man in the boat spoke with a voice fitting his grave and weathered-looking face as he told the story about the last woman in Norway to be executed. He then adjusted his position so he could face Jenny eye-to-eye to watch her reaction.

Jenny Mohr appeared unmoved, but felt a chill and wrapped her coat closer to her body, avoiding his looks. Watching the shoreline, she wondered what the young man must have felt when his love was executed so brutally and did he know of the children she had murdered and if not, how did she keep her pregnancy, not once, but twice, a secret?

"Her long blond hair blew in the wind," the man continued. "It was the summer of 1724. Dorte was a beautiful young woman, who climbed the mountains, going from farm to farm, looking for work. She eventually was hired by a farmer who was trapped in a marriage of convenience with a woman twice his age. The farmer fell in love with the much younger, beautiful woman and she soon became full with child. In a desperate attempt to hide her condition from the villagers and the farmer's old, bitter wife, she killed her newborn. It had happened twice. The lawmen found two tiny skeletons in unmarked graves beside a path not far from the main farmhouse." The old man pushed extra hard on the oars as if he wanted to underscore his favorite story.

Jenny would soon learn that the people who live above this meandering waterway, clutching on to the small ledges, were as full of mysterious and dramatic stories as the surrounding mountains were full of ghostly ravines and gorges.

As they passed the execution site, an inhabitable tongue of land only accessible by boats, Jenny changed her focus and began to look at the outline of the mountain peaks wondering how such a spectacular mountain ridge had ever come about, realizing that its creation had not happened over night. It had actually taken millions of years when heavy clouds off the Norwegian coast pushed against the mountains turning moisture into snow, creating an ever-accumulating snowcap. Then the tremendous pressure transformed the snow into solid ice, which at the mercy of its own weight, carved and gouged the landscape while slowly moving back down to the ocean. Some eleven thousand years ago, the ice retracted uncovering a hidden landscape of deep-trenched fjords and steep mountains.

Jenny felt like the young and beautiful Norwegian princess forcibly taken against her will by an idiot of a Prince to an impregnable castle on a secluded mountain, feeling so small in comparison to the massive mountains surrounding the rowboat. She felt the need to explain her feelings in words to her mother, to say how sorry she was about the impending drama her life had become and how this silent fjord's serenity and waterfalls made her feel at ease. Everything seemed so jumbled. Words were insufficient to capture this moment moving through the water, witnessing the extraordinary art of creation while pondering the trials of lost love. The depth of her 22-year-old eyes reflected a sadness beyond her years, giving her countenance a gentle, quiet dignity. Her grief could not diminish her beauty; in fact, it made her all the more vulnerable and appealing. As the only daughter of Christian and Marion Elizabeth Mohr, she had been protected inside their large estate in Kristiania ever since she had seen the first light of day.

"The girl is overprotected" her aunt had repeatedly remarked, but it had always fallen on deaf ears. "Overprotected" was not a word in Marion's vocabulary and she had no idea what her sister was talking about.

"Can't you see what you are doing to the girl? She will be unable to take care of herself once you're gone. It would be like keeping a bird in a cage, feeding it every day until you suddenly release it in the wild. The bird would not know how to find food on its own and would die."

Marion had just walked away; comparing her dear daughter to a bird in a cage was just too much. How dare her sister talking about Jenny like that? Jenny had everything she needed and as the heir of their estate, she would never have to worry about anything.

Jenny began questioning her reasons for leaving Kristiania; were they well founded? The fact that Robert Blackstone, an English businessman she had fallen in love with, was twice her age could not be the sole reason her father had persuaded her to leave; it had to be deeper. Like a tug of war her emotions began to fight for attention. Days of her childhood, adolescence and young adulthood flashed before her, moments of trust and moments of doubt, moments of happiness and moments of joy, moments of lies and moments of truth. She didn't understand why she had to leave her secure home to get away from Robert - why couldn't she just stop seeing him? "What do we need the gate and guards for then?" she had asked her father while arguing about her leaving.

"Any security system is usually sufficient for most people; unfortunately Robert is not among those," he had answered.

"Wouldn't it be enough to just stop seeing him, to say it's all over?"

"No my dear, not with Robert Blackstone," was the replay she got.

No man alive hated Robert Blackstone more than her father. Christian just shuddered at the sight of Robert; imagining his daughter going with a man like that made him want to vomit. He was certain he had made the right decision for both her and the family to send her away for a while. Sooner or later Robert would give her up and return to England. He couldn't imagine a woman, or anybody for that matter, would come before Robert's business. With Robert, everything had a price tag, whether it was people or things, so for Christian, it would just be a matter of keeping Jenny out of his hands long enough for Robert to consider the search to be not worth it. Since Christian had started to climb the ladder in the Norwegian army, he had learned that everything he said and did would be used against him, so the less people knew, the better. Not even his wife knew all the details about his past endeavors with Robert and regardless of its innocent appearance, the circumstances had pulled him into something he had no control over. Revealing it to Marion wouldn't gain anything. It would only stir up speculations and suspicions.

It was his wife sister that prompted Christian in a direction of hiding Jenny on a remote mountain farm. She had met Marta Holseth at the hospital while nursing her after eye surgery. The woman, the sweetest, kindest soul, had shared wonderful stories of her family and their farm, she told him.

"Marta seemed perfect, a total stranger to our city returning home to a hidden farm, Blackstone would have difficulty finding Jenny there." She continued.

"And did the woman from the farm agree?" Christian wondered

"Yes, the family owns two farms. Marta is widowed and lives with her father and a few of her children at one farm, while her son, Iver, who accompanied her to Kristiania, lives at the other. They call the mountain farm Holseth. There's a small room for Jenny at the main farm, though it didn't sound like she'd have the privacy she's accustomed to, well then it's only for a short while."

"Do you feel the family's respectable, what I meant to ask is do you know anything more about them?"

"Yes, I've done some checks on them and found out that I know the doctor in Stranden, he had an internship at the hospital while working on his degree. He sent me this telegram stating they're a fine family. Here, read it for yourself."

"No need, as long as you're satisfied."

Jenny's thoughts continued to swirl around the last days in Kristiania, remembering how stunned she became when her father gave her a hug and said he loved her; it was then she really began to understand he was serious. Christian was not among the hugging fathers; neither did he overuse the words "I love you." Such manners never fell naturally to him as to most Norwegian men, and even though he loved his daughter, he never told her. Many men in Norway do not say "I Love" you to their wife or daughters. Somehow it is expected that they know they are loved. For a father to say "I love you" to his son is even rarer; if that happens, there's a high probability that one of them is dying. Christian was never mean to Jenny; it was just that he didn't express any feelings. Sometimes she could see restlessness in his eyes; they flickered without focusing on anything. She wondered many times if he was hiding something and wanted to ask him, but the opportunity never came. When she was a young girl he was an officer in the Navy and could be away for weeks at a time and the short moments he was home, he never found time for her. Could there be any truth in the belief that the kind of relationship a daughter has with her father will reflect the relationship she will have with a future husband? If so, Jenny would rather stay alone.

She thought about the conversation she had overheard in Robert's office, where he threatened to kill her father if he didn't let him marry her. Maybe Robert was just trying to make a point. Jenny believed that some people, especially men, tend to exaggerate about what they would do if they don't get what they want. She couldn't imagine Robert would kill her father! Although they probably had some unsolved issues from the past, she didn't think they would kill each other. She could always go back and maybe she could use some time to really make up her mind. Robert had, after all, moved too fast the last couple of weeks, as if he was in a hurry to get married. Men are not easy to understand; it's like they have hidden agendas. They say one thing and mean something else.

Iver Holseth sat in the back of the boat, keeping up with his neighbor's rhythm of rowing, all the while studying Jenny, occasionally getting a glimpse of her profile. He wondered what kind of man would send a woman like this into hiding. He had a rough look, not fair-haired like his siblings or dark like his deceased father; he had an earthy brown color. Strong like all the young men from his region and blessed with his grandmother's unassuming nature and self-educating prowess, now a widower, he was still considered a prize by the young women of Stranden. He spent his days working and his nights reading, preferring quiet company, usually his own and could lose himself in a book, where he believed men's thoughts were carefully set down, unlike the mindless chatter of men's speech.

"It was the Germanic tribes who created the first settlements nine thousand years ago and there is a theory about my ancestors who fled the Viking Chieftains to maintain their independence," he begun

Vikings, Jenny thought. How many times had she heard about her father's great heroes and his admiration of the circular stained glass window above their front entry? He had found an artisan who could replicate in colored glass a Viking ship. Her father associated the ship with power and believed the Vikings' superiority in battles was strongly attributed to their lightweight, high speed ships and their tactic of using the element of surprise, gliding like a leopard around the corners and striking while the prey was sleeping. The Vikings defended their outlaw behavior by classifying their victims as enemies and believed that no one should be prosecuted for an unlawful deed before a jury of twelve civilians had heard the case. In addition to a civilian jury, an accused had also the option of using a type of lie detector to prove his innocence by walking barefoot twelve steps, one for each jury member, on a red-hot plow iron. His feet would be examined three days later and if the wounds were free of infection, innocence was proven. The biggest and most feared Viking was Jenny's father's hero, Ganger-Rolf, whose name meant "Rolv who walks." He was so big that a horse couldn't carry him, but in spite of that handicap, he raided and conquered Normandy and became the forefather of William the Conqueror. When her father bragged about his hero, Jenny used to argue that it wasn't Ganger Rolv who was big; it was the horses that were small, ponies imported from Iceland. Oh, Jenny had heard the story quite a few times; it seemed like her father, although only 45 years old, had begun to tell the same stories over and over again as older people do. She turned her attention to Iver again as he began to speak.

"On these mountain ledges, my ancestors found safety by working with the natural elements and harvesting what they sowed."

"Sow, where?" asked Jenny. "Looks like only rocks and mountains."

"They located every piece of usable land, a lot of tiny pastures, some only a few square yards wide, but it all adds up. Like a water ore - you might not see it, but it's there. And sometimes it's not always what the eye sees that gives the greatest harvest."

"How long has your farm existed?"

"More than three hundred years."

Jenny noticed that the man by the oars was scrutinizing her again. It is easy to see when a man is measuring a woman and he had probably not seen a stranger for months and surely not a woman from Kristiania. It was something about his look, deviating and at the same time, attentive. As soon as she looked away, she could feel that look like a cold draft down her neck. She leaned over to her side to avoid him by getting Marta in between them. But it didn't take long before he had repositioned himself in a way so he could continue his secret scrutinizing game. *Ok,* thought Jenny, *if you want to play that game, fine with me.* She pointed her nose toward the sky and looked down at him the same way the high society class did back in Kristiania to emphasize its pecking order. It did not surprise her that it worked; it usually did if you were dealing with people who didn't think much about themselves. Maybe he was a bachelor with few opportunities to meet women. He immediately turned away and looked alternately between the bottom of the boat and the mountainside.

Iver's mother, Marta, had been dosing on and off the last hour; the long trip back from Kristiania had taken its toll on her. Her hurting eyes were still light-sensitive from the surgery she had left her home to have, so she kept a hat pulled down over her eyebrows to shadow her face. A simple woman in her late forties, Marta had a pleasant face and a kind demeanor; nothing about her caused attention until she spoke up. Now she could smell the fragrance of home and straightened herself up. "We are almost home. Look Iver, I can finally see the ledge."

It was difficult for an unfamiliar eye to see the two specks on the small pasture in the middle of the gray and black mountain wall, dotted with only a few patches of pine trees and dwarf birches. Jenny spoke up. "Up there is Holseth? I never dreamed it would be so far above the water. How do we get up there?"

"When we get closer to shore you'll see the path."

Jenny scanned the mountainside for the path Marta talked about and in between bushes she saw part of it. "I guess the coach man needs to steer the carriage very carefully not to going astray."

"Coachman, carriage? We have no coachman and no carriage."

"Oh, so all of us ride horses then," said Jenny, glad that she had taken riding classes when she was a teenager, so now her riding skills should come to the test.

Marta faced her. "Dear, a horse can't walk these paths. We walk, climb, crawl or whatever you want to call it."

"What? All the way up?"

"Yes my Dear, all the way."

Jenny sighed. "How about all the stuff? I mean bags - who carries that?"

"We do, one for each."

Jenny didn't understand how people could live in a place where everything had to be carried to the farm by hand. Surely they would soon learn how to pack light when they went somewhere. She thought about the books and extra shoes she was bringing; maybe she ought to leave some of it behind.

It was as if Marta read her thoughts. "You know, Jenny, sometimes we have to leave something behind to take it with us next time or if some one else in the family comes up. There is a place by the boathouse where we place all goods that are going to the farm and a place where we leave things that are going to the village. It is simple; we just have to apply to certain unwritten rules."

"What kind of rules?"

"Everyone must do his or her fair share. No one may go up or down the path without carrying something; like my father said once, if we were ever in the fields and needed to run for cover from a falling rock, we were to grab onto a hay bail or something and run for our lives, taking cover."

"A hay bail - to protect your body from falling rocks?"

"Oh no, it was just my father's way of telling us no matter the circumstances, you always carry something."

Jenny realized the stories she had been told about these farmers must have been true; they did indeed live like eagles above the clouds.

Iver waved. "I'll bet Olaf and Grandfather are watching us."

"Olaf, who is Olaf?" asked Jenny.

"My son," replied Iver, glad to be home and impatient to get on land.

Jenny remembered her aunt telling her that Iver was single; no one mentioned a son. Of course he was not single - she couldn't imagine a man could make it up here alone; he would have to have someone to cook and take care of the house and the children. And by the way, if it should come down to it, there was no way she could ever stay with a mountain farmer! She shook her head in amazement at her own thoughts. Why in the world would she even think about it?

When the boat bounced against the small dock, everyone instinctively grabbed on to the its rim to regain balance. A few logs tied together with wire and bolted to the bedrock made up the primitive dock connected to the boathouse. Iver reached out for the rope and threw a loop around a pole, pulling the boat securely to the dock. With everyone safely on shore, Marta thanked the man for taking them from the village, promising him a favor in return.

"Marta, the only favor I want is for your son to make up his mind which of my daughters he's interested in. There's fighting going on at my house over that young man." He pushed the boat away from the dock and waved back at them.

Iver noticed Jenny's curious look and shrugged. "It's not me he's talking about. It's Lars, my younger brother."

"Couldn't you have picked another person to take us? He's the biggest gossip in the village," said Marta, looking quite agitated at her son.

"He never asked any questions."

Marta nodded. "Silent like a grave, making up his mind, I'll have more visits now from neighbors snooping around than ever before. I wonder what the boy has done now. I'm gone just three months and I told him to stay put on the mountain and help his grandfather. It's not my son's fault that every young girl in the region is after him."

If girls were attracted to the younger brother, thought Jenny, he must be entirely different than Iver. She couldn't imagine someone would fight for Iver - be with him, yes, but not fight for him. Although it would depend on how many bachelors there were around and how desperate the women were to get married. She was standing at what appeared to be a never-ending horizontal wall of solid granite, wondering where the path might be, when she noticed that Iver was pointing at her feet, shaking his head.

"What's wrong?"

"You can't walk the path in those."

"What do you mean?"

"Your shoes, you can't get up the hill with high-heeled shoes!"

Jenny opened her bag and rummaged around, pulling out a similar pair.

Iver frowned. "You have no shoes without those stupid heels?"

Stupid heels! What kind of man was this Iver anyway? Jenny wondered. The last thing she needed now was an arrogant man picking at her. "Not with me. I must have left them behind in Kristiania."

"Give them to me," Iver demanded, grabbing the shoes and heading toward a nearby shed-looking boathouse.

A stunned Jenny followed close behind and walked into the sparsely lit boathouse. When her eyes had adjusted to the darkness, she noticed old fishing rods, splintered oars wrapped in cobwebs, pieces of timber stacked to the ceiling, broken furniture, and rusty farm equipment. Directly above her head dangled a large fishing net, smelling of seaweed and rotting fish, and on the walls hung old jackets, misshapen hats and moth-eaten sweaters. Nothing seemed organized and everything smelled like old men. She picked up a ball of twine, looked at it for a moment and laid it on top of a wooden bench.

"I wouldn't do that if I were you. It's best to leave it on the floor where Grandfather has left it. Even though it looks unorganized here, the old man knows where everything is." Iver took the ball and dropped it back on the floor, grabbed an axe and swiftly cut the heels off Jenny's shoes. She opened her mouth to protest, but didn't get a word out before Iver quickly ushered her out, closed the door and handed her the shoes.

Jenny snatched the shoes out of his hands and gaped at him. "You've ruined them! I can't walk in these."

Iver shrugged and turned his back to her. "Walk without, then." He wrapped a rope around his arm and moved quickly toward the path's incline, then dropped his bundles down on the ground and looked back at Jenny. "You should walk ahead of me and I'll try to stop your fall. My mother would never forgive me if I let you slip down the mountain."

As Jenny came, dragging her stuff, Iver raised his hand. "Hold it! You'll have to leave the larger bag behind."

"No, I'm taking it with me." She firmly held onto the suitcase.

"No, you're not. Understand, this path is treacherous and I do not want to be responsible for what may happen to you."

Jenny stomped her foot. "You aren't responsible for me! You will never be responsible for me and I am going up the mountain with all my bags." She stormed a few yards up the path to get away from him, then realized he was right. There was no way she could carry all her stuff at once. Looking up, she didn't even know how she could get up with just one bag to carry and wondered why she had reacted the way she did. Usually she felt safe under the protection of a man, remembering how she felt when Robert wrapped his strong arms around her. Now, no matter how she hated to admit it, she was literally in the hands of this man who had cut the heels off her shoes and just one more glance up at this horizontal wall of granite made her realize she could not scale this mountain by herself. She noticed Marta, who had started ahead of them, was now waving at her from a boulder further up the path. It seemed so far up to where she was standing, but as Jenny turned down toward the fjord, she realized a given distance might look much longer vertically then horizontally. Even though it appeared that the dock was way down there, she knew she hadn't gone very far. It was probably the same effect as when you stand on top of a building looking down; it looks far down even thought the height might not be more than the width of street.

Iver quickly picked up his bundles and ran to catch up with her. He wondered why this kept happening to him; he didn't mean to be rude. He could have been much more gentle but it was like something exploded inside when he saw how misplaced this vulnerable city girl was, standing on the wharf with high-heel shoes. As he got closer to her, she tried to ascend further up to keep the distance between them, when she suddenly lost her foothold and slid down, landing against a tree. Still holding onto all her bags, she grabbed the branches of a bush to get upright and moved up the path again.

Iver thought he would watch her struggle a little bit more before he intervened. She seemed to be of the stubborn kind, the ones who have to get it all the hard way. As he watched her inching up the path, she suddenly lost her foothold again, slid down and stopped against his feet. He grabbed her around her waist and carried her up the incline to solid ground. "Got enough? Keep in mind over the centuries many have died on this mountain. Pay attention to your step. Go slow and breathe deeply."

After regaining his own breath, Iver grabbed the suitcase away from her, cut a piece of rope, tied it to a tree and waved at her. "We will pick it up later, so let's get moving while I'm still young." He waited until she has passed him then followed close behind her.

Around a bend, Jenny stopped a moment and shuddered at the sight of a massive ravine unfolding in front of her, reaching thousands of feet up from the fjord to a place way above the timberline where the mountain had no moss or earth. Steams of water ran over the gray bedrock and merged into a roaring river that rushed through a cleft before it poured into the fjord. Her knees went numb when she noticed the path went across the ravine, right into the heavy spray from the river. *There has to be a way around*, she thought. *No one can walk across that*! Her father could not possibly have any idea of what this was all about! No one in their right mind would send their daughters to a place like this! Actually, most would do whatever they could do to stop an adventuresome daughter from such an expedition.

Iver, who was only a few yards behind her, suddenly moved forward, pushing his body into hers, pinning her against the mountain wall. Shocked, she tried pushing him away until she heard a rumble. *Was the mountain crashing down on them*? she wondered. Then, a large boulder rolled past them, leaving behind dust and chipped rock floating through the air before it hit the fjord with a splash.

As soon as the vibrations stopped, Jenny felt uncomfortable with Iver's grip around her and asked, "Will you let go of me now?"

He pulled away a few inches, looked up, then moved his body closer. "Not yet."

Just then, another boulder crashed against the bedrock close to the waterfall, causing a cracking noise to echo between the mountains. Afterwards, settling against the mountain, Iver released his hold. "Now you can go."

Shaken by the falling rock, Jenny grabbed hold of Iver's coat and yelled at him, "Is there any safe place on this mountain?"

"No," he said with a grin.

They came to a small, rustic bridge being showered with water from the river. Jenny backed off a couple of yards. She had had it - she was not going to cross that! Her father would understand if she returned to Kristiania. There had to be other places in the country to hide. After all, she was not an outlaw running away from the executioner; just a young woman running away from a man who loved her. So how bad could that be? Her father had to be wrong;

Robert couldn't be that bad. Everything would be better than what this appeared to be.

"I am not crossing that! I am going home. Take me back to the village," she yelled

"What? I can't hear you," shouted Iver.

"I am not crossing that bridge! I want to go back," yelled Jenny, dropping her bag and pointing at the primitive bridge which consisted of five logs with no railing, just a loose wire strung from tree to tree to hold on to and a dangerous drop below.

Iver ignored her remark, moved her aside and took a slow step on to the first log.

Standing safely on the other side of the bridge, Marta shouted, "Be careful of the left log. I almost fell through."

Iver stepped back and collected their bags, then reached out for Jenny's handbag.

Jenny retracted her hand and snapped, "I can carry it myself."

He turned around and disappeared into the mist. Dripping wet and safe on the other side, he dropped Jenny's bag, straightened the rope and began to tie it around a tree trunk. "What are you doing, Iver?" asked Marta.

He finished the knot. "There is a stubborn mule on the other side." He took hold of the rope and walked back across the bridge.

Marta yelled, "It's all right Jenny, don't look down," but her voice was drowned by the roar of the waterfall.

Iver swiftly tightened the other end of the rope around Jenny's waist. "Jenny Mohr, you are going across this bridge. You can either walk across or I'll carry you over. Take your pick. Step slowly and don't panic. If you get frightened, kneel down and crawl. If you fall, the rope will hold you."

He called out across the ravine, "Mother, keep the rope tight." Then nodded at Jenny,

"Go on I'll be right behind you."

She hesitated, stepped onto the first log and held on to the wire with one hand, clutching her handbag with the other. Slowly she moved forward. Never had she been so frightened! She cursed her father and everybody who had been a part of this ridiculous hide-away operation. Her heart beat harder and harder and she felt its pounding in every limb in her body. Just as she reached the middle of the bridge, the ever-pulsating river doused her with ice-cold water, causing her to slip and fall to her knees. In a frantic move to hold on, she lost her grip on her handbag and watched it slide outside the bridge. She screamed out as all her personal possessions disappeared into the abyss. She shivered and felt her body wouldn't move. She looked down and began to cry.

"Don't look down," yelled Iver, "look straight ahead and keep moving."

Jenny remained on her knees, shivering. Iver knew it was too dangerous for two people to be walking on the bridge at the same time, but if she didn't get across soon he would have to try their luck and carry her across. He shook his head and flung his arms in pure frustration. It never fails that terrified species just freeze in their tracks.

Jenny looked back at him screaming, "I can't, I can't!"

"Yes you can!" yelled Iver. "Look ahead and begin to crawl, damn it."

Jenny took a deep breath, focused on Marta and began to slowly move forward. As soon as she was out of the wet part of the bridge, she struggled back on her feet, held on to the wire and took a giant leap to the opposite side, landing safely in Marta's arms.

"I've never seen anyone jump so high; I thought you were going to fly!"

"I wish I could, I wish I could," said Jenny, relived but still shaking after the scary walk. She was amazed at how close the path of life and path of death go sometimes.

The mountain path had evolved throughout the years as opposed to being made at a certain point in time and was based on old animal trails. The villagers used to joke about the path to Holseth, arguing it was so steep you got several mouth-fulls of grass and dirt before you even got halfway. Even though falling rocks and numerous avalanches had forced them to reconsider its course, they always ended up with its original direction after securing the most dangerous places. When animals wander the mountainside, they make their trails pass by places to hide and rest, so by following an animal trail, you can count on the fact that sooner or later you will come to an overhanging rock or a cave where you can rest, be safe and dry. From the very beginning, even before the first turf had been turned of what would be the future farm, the villagers took advice from those who knew the mountain the best - the animals. And by adhering to that philosophy, they could survive in places that from the surface would appear inhabitable. As civilization had continued to evolve in these villages, and the need to protect themselves from criminals, the tax collector or any other unwanted visitor arose, they would use certain parts of the path as a gate. Holseth's gate was a wooden ladder raised up against a vertical portion of the mountainside. When they pulled the ladder up, they kept all wingless creatures out of their property.

Neither Jenny nor Iver spoke as they one by one climbed this natural wall of protection; they needed all the concentration they could get and just one wrong step could easy be the last. Finally, safely on the small pasture above, they were met by Iver's son Olaf, his brother Lars and a dog that almost pushed Iver back down in his eagerness to welcome his master home.

On the final walk up to the farm, Jenny could feel Lars' eyes scrutinizing her as he took hold of her bags and chattered with his mother. Not at all like Iver, he was fair and handsome with light blonde hair and the most beautiful blue eyes had she ever seen on a man. He was strong like Iver and yet softer. His eyes sparked when he spoke with his mother and he made her laugh. It was obvious that mother and son were very close. After Marta shared with him a little about their trip and her eye operation, she asked, "Where is your grandfather?"

"At Iver's farm. He wanted to take another look at the damage."

"What damage?" Marta abruptly stopped and looked at him.

"A day ago Iver's barn was hit by a boulder."

"Did you hear that, Iver? Your barn has been hit by a boulder," she hollered at him.

He hurried to catch up with them. "What boulder?"

"You were lucky this time, Brother. It could have been much worse; if it had hit a few yards closer to the roof, your hens would have counted stars all night. It was part of the north wall that was hit; should be easy to repair. You will have a much tougher time dealing with your grandfather who didn't want you to build the barn there in the first place."

After Iver wanted to start a family on his own, Holseth had become a two-farm community with the buildings only a few hundred yards apart, separated by a dangerous ravine. After his wife died, falling prey to the mountain, danger began to lurk around him. Boulders tumbled down frequently, barely missing the farmhouse and it seemed like they got closer and closer every time, as if nature was telling him to move, but Iver felt he had put too much time and effort into the place to just let it all go. It turned out that his sister, Anna, and her husband Jon moved in to help him out.

"Anything else happened while we were gone?" asked Marta almost afraid to ask.

"No, just the usual squabbles with Grandfather."

"What about the neighbor's daughters?"

"Which ones?" laughed Lars.

"Well I guess I will hear about all your antics the past three months from the village, especially if something is brewing."

The path continued up through a sixty-yard long by thirty-yard wide pasture, broken in sections by large rocks and boulders. Although not flat, it was truly the most horizontal piece of land Jenny had seen since beginning the climb and she looked forward to planting her feet firmly on solid ground. Partly hidden by fruit trees and bushes, under a large over-hanging rock, she spotted the farmhouse with its curved roof covered with small rocks and debris, all of which were an accumulation from the last winter's snow avalanches. Jenny was stunned to hear that snow avalanches went straight over the house, but Marta comforted her by saying although it was frightening when the whole house rumbled, no one had ever gotten hurt once they were inside and she claimed that their small house was the safest place they could be during bad weather. It had been built at a place where wild animals used to seek shelter.

A fair haired woman stood at the front door on the stairway of moss-covered natural rocks. She resembled her brother, Lars, in her fairness and carried herself with the dignity of a Viking princess as she graciously walked down the stairs and moved toward the group, wrapped her arms around her mother and nodded at Jenny. Marta, amidst the hugs and kisses, introduced her oldest daughter, Anna. She smiled at Jenny, a smile that included her entire face and emitted a kind of love Jenny had never felt before. Anna's blue eyes sparkled like sapphires under the most perfect shaped eyebrows. When she blinked, her eyelashes bounced softly like the wings of an eagle. A row of sugar-white teeth were framed by plump natural-colored lips. Jenny was awe struck by her beauty and knew that if she were left alone in Kristiania, there would be many men fighting for her. Jenny brushed the dirt of her dress, straightened her hair and excused herself for how she looked.

"It's ok, Jenny. Up here we rarely care how we look on the outside, as long as we look good on the inside. You know if you have a good heart, your love will shine through you and a loving person will always look good."

It was hard for Jenny to imagine those words came from Anna; in Kristiania, such a beauty would be so preoccupied by her looks that she wouldn't have time to be loving and nice toward others. Jenny tried to imagine Anna with a long, beautiful dress in a ballroom - wow what a stir she would make! She glanced briefly at the house, wondering how a whole family could fit; even their own guesthouse in Kristiania was bigger than this house. The horizontal timber logs were weathered and at one corner, the layers of flat rocks that served as its foundation had sagged so much that the whole frame had become lopsided. Pieces of splintered rocks, a plank, a sledgehammer and some other tools lay on the ground, giving witness that someone was working on it.

While the others went inside, Jenny expressed her wish to remain outside for a moment to get a view of the farm. She sat down on the stairs to get a well-deserved rest and reflect. The journey had been long and tiring, but after all, she was relieved she had at least arrived safely. Looking around the isolated place hundreds of yards above the fjord, she was actually surprised that she didn't feel worse than she did, but the reactions might come later. But one thing she was certain about, if she had seen a picture of this place back in Kristiania, she would rather have fled the country.

A loud chirping bird caught her attention. In a birch tree nearby, she noticed the bird stretching its beak toward the sky, emitting a series of short crispy sounds. *Got to be a finch* she thought, remembering her biology classes as a child when the whole class went out into the woods to study birds. After repeating its call a few times, the bird flew in a looping formation into a thicket. Seconds later, a flock of other birds flushed out of the thicket and flew away. It seemed like something had scared them; then she saw it. A lone sparrow hawk was circling above the trees. Suddenly the hawk nose-dived with wings pointed upward while adjusting its speed and course. His sharp and powerful claws opened up as he dropped just inches above the ground, snatching something. Instantly the hawk's body shifted movement and with a powerful pumping motion, he gained altitude, heading to a nearby boulder, leaving behind a thin cloud of dust. Clucking hens ran for cover and a cat sought rescue under the stairs. Bewildered by the scene, Jenny realized that even though the place was isolated, it was definitely not dead.

A moment later, she stood up to Anna's call for dinner and walked with her into the house. The doorframe reached only to her shoulders, so she needed to bow deeply to get through. She wondered why they made the doors so small; it gave an impression that there were only dwarfs living there, but the family all seemed to be of normal height. A long table with a variety of foods had been arranged in the living room. Customs dictated that in the event of having guests, especially from far away, you brought out the finest food you had. Anna must have spent hours and hours making it. There were several kinds of crisp bread, pancakes, cheese and butter. She had also prepared a large plate of sliced, cured ham and dried lam.

"You have been busy, Anna. You did this all by yourself?" said Marta as she leaned forward in progress of lighting the row of candles in the center of the table.

"Kari helped me, so I am much grateful to her," Anna said, nodding at a young girl by the fireplace. Kari was eleven and the youngest of Marta's four children.

Jenny nibbled at the food and ate out of politeness rather than out of hunger and she was glad when an appropriate time to leave the table came. She was so tired she could barely keep her eyes open.

"Anna will show you where you can sleep," said Marta as she courteously pulled out the chair for her.

Anna ushered her into a small closet of a bedroom next to the kitchen where she stumbled toward the bed and fell asleep as soon as her head touched the pillow.

Hours later she awoke; the unfamiliar room caused a great deal of anxiety as she watched the shadows from an oil lamp dancing on the timber walls. She struggled to move herself to a sitting position, finding that every muscle in her body ached. Through the small, plain window, she saw the sun illuminate the mountains, showering them with its last light for the day. Homesickness took hold of her and soon tears flowed down her cheeks.

Marta found her crying softly into her pillow. She sat down beside her. "Crying helps. I usually do it while talking to my aging cow. The two of us get going and we make such an odd sound together. Often her milk flows after all that lowing." Jenny started laughing at the idea of crying with a cow. She wiped off her tears and sat up in the bed. "I didn't know you had cows up here."

Marta stroked Jenny on the forehead and pushed her hair away from her eyes. "We had one; bought her in from the village as a calf. My father rowed her all the way." Marta shook head and smiled. "You know, to keep her calm in the boat, we had to make sure she had enough to eat and you know the mixture of flour, grass, manure and sea water makes a mess."

Jenny's face turned into a grimace; she could almost smell it. "How did you get her up the path?"

"The path wasn't the most difficult. When we first found a method that worked, it was just to take one step at the time. Two of us were pulling a rope attached to a halter we made for her and two others were pushing from behind, but the biggest challenge was to get her out of the boat and up on the wharf. We had forgotten to time her arrival with the tide."

"Time it with tide - what do you mean?"

"With high tide, it wouldn't be so far from the boat and up to the wharf; she could almost have leaped her self, but this time it was low tide. And with four sprawling kicking legs, that was a challenge. My father would be happy to tell you the whole story later." She patted Jenny on the arm. "I know what you're thinking. It might not seem like much up here, but we have plenty to eat. Tomorrow you will meet the rest of our family and they are a good bunch. Lars brought you clean water and towels so when you are ready, the basin is on the night stand."

The next morning Jenny awoke rested and opened her eyes to Iver's son at the doorway. She motioned him to come in but he ran out calling for his grandmother.

It was first when Marta come into the room that Jenny realized how much the floor planks creaked. For every step she took, it was like the entire room vibrated. It would be impossible to sneak back in after a late night without anyone noticing it. Privacy in the house was probably unheard of in this family.

"Good morning Jenny. I hope you have slept well. Anna has kept the kettle of porridge warm for you."

"Yes I feel better now. I will be out in a moment."

She got out of bed and moved to the small nightstand which was only a fraction of the one she was used to. Her legs ached from the day before, while her mind seemed a bit confused as if she didn't really understand what was going on. She repeatedly flushed her face with cold water before drying herself; the face in the mirror looked tired. How in the world could she have gotten so old in just a couple of days? She pulled out a dress and after putting it on, she noticed how wrinkled it had gotten. *Oh my, how I look! I can't wear this.* She took if off again, put on another that hadn't gotten so beaten during the journey and sat down in front of the mirror. Quieted, she lifted her long arms above her head and untied her ribbon, allowing her red curly hair to cascade over her shoulders. Picking up the hairbrush, she began to comb out the curls. Her thoughts went back to favorite moments when her mother would comb her hair, Jenny sitting in her lap while she spoke about the gardens. "Jenny, you have your grandmother's hair"....and then her mother would tell the story of Grandfather falling in love with Grandmother. One day he saw her with her hair down and realized he was in love; they were married within the year. Jenny loved this story because it connected her to her grandparents whom she had never met.

The chattering ceased at the table and all eyes were on her as she stepped into the living room. Marta came up beside her and introduced her to Kari who was playing in a corner of the room.

"Kari turns eleven next week."

Kari smiled a big toothy smile; she was a miniature of Anna.

"Excuse her bashfulness; it doesn't last long." Next she motioned to a man who had just walked into the room. "This is Jon, Anna's husband."

Jon came from a similar farm as Holseth, another nest clutching onto a shelf more than thousand feet above the fjord, from a family that was known for their gentle spirit and kindness. His aging parents had just recently moved to the village while his oldest brothers took over the farm. Marta knew about him long before he had met her daughter and prayed that her Anna would one day accept Jon's attentions

Jon didn't say a word, nodded and walked back outside. He was as dark as Anna was fair and they both had the same sparkling eyes. Jenny could see why Anna had married him.

"He's not shy, just a quiet man, but once you learn to know him, you will see the light in him."

Jenny sat down next to Lars who was finishing his meal. She looked briefly about the room and could see a glimpse of the barn through the only window in the kitchen, a rectangular frame with six square glass windows embedded into the wood. The kitchen was partially separated from the living room by a wood stove sitting on a flagstone.

"Did you sleep well?" asked Lars.

Jenny acknowledged him with a smile.

Anna placed a bowl of porridge in front of her. She picked up the wooden spoon and examined it for a long time. She had never used a wooden spoon and had only seen them in the museum, old spoons with crosses or symbols burnt into them, relics from the old days.

"It's barley porridge, very good," said Lars as he excused himself, anxious to get outside.

A moment later, the back door was flung open and an older man came hobbling into the kitchen with a crowbar in his hand.

Marta looked at him. "Finally. I wondered when you'd show up. Why didn't you come back last night?"

The old man didn't answer. He left the crowbar by the door, dropped his hat on the table and walked straight to Jenny, looked at her for a long time, shook his head and said, "So this is the lady from the city Iver spoke about. Has my daughter been nice? You see she treats me, her only father, terrible at times, but I always suffer through." He looked at Marta. "But I am glad you're home, Daughter. I missed your cooking."

In spite of his seventy-two years, Andreas wore his age well and appeared not to be a day over sixty, a quiet man, long, lean and handsome, born with a natural ability to work the earth and tame the animals. Fearless, stubborn and in his youth, an adventurer, only his deceased wife could soften his ways. The years since her death had made him ever so quarrelsome. Many times his only daughter Marta took the brunt of his loneliness that showed up in his sarcasm. Marta loved him dearly and oftentimes overlooked his shortcomings. When those feelings about his deceased wife surfaced, his entire body cried out and he remembered how he had held her, clutched her, almost suffocating her by holding her so close to his chest their hearts would beat together. He felt strong with her by his side, even as an old man. How odd after all these years he could still remember how difficult it was to breathe and swallow when he first saw her, like time had stopped. He could still see her flying past him, running down the path with her long wheat-colored hair bouncing back and forth off her shoulders. Flushed from hurrying, she had only turned for one brief second to look his way and smile as she hurried away. He knew in that brief second, nothing would ever be the same and they would meet again. Now, half a century later and seven years after she died, he could still feel her presence in the house, her smile lighting up her round face, her blue eyes looking at him through their daughter's eyes.

With the day's chores completed and the evening meal at an end, the family found a moment to sit quietly by the fire before retiring. Jon, Anna, Iver and Olaf were back at their own farm while the rest of the family gathered in the small living room with their guests.

Andreas had brought up his beer from the cellar to share with Jenny; customs dictated you would share your beer with every visitor, woman or man. The moment Andreas shook hands with Jenny, she knew he was a man who toiled the earth. Marta, sitting comfortably in an overstuffed chair, clicked her knitting pins in a quiet and soothing rhythm. She frequently put the pins aside to help her daughter Kari unravel the wool from the spinner. The day had gone by just cleaning up the mess left after her father and Lars had roamed around on their own; two men should never be allowed to be alone in a house beyond a day. Her thoughts where interrupted by Iver coming into the house with a lantern in hand.

"What are you doing here? You never come over after dark," asked Andreas.

Iver extinguished his light and placed it by the door. "Why am I here? Ah, just to talk to Lars about how to best repair my barn," he said as he fumbled to pull out a chair and sat down across from Jenny and Lars. He hardly talked to Lars, and his occasional looks at Jenny made it quite obvious that talking to his brother was not the reason he had come over.

Jenny, sitting by the fire, noticed how different he appeared among his family members; he seemed misplaced in a sad face. Looking into his face was like looking at a blue lake surrounded by the havoc after a forest fire, a lake where you would have to dive deep to get to its bottom.

Lars seemed miles away, working on a paper. Jenny interrupted him, "By the looks of your paper Lars, you must be inventing something."

"The boy has been inventing since the day he fell out of his crib," replied Marta, looking down at her son with respect.

"Thank the heavens none of his schemes have killed us all yet," quipped Andreas.

Marta asked Lars to light another oil lantern.

Lars fumbled with the matches and after a few unsuccessful attempts; he flung his arms out in pure frustration.

"Pump the oil and turn up the wick. Why are you making it so difficult?" said Iver sarcastically.

Lars pushed the pin several times, turned up the wick and lit another match. Flames flared up and black smoke wafted toward the ceiling. He instinctively pulled his head back to avoid getting burned.

Iver shook his head, "You seem to need a course in lighting oil lamps."

Lars threw the matches on the table. "I'll tell you one thing brother. In the future, we won't have to fiddle around with matches and oil wicks. We can just say as in the Old Testament, 'Let it be light and it shall come."

"I didn't know a heathen dog like you read the bible," said Iver.

"Heathen dogs read between the lines Brother, but this is something new. They call it electricity. You just do this," he snapped his fingers, "or you turn a knob and this room would be bright as daylight. One day we can throw out the oil lamps and the wood stove."

Marta frowned. "That kind of witchcraft isn't coming into my house."

"It's not witchcraft Mother, it's science."

"You're losing prospective, Lars. New science will never replace oil lamps and wood stoves. They have worked for hundreds of years," said Andreas.

"It's the future; we need to move into the future."

Marta crossed her arms in front of her. "I am not moving anywhere. By the way, who feeds your mind with all this?"

"Heard it in the village, but now listen to this, this is even more fantastic. An English man with the name of Bell has invented something he calls a speaking machine. You can talk to a person not even in the room with you without hollering. Just crank the handle of a wooden box and speak into a spout."

"Speaking machine?" Andreas laughed. "That is the stupidest thing I've ever heard. It's bad enough having to talk to people let alone speak to them through a box. How do you know what a man is really saying if all you can hear is his voice? You need to see his eyes, facial expression and gestures, otherwise what's the use? I bet it's the grocer who has been spouting with his loose tongue again. You never know when he lies or speaks the truth. You said the man was named Bell; well I'd say he's appropriately named. He must have bells ringing between his ears to come up with such a device." He turned toward Jenny. "You, a young woman from the big city, what do you make of the boys' stories?"

"I've seen the box once in my father's office and I think it's a nice thing to play with, but I don't see it will have any practical use. So I agree with you, I want to see a man's eyes when he talks to me."

The villagers had many times predicted that Lars one day would invent something that would benefit the whole region as long as he stayed far away from dynamite. The dynamite story at Holseth had spread through the village like wildfire. Andreas had gotten a case of dynamite from a friend who had recently returned from America, but no one knew how to use it. The only thing they knew was that it somehow blew things up. The memorable day at Holseth was a rainy and wet October morning, a perfect day to fertilize the fields. The manure had been carried out from the barn and assembled in a huge pile and Lars had gotten the task of spreading it out, a literally dirty job nobody liked doing.

"The more I looked at the pile, the more I hesitated to go out and dig into it," Lars told his friends afterwards in the village. "Then I got the idea of trying the dynamite. I buried it in the manure pile. I didn't know how much to use, so to be sure, I used all of it. I lit the strings and ran for cover, waited and waited, but nothing happened. I was on my way back to see what went wrong when it suddenly exploded, knocking me off the ground. It happened so fast! I was covered in manure, every window on the south side of the house was shattered and the entire front wall had become brown. Needless to say, after that day, I became the least appreciated person at Holseth." Lars could have limited the damages by beginning to clean up the mess, but instead he took off to the village and hid with a friend for several days, leaving the clean-up to Iver and his father.

Jenny chuckled at the story and grabbed the bowl of beer handed to her. She took a small swallow and tried her best to hide her dislike of its unpleasantness taste and drinking from the same bowl as all the others, but the politeness and respect of other customs she had learned from her mother prevailed.

"Seem like Lars could do a lot for the future advancement of Holseth, but it still baffles me how generations have lived on this isolated land. What do you know about your ancestors?" she asked.

"We know quite a bit."

Kari lit up. "Tell her about the diary, Grandfather, the diary we found."

"A diary?" Jenny loved looking at old documents.

Andreas leaned back in his chair and cleared his throat.

"The first settlers to Holseth, my great, great grandparents, were young and eager to be married. They wanted to live as man and wife, but neither of their parents had a place for them, forcing them to stay away from each other until they had a foundation; getting married without a source of livelihood was strictly against the customs. The man's father suggested he work and lease land from a nearby landowner, but the stubborn young man refused to lose his freedom and kept dreaming of his own farm. His desire for his girlfriend grew strong and their secret encounters became difficult to hide, so he would soon need to do something or lose her. One summer morning, he borrowed a boat, left the village and headed aimlessly in through the fjord. His life flashed before him as he rowed through the silent water until he noticed a sparrow hawk that dove close to his boat before soaring and flying further down the fjord. Before he knew it, he found himself following the bird. When he no longer could see the hawk, he sat near the mouth of a ravine, surrounded by mountains so steep goats could hardly find a foothold. He cursed both himself and the hawk for getting so far into no man's land and planned to return home when he thought he heard a voice telling him not to give up.

He docked at the only shallow place he could find and jumped ashore, clinging to the wall of the mountain. With unyielding determination and a hunch he would find a place where he could build a farm, he climbed up the steep slope before crossing the ravine and finally reaching a plateau covered with grass and wildflowers. He found the soil, although shallow, unusually rich and when he located a brook nearby while taking in the magnificent view, he must have decided that this would be their home.

Back in the village, he saw the man of law and found out that this area had been written up as worthless land and decreed free for any one who was dimwitted enough to live on it. He signed the property registration document, blessed the antics of the sparrow hawk taking him to the Bluehorn Mountain, and went to tell his future wife. For two summers he worked the land, cut trees, tore up bushes, turned rocks, and around the clock tilled the turf, taking advantage of the light summer nights. When the winter prevented him access to the mountain, he made wood benches, cabinets and counters in his father's cellar.

A spring day, two years after he broke the first ground, he carried the love of his life across the doorsill of their new home that would, in later years, swell into several rooms. It had a kitchen at one end and a bedroom at the other, separated by a flat rock fireplace. Above the fireplace, his wife hung an antique kettle to symbolize that no one who entered that kitchen should go hungry. The warm days came and went and by the end of summer, the farm boasted goats, chickens, pigs, a sheep and one feisty calico cat. The entire fall they dried fish, stockpiled food and remained forever thankful to have each other."

Jenny shook her head and asked, "I still don't understand why he chose this place so crammed in between these mountains. Since the Viking chieftains were no longer a threat, wouldn't it have been easier to get land in the coastal area where there's more space?"

"Indeed, they have more space, but do you know

what those coastal people eat?"

"The same as we do, I guess."

"No, they eat herring and potatoes one day and potatoes and herring the next."

After the laughter had settled, Jenny asked, "Did the diary say anything about their feeling of isolation and being so alone?"

"They do talk about that a little and like all diaries, you can read between the lines and get an idea of how they might have felt. The best-preserved pages are where the young man writes about their first Christmas Eve. He took down the diary from the shelf, opened it and turned the pages carefully until he stopped in the middle. He moved closer to the oil lamp and began to read.

Christmas Eve, 1604. The fire is burning. I have chopped juniper limbs and spread them across the floor. Outside, the cold north wind howls and is building huge snowdrifts. The windows have frosted over. In some corners, the snow has found its way through small cracks. I told her to ignore the wind. She is safe as long as we have wood for the fire, food in the house and each other. Every time she looks at me and smiles, I am a content man. Afterwards, we ate and I read a passage from the bible and then we sang hymns. When the fire died, we got cold and I gathered up the sheep hides and wrapped them around us, pulling her close to me.

Andreas handed the diary over to Jenny. "Be careful, the pages are brittle."

While Jenny looked at it, Andreas continued with the story.

"A wonderful story! Did he ever write about the hardship?" asked Jenny.

Marta spoke up, "All of our ancestors have gotten their fair share of pain and suffering. We have all had good times and bad times. The part that is the hardest is the waiting. You have a feeling something bad has happened to a member of the family but it takes days or sometimes weeks before you know. The men have always worked somewhere in the mountains or been fishing in the fjord in all kinds of weather. Being home, keeping the house up and caring for the animals, you have more time to think and worry."

"Yes; the unknown is sometimes harder to live with than the known."

Lars broke in, "And mother is the best worrier."

Marta snapped, "Why don't you go, Lars, and make sure the hens are in for the night and close both gates. Remember they can fly, so you need to close the top gate too."

Lars flung his arms about, "I know mother, hens do fly, at least they did when Olaf let the dog in last summer."

"Don't blame it on Olaf! You know as well as I, it was one of your experiments."

Jenny was surprised at the calm atmosphere within the family; was it only on the surface or were they all so rooted in the ground as they appeared to be? There didn't seem to be any major conflicts, other than between the two brothers. Lars was the light one, full of jokes and always laughing, an unafraid risk taker who hardly took any thing seriously. He spoke with a wide-opened mind and was a person you could learn to know within days. Iver, on the other hand, seemed to be the dark person in the family, serious and careful as if something was constantly haunting him. He seemed to choose his words carefully and be a person it would take a long time to know. So maybe it was this major difference that had forced Iver to get his own place. The more she thought about it, the more she realized that had to be the case; two people like that can't live under the same roof. She tried to visualize the two brothers side by side - who would she pick if she happened to be in a situation to choose between them? Even though the answer seemed to be given, she wasn't so sure that she would pick Lars. Why she didn't know.

"You are so quiet Jenny. What's in your mind?" Marta asked

"Oh I was just, just wondering about your eye. What happened?"

"I got an infection that wouldn't go away. The doctor said he couldn't do anything and an operation was the only way; to do that, I had to go all the way to the National Hospital in Kristiania. We had a long discussion about how to get me there, since we didn't have money for the trip."

"How did you pay for it?"
Marta became thoughtful. "We had to sell our cow. Took it with us to Trondhjem."

"I remember you talked about a cow last night - that cow?"
Marta nodded. "Yes my only dear cow."

"How did you get the animal down the path?"

"We didn't. We ushered her over the Blue Horn Mountains," said Lars, standing in the doorway. He moved across the room, sat down next to Jenny and continued. "Oh my, what a ride! You should have been there when Iver and the cow lost their foothold on the wet, steep pasture. They didn't stop before crashing into the hay barn at a farm on the other side of the mountain." He shook his head. "It didn't work as I planned it. The cow became so frightened that it took us an hour to finally get her to calm down so we could continue to the village and bring her onboard the steamboat."

"Why did you have to take her all the way to Trondhjem?"

"Much better price there."

"Oh, I understand, and then you took the train from there." Jenny looked at Marta. "And now, everybody knows that you're back from Kristiania, I guess, and not only the ones that you talked too."

"Certainly."

"I noticed that people seem to be very curious around here. When we walked off that steamboat, I could feel every eye on me and hear the silent whispers, almost like leaves rattling in the breeze."

"There are two major kinds of people; you have the curious and compassionate ones who are truly interested in you, what you are doing and who want you all the best. Then you have the second group, the rumormongers, who don't care about you at all; they just want to have something to tell others and the worse it is the better."

Lars spoke, "Especially everything that has to do with relationships, who's sleeping with whom, so now everybody knows that we have visitors and some have already began to speculate about who is sleeping with you, Jenny."

"You've got to be joking."

"No, this is what people are talking about."

"So who told them I am here?"

"Remember the man who took us in through the fjord? As soon as he got back to the village, he would go right up to the grocer, a meeting place for rumormongers. They all meet there almost on a daily basis, and especially after the arrival of the steamboat."

Andreas spoke, "Gossip is not only bad. It has been and is an important part of our lives; it protects us, satisfies our curiosity and bonds us together. It's the way we communicate. It's how we get the assistance of a doctor or a midwife. It's how we know when a neighbor needs help; it's how we're notified about a missing animal or told about the best places to harvest wild berries. Gossip is everything, good or bad. We care about each other and an erroneous story on the loose is just part of it all, but sometimes the tongue of the viper may become deadly. It happened to a young and beautiful woman deeply in love with a man from a neighboring village."

Lars leaned over and whispered to her, "Here he goes again, the story about the young woman jumping off the cliff. I have always wondered why old people tell the same story over and over again and repeat themselves so many times."

"With the wedding plans set, she was the happiest girl in these parts. But one day she found out that her betrothed had fallen in love with another. She became heartbroken and cursed them. A year later the young man and his new sweetheart were married and on the way home from the church, their boat sunk and all onboard drowned, including the bride's family members and a few of the wedding guests. The villagers remembered how the young woman had cursed the two and stirred the pot. Was she a witch? Did she cause the accident? The day after the accident, evil tongues said they had seen the young woman earlier, paddling around in a dinghy at the same spot where the wedding boat had sunk, stirring up the water. The villagers turned away whenever she passed by; no one spoke to her, touched, listened, smiled or greeted her any more. She had been decreed an outcast. The shopkeeper wouldn't even take her money. He just threw food on the counter and spit on the floor to ward off any evil. She became a stranger to her parents, an aimless wanderer during the day and a hideaway at night. She thought about leaving and starting a new life, but she had no place to go. The gossip spread like a plague in record time. She lost her ability to talk, forgot how it felt to be loved, touched or cherished. The trees whispered behind her back and the birds seemed to disappear from her path. All about her life was still.

One night, she crawled out of her hideaway long before anyone else woke up, carrying with her a doll her grandmother had given her on her fifth birthday, and walked up the mountainside. When she reached the cliff, she looked down on her home far below and jumped. Below her stood her parents who heard their daughter's screams echoing between the mountains before gradually vanishing with the wind."

Jenny shook her head. "What a sad story, Andreas!"

"You see Jenny, we can't prevent an evil tale from spreading, but we can make a significant influence when a tale is conceived. We can speak the truth. We need to direct gossip to our advantage and feed it with love, truth and compassion. I believe the more facts we provide, the less imagination and drama will be created.

Jenny excused herself and went to her room. *So much gossip and talking about what other people did and said,* she though. They never seemed to talk about themselves and how they felt about each other. With scientific precision, they could lay out the entire family tree of a person they happened to meet in the village and see how they were related. Even though they knew that the only way the village could have survived was through inbreeding, such discussions just brought out the details like finding one who had been labeled as insane and seeing how that insanity more or less would reappear in the following generations.

The next morning, Jenny wandered about the edges of the mountainside. She hoped by now Robert would have put his desire for her to rest and she could go home to Kristiania within a few weeks. She liked everyone except Iver, but she was still homesick. Anna was close to her age and she lifted her spirits, always in a happy spirited mood like her mother. Thinking about Anna, she turned around to the sound of the front door opening and saw her walking out of the house with a tub of clothes in one hand and holding onto Olaf's hand with the other. She had decided to stay with her mother another night and help her with some extra chores.

"Good morning, Jenny. Did you have a good night's sleep?"

"Yes, thank you."

Anna dropped the tub on the ground and tethered the boy to a rope, hooking it to a wire lined up between the barn and house. She noticed Jenny's curious look.

"Oh, just protection. Olaf nearly fell off the cliff last summer and Iver has been overly cautious since. He asked me to look after him today and even though I think he's old enough to go about on his own, I wasn't going to upset his father." She touched Jenny's hand. "Come with me. I want to show you something."

Anna led her across the small pasture toward the cliff. She stopped, leaned down on her knees and waved at Jenny to join her. "Do you see why we need to secure our children?" Anna pointed at a tree leaning over the cliff. "Olaf climbed it last summer."

Jenny thought it was odd to tether children like cattle, but what other option did they have when the mother was forced to work on the farm from early morning to late night, seven days a week? And you couldn't lock them in the house forever.

"I'm sorry if you were uncomfortable about the conversation last night about gossip. We all understand why you are here and our village is a very tightly knit family of extended family and friends. You will be a wonderful addition and you must expect that our best way to keep you safe is to share the truth with the villagers. Mother and Andreas can get more done through whispers then you can ever imagine. Sure there are some mean spirited folks but they are the few."

"I understand; just bear with me Anna. Everything is so new to me and I miss my home. I cannot imagine that Robert Blackstone would go to that much effort to find me. It is my father who has voiced all the concern." After they had chatted for awhile, Anna went back inside. Olaf played with Iver's dog in the grass and Jenny walked across the pasture. She sat down on a boulder and watched a distant waterfall that looked like a bridal veil. Try as she might, she couldn't quit thinking about Robert. He was the reason she had to flee her home. She thought about how he had aroused her. She recalled his first kiss. Robert had never been a man to take his time with women; he had kissed her long and hard, releasing her only to stand back to relish the hunger he hoped would be reflected in her eyes. Pleased, he moved his body into hers; his fingers touched her face and gently followed the soft line of her neck across the contours of her breasts to stop above her pounding heart. He had laid his head against her breast to listen to her beating heart. Exploding with desire, his mouth found hers. *A memory, a memory,* she gasped and caught her breath, her heart pounding; the aching moistness in her body returned a flood of emotions. Flushed, dizzy, a heat swept through her and she cried to taste such passion again. Her arm covered her eyes from the tears. She sat up and looked back over the beautiful fjord wondering *Why,* why did it have to be so complicated? She thought of her parents and her promise to them to never see Robert again. Then she remembered that her mother once said, "Everything has a reason, Jenny, no matter what. You just don't see it when you are in the middle of it." Maybe mother was right or maybe not; maybe things just happened at random. She wondered if Robert would ever come and look for her. The way she knew him so far, she would not be surprised to see him climbing this mountain.

A couple of weeks later, Andreas and Iver returned from a trip to the village and handed Jenny a letter. She was overjoyed to see her father's familiar handwriting, expecting her first letter to be from her mother or aunt. She rushed into the privacy of her room and opened it; she could only imagine what had happened to her parents the day she left Kristiania.

My dearest daughter,

I must confess just hours have passed since you left your home and already missing you has greatly wounded your mother's heart and mine. So know that we love you dearly and excuse me if I move straight on to my reason for writing. In our last conversation before you left for Holseth, I only skirted over my past relationship with your Mr. Blackstone. Having since regretted not telling you all the specifics, I will now attempt to share with you a part of my history that I wish never had to be uncovered.

My experiences as a young man at sea were noteworthy. They set the stage of my formidable years and helped transform the man you know to be your father. Like many young men, I sought an adventure outside my native land. Eighteen years ago, when you were just four years old, I left your mother to make a fair sum of money as a sailor, traveled to England, signed aboard a beautiful schooner setting sail for Dakar in West Africa; it was a true adventure. Unfortunately while in Dakar, I cut my hand and an infection set into it whereupon I was hospitalized and my ship sailed on without me. After I recovered, I went looking for work and was abducted by Captain Robert Blackstone. His ship carried live cargo from West Africa to West India. Your Mr. Blackstone, my Captain Blackstone, was my past, and I pray not your future. I sadly repeat the worst of his crimes: he demanded slaves to be housed in coffin-like fashion on a terrifying month-long voyage; he laughed while ordering men to be tortured; he refused to pray over men who suffocated under his care. But the horror of horrors was watching him ruthlessly prepare to kill all the slaves off the deck of the Drayton. No man was ever less remorseful or cold-blooded than he who demands to win your heart. I know your heart; it is a combination of your mother's and mine, a kind heart. And ours will be broken until you return safely to Kristiania forgetting Robert Blackstone forever.

Your father,
Christian Mohr

The Mountain Ledge

"The afternoon knows what the morning never suspected." Swedish Proverb

During the first few weeks after reading the sobering letter from her father, Jenny wandered about the mountain. A guest at the Holseth farm had little to do other than stay out of the way. The family was generally busy from sun up till sun down. She wrote a little and read several of the books she had brought. She also had a passion for drawing and found she could sketch members of the family in the evening at the fire, the only time they sat for any period of time. Olaf was most impressed at the likeness of his picture and had brought her his menagerie of pets - turtles, spiders and the like. He was oftentimes quiet like his father and the most she could get out of him was a smile after handing him renderings to decorate his wall. Often she thought about wandering off to be alone; unfortunately Holseth wasn't a place where she could easily find sanctuary without curious eyes watching her every move. But most of all, she spent a whole lot of time thinking about her father's association with Robert and how it would all end. The most memorable day of her relationship with Robert had been when she was going to surprise him in his office wearing the summer dress he had bought for her. As she, in her childish manner, cheerfully had tiptoed down the hallway thinking how she would slowly open his door as if she were a ghost and then scare him, she noticed that his office door had been left ajar and she heard voices from inside.

"Make it look like an accident. Even though it takes a little more planning, I know you're the best for a job like that, Chen. I do not believe in people vanishing; the family will never stop looking and after a while they become suspicious. An accident my friend, funeral and the whole package - that's the way to go. He would be safe under the turf and we would be safe on top of it." Jenny's body had stiffened upon hearing Robert's voice and she moved a little closer.

"Why do you have to get rid of her father to marry her? "

"You don't understand. Her father knows my past and he will never let me marry her. I have only two options: take her with me to England or get rid of her father, or maybe both." She remembered her heart had pounded so hard she was afraid the men inside would hear it when she had slowly pulled back from the door, but she didn't remember how she had got out of the building.

Voices from the kitchen brought her back to the present as she was about to get out of her room, but after hearing Iver's voice, she sat back on the bed to wait until he had left. After half an hour, she became impatient and hungry and as she stepped into the narrow hallway, she heard him say, "Tar the boat? It doesn't need it until next year."

"Another year that boat will be so waterlogged it wouldn't be able to float a cat," snapped Andreas.

Both men looked up as she walked into the kitchen, greeted them and went about looking for something to eat.

"Did you sleep well?" asked Andreas, helping Iver untangle a fishing line.

"Yes, thank you," smiled Jenny, wondering if Iver would acknowledge her presence.

Iver both saw and heard her, but acted as if he didn't. He appeared to be anxious to get on with the day as he wrapped the line around his shoulders and spoke to Andreas. "All right, you win. Let's tar the boat."

Andreas began to clear the table when Jenny interrupted him, "Where is Marta?"

"Don't you remember Lars took her and the children to the village early this morning? Iver and I will be back late this afternoon. Most of the chores have already been done and Marta left the evening soup for when they return. Enjoy the peace and quiet. Anna might come over this afternoon to see you." He winked at her, then followed Iver and his dog out of the house. Iver barely acknowledged her presence.

Her prayers had been answered! An entire morning alone and she knew exactly what she would do. Plant the flower seeds from her mother's garden. She had found them in the pockets of one of her work dresses and if she were still at Holseth when they sprouted, it would be fun watching the surprise in these dear ladies' faces when the flowers matured and bloomed. With limited area of cultivable earth, she suspected the Holseth men would mow every square inch of the pasture, including the bedding in front of the house and around every rock and boulder. She would have to go elsewhere to find a spot and had noticed a small pasture up the mountainside that might escape the men's scythes. Before she knew it, she was outside enjoying the crisp, beautiful May morning.

She stood by the Outlook Boulder; how different it felt now after three weeks of living with the Holseth's! She watched the men walk down the path and wondered for the hundredth time why Iver disliked her so. She looked up at the snow-capped mountain peaks, over white-spotted meadows anchored in the hanging valleys, to the timberline where the final battle between winter and spring unfolded, creating a network of white foamy creeks. She scanned the mountainside over the seemingly bottomless crevasses, absorbed the beauty of the silent fjord, and rested her eyes on a cluster of white anemone growing at the banks of a nearby brook. The night had been cold and covered the brook with a thin layer of ice; she watched tiny drops of water forming under the ice. Like a dance, the drops merged with one another and dripped into the stream meandering through the pasture before it floated over the face of a cliff. Like a flapping curtain, the mist from the waterfall drifted toward a birch and doused the mouse-eared leaves where they sparkled like green emeralds. As the sun broke through the clouds, a beautiful rainbow appeared in its entire splendor, framing the scenery. Spring was the Holseth's family payoff for enduring the long, harsh, dark and cold winter.

Jenny couldn't get enough of this dazzled beauty, its contrasts beyond imagination. It was a timeless moment when she felt she was more than alive, when all her senses were tuned in to engulf nature in its purest form.

An hour later, with pickaxe in hand, she followed an animal trail heading up the mountainside. The beautiful morning and mystery about this mountain had awakened her adventuresome spirit to explore the unknown, a spirit she didn't know she had after being overprotected all of her life. Jenny didn't know the old stories of this area telling of strange sounds or bats and owls flying about in daylight. Some believed the ledge was haunted by an evil spirit; others were certain the devil himself lived deep inside a nearby crevasse. Whatever happened here, it was the most spectacular viewing point in the region but had become the forbidden side of Holseth under the name "The Ledge". Although there were many mountain ledges around, when The Ledge was mentioned, everybody knew what that meant. Jenny was too new to the land to know that you don't take on any path without knowing where it leads or how to get back. The old-timers knew that a trail to a place is not always the same one back.

The incline became steeper and Jenny's breathing increased as she ascended the slope, reminding her that she was not in such a good shape anymore. She had to slow down and take frequent breaks, making her question whether she should continue or give it up, but for every time she stopped and looked back, the panoramic view become more and more spectacular. She went on and on, higher and higher, steeper and steeper. It became like an obsession, just a few more steps until she could stop and admire the view again. Her feet began to slip on the loose gravel, creating small avalanches of dirt and rocks that tumbled down the mountainside. Old tree trunks crossed her path, hanging limbs scratched her face and slippery bedrock appeared in front of her like a stop sign, but oblivious to the danger signs nature provided, she continued toward a huge boulder she had pointed out as a place to rest. If she could just get up there, she promised herself she would return to the farm. As she reached the base of the boulder, she had to use the pickaxe to ascend the last few yards. She anchored the pickaxe into small cracks in the rock with one hand and grabbed on to heather and small bushes with the other and like a slow moving spider, she managed to drag herself to the top.

After regaining her breath, she looked down at the mountainside she had just conquered and it amazed her how far she had gotten. Climbing a steep mountainside gives the impression that you have gone much further then you would do on a flat terrain. She saw Holseth way down there, which reminded her of the playhouse Christian had once built for her back home. Jenny was proud of herself and felt a sense of accomplishment for the first time for as long as she could remember. She wondered what her mother, who wouldn't even allow her to climb the trees in their own backyard, would think if she saw her now. Would she finally be proud of her for accomplishing something or would her excessive cautiousness overrule all common sense as it had done for the last twenty-two years? Most likely she would be terrified if not hysterical.

The warming rays from the sun and the magnificent view over the meandering fjord tranquilized and energized her body in such a way she forgot her own promise of returning to the farm; instead, she looked up, trying to get her eyes on her next goal.

Nearing the boathouse, Iver and Andreas instinctively stopped to listen. Both were in tune with the sounds and vibrations of the mountain. Rocks were falling. Worried, Iver looked back at Andreas. "The Ledge."

The old man nodded in agreement.

"It's getting worse," said Iver hurrying down the path for a better view.

Andreas called out, "Would the goats be up there?"

"No, they know better, but it could be your sister."

"I don't think so. She moves around only at night."

Gusta was Andreas' youngest sister, born to their mother late in life. Frail at birth, she grew into a beautiful girl with blonde hair and intense blue eyes who had the habits of a butterfly, fluttering about, moving from place to place, never settling in one spot and always disappearing for days. At night when everyone was asleep, Gusta would waft about like a ghost, and in the morning the family could follow her trail by the crumbs she dropped. This did not unnerve her parents as much as her silence - she never spoke.

For sometime Andreas and Iver stood looking up at the mountain waiting for any more signs of trouble. Something other than water must be triggering the slide since it hadn't rained the last few days. It was usually the moist ground that set off the rocks.

The two men worked well together pulling the boat out from the boathouse, turning it upside down. It took only a few minutes to warm up the tar so it could be soft enough to smear it on the boat's keel. Andreas made the tar and what he didn't retain for his own use, he sold in the village. His small distillery consisted of a millstone, a wood keg, a two-yard long gutter, a large dome-shaped iron kettle and a pile of fir logs. Although a simple process anyone could do, he considered it an art, the same as brewing beer - every man had his own technique. There was good beer and there was bad beer; he believed it all depended on the ceremony and a few family secrets. The millstone had to be placed in a precise horizontal position with just a little decline toward its eye so the liquid could be collected. The first task was to locate premium raw material, fir rich in sap, preferably a damaged tree that couldn't be used for anything else, chop it up into small sticks and place it on top of the millstone. He'd light it and quickly cover the kettle - now came the trick. The inexperienced either burned up the wood too fast, producing very little tar, or they'd extinguish the fire and get nothing. Andreas would watch the fire like a mother watches her new born babe, letting in just enough air to keep it burning without extinguishing it. The exact amount of heat caused the wood to sweat out its moisture, which oozed through the eye of the millstone, into the gutter and collected in the keg. When all the tar dripped out of the wood, the fire died. After a while, the tar separated naturally from the water and sank to the bottom of the keg. The brownish colored water he would give to Marta who used it as a remedy for colds.

As soon as they started the tarring, the rumbling sounds returned. This time larger rocks tumbled down the mountainside.

Iver told Andreas that he wanted to check out what was up there and if he wasn't back in a couple of hours, he should just cover the boat with the canvas and leave it out until tomorrow. With his dog in hot pursuit, he started running by leaning forward and taking small steps, more tiptoeing than leaping which is the easiest way to run a steep slope. He hoped this did not involve Jenny and that it was just a goat that had gone astray as Andreas had suggested, but something inside of him told him it was Jenny. Why, he didn't know.

Further up the mountainside, Jenny had left the sturdy boulder and moved on to the erratic territory again and before knowing it, she ended up teetered on a narrow ledge, wondering how she had ever gotten there. What a frightful mess she was in, all for a few flower seeds! She was caught with no way back and no path down. How sudden the conditions had changed as they always do in the mountains. A chill flowed through her when she realized she had reached a point of no return. Fear and agony spurted over her like a sudden rain shower. Her body stiffened. Her heart was beating faster and she felt her knees could buckle any time. Instinctively she screamed out, "Anybody there? Hello, help me." But the only ones responding were the mountains with a ridiculing echo. It was like they were making fun of her. Thoughts began flowing through her - was she going to die up here in the wilderness? Become just another number claimed by nature? Marta would write to her mother telling her, "I am sorry but Jenny has died in an accident up in the mountains." Her eyes watered at the thought of seeing her family in the cemetery, watching them lowering her coffin into the ground. She imagined her crying mother, covered by a black veil, standing next to her unexpressive father. Would he ever cry or show any feeling at his own daughter's funeral? Images of the time when she wanted to commit suicide came back. She had felt she wasn't loved or cherished by any one and no matter what she did, nothing made any difference. She had been just like a fragile, fancy, dressed-up puppet sitting on top of their massive mahogany bookshelf, glancing out into the large and cold library. So why had she now gotten such a strong will to live? At least she felt alive, very alive. The blood flooded through her veins, putting all her cells on high alert by giving them an injection of adrenaline.

Survival is obviously not something we plan in the same way as we may plan for suicide. The survival instinct is somewhat similar for most living creatures and a person may attempt to commit suicide many times, but in the event of facing death outside one's own will, the body inhibits the thinking part of the brain and takes control.

Jenny began taking deep breaths and exhaling slowly, the best remedy to prevent panic her aunt had told her. Amazing how those small, but crucial details aid in a critical situation. Her aunt had told her time after time how important it was to try to stay calm by taking deep breaths when facing danger. Now, for the first time in her life, Jenny could use those words of wisdom and already after a couple a minutes she began to feel better, as though the fear and agony had been replaced by just uneasiness. She pressed her body against the bedrock and tried to figure out her next move when an obnoxious raven broke the silence. The squawking bird sat on a bough of a pine tree not too far from her.

Jenny had been told that ravens are messengers from the spirit world and when they appear, they have something to tell you. It might be a warning or just to light up the way. The raven remained Jenny of the old tale about a boy who had gotten lost in the woods. Hungry and scared, he had walked further and further away from his village. While sitting on a tree stump crying, a raven appeared above him. The bird had begun to jump between two branches, back and forth, back and forth like a dance. The boy had never seen a raven behaving like that and forgot for a moment his misery. As the raven moved on to the next tree and repeated his dancing game, the boy followed. This was getting fun to watch for the boy and just before the night totally encapsulated the forest, he saw the lights of his house.

Maybe the raven is showing me the way out of this Jenny thought. As she looked in the bird's direction, she noticed animal droppings on a narrow horizontal ledge of the bedrock. She believed that if an animal could get over there, she could too. She found a crack to anchor the pickaxe and tried to reach the other ledge by keeping her body close to the bedrock and moving slowly alongside the swelling.

She held her breath and told herself there was nothing to be afraid of. As soon as she began to move, the raven flew away and the mountain became silent again. In the middle, between the two ledges, she suddenly froze in her tracks; she could have sworn she heard another person climbing right behind her, but when she stopped, the sound behind stopped. She started laughing to overcome her fear, an artificial and heartless laugh that came from somewhere far from her heart. Of course it had been the sound of her own foot steps and body's stroke against the bedrock that she had heard. But as she begun to move again, so did the sound. "Stop it! Get away," she yelled.

"Get away, away, away," the mountain responded.

"You're a fool," she screamed.

"A fool, fool, fool, fool."

As the mountains became quiet, she inched her body as silently as she could with sudden and abrupt stops as if she wanted to surprise the invisible behind. Then she heard something she hadn't noticed before. The sound behind her was out of sync - it was delayed. When she stopped, the sound behind her stopped a fraction of a second later. She tried to laugh again, the same heartless laugh, but it soon died and the only thing she heard was her own heartbeat. Was she hearing just imaginary sounds? Maybe her mind was indeed playing a game with her. "I don't want to play this game anymore," she yelled.

"Anymore, anymore, anymore," the mountain responded.

Jenny took a deep breath and moved quickly over the last part of the swelling, took one last leap and landed safely on the other ledge. She looked around wondering, *What now?*

By the time Iver reached the ladder, he almost tore it down as he tripped and dived headfirst into a thicket. Back on his feet, he scooped up his dog and rushed up the ladder, running the rest of the way to the house. "Jenny, Jenny, are you there?" He stormed into the house and opened her bedroom door. Finding no trace of her in the house, he headed to the barn, but with same result. He looked up the mountain path. "No, this can't be happening again!" In sheer frustration and fearing the worst, he kicked an empty bucket so hard it tumbled across the pasture, scaring the heck out of a cat that hid under the front steps of the house. His dog backed off while a flock of clucking hens sought refuge in the barn. They all seemed to know that when Iver was in that mood, they better stay far out of his way. Iver took off up the mountainside, wondering about how far Jenny had gone. If he knew for sure, he could take a shortcut and cut her off, as he would do with any animal, preventing it from running into a deadlock. He thought about yelling at her, but then remembered his first impression - stubborn as a goat, so it would be best to just treat her like one. Why couldn't she find another place to go? Why do they all seem to want go up there? He could understand that animals would be drawn to the green pasture, but not people. Especially after his wife's death he never went to The Ledge. The morning of her death, he remembered seeing her climbing up there while he was hauling timber below; he had yelled and motioned to her to come down. By the time he made it to the ledge where she sat, at the edge of a boulder looking out over the fjord, it was already too late. Within seconds the earth moved under her and the boulder went tumbling down the canyon. Her last look, outstretched arms and pure terror, was the last time he had seen her alive and her body had never been found.

Iver's trained eyes scanned the slope in front of him for fresh footprints. He looked for broken twigs and rocks that had been moved out of position. He had long ago lost his confidence in his dog's ability to smell;

Andreas argued that he didn't even smell his own pee. And to a certain degree, Iver must admit his grandfather was probably right. But he loved his dog and he would let him follow him to the bitter end. Now the dog was running back and forth in front of him, poking his nose into everything. Iver would let him at least believe that he was helpful.

Standing on the ledge looking at the area around her, Jenny realized there was no way back, no way forward and no way up. Luckily for her, the ledge was wide enough so she could sit down and at least feel safe there and then. She could even sleep on the ledge if she had too. After a while, the fear had almost disappeared and she began seeing the humor in it all. She tried to push the fearful thoughts further away by amusing herself with some of Andreas' stories where she felt just like the goat the fisherman once spotted on a tiny ledge about ten yards straight up from the fjord. After several unsuccessful attempts to rescue her, a person went down in a rope to scare her to jump into the water where two men hauled her safely into to a rowboat. As a thank you gesture, the cold, wet and frightened goat made such a stir in the boat that they all ended up in the cold fjord. Jenny prayed she would find a way out and get safely off the ledge in such a way that this moment would later just become a good story and she could be the one telling it. It is often the best stories that contain the most frightening moments. She looked one more time at the branches of the spruce that almost reached her; if she jumped, the branches would cushion her fall, but would they cushion enough? There was only one way to find out. She took a deep breath, made a silent prayer and jumped as far as she could out from the ledge. The echo of her scream reached her as the branches scraped her face with their sharp needles and tore her clothes. Just before hitting the ground, her dress became entangled in the branches of the spruce and for a moment, she swung upside down like a doll before her straps tore and she fell headfirst into a thicket. Her drama was over almost as suddenly as it began. She was safe with just a few painful scratches. She looked up at the ledge and began to laugh, realizing that fear and laughter do indeed go hand in hand sometimes.

Loaded with self-esteem about her climbing abilities, Jenny decided she would try to find a path and continue to the pasture and plant the flower seeds. Half an hour later, she stood on a ledge overlooking the most beautiful view she had ever experienced. The breathtaking scenery made her forget herself and the drama she had just gone through for a moment. She untied her hair and allowed the gentle breeze to blow her curls apart and found herself in a world of complete stillness and peace. If she could divide herself like a cell into several identical elements, she would be at many places at the same time, breathing in the intense beauty.

Suddenly, a tormented moan came from the ravine below. Jenny crept close to the ledge's end to get a better view when a sudden and powerful cold wind caught her off guard, pushing her back. She kneeled, crawled forward and looked deep into the ravine, but didn't see anything other than black bedrock all the way down to the fjord. Then she heard a flapping noise behind her. She turned around but saw nothing other than a raven restlessly turning its head back and forth.

"Was that you stupid bird trying to scare me?" She clapped her hands and the raven took off, making no more noise than a feather falling to the ground.

"Ho..ho..ho..ho..." she heard from the ravine. The deep, growling, cruel-sounding laugh echoed between the mountains before it faded away. Confused and scared about all the unfamiliar sounds, she searched for a higher place to sit and climbed up on top of a tall boulder. She would sit quietly and get her bearings before finding a spot to plant her seeds. She heard a stick crack once, then a second time. It must be footsteps. At first she tried to look as far back as she could; then she spun around finding nothing but the small brown pasture covered with scattered rocks. This place seemed very odd. It felt like people were all around her, making all sorts of frightening sounds and yet, she was alone with only a scraggly raven.

Iver found Jenny at the edge of the pasture and he broke out in a sweat. His first instinct was to scream at her to get back, but he stopped himself, afraid he might startle her, causing her to fall. He began to slowly walk behind her, praying she would remain still until he could pull her to safety. Before he could softly call out her name, his vision became unclear. He blinked several time trying to regain his sight, wiped his eyes with his shirtsleeve and instead of Jenny sitting before him with her red curls about her, the hair was blonde; it was the silhouette of his wife. Her ghostly image flashed in front of him as he dropped to the ground. This *is not happening to me*, he thought as he painfully wiped at his eyes and the vision disappeared, leaving Jenny before him. On his knees he felt the earth move ever so softly and saw small pebbles of rocks and dirt began to slide on both side of Jenny's boulder. "Damn it," he whispered, realizing the boulder was coming loose. There was not much time left. He approached her like a skittish deer, walking softly across the small pasture. When he was within arm's length, he leaned down and with a snake-like swiftness, he wrapped his arms around her and yanked her off the boulder.

Jenny screamed out, kicked her legs in the air and swinging her arms at him.

Iver told her to shut up and while taking a couple of leaps, he tripped and fell with Jenny ending up in his lap. His anger erupted, "What in God's name were you thinking to come up here?"

"I am thinking? What are you thinking, scaring me like this?" she snapped, trying to get away from him. "Let me go, let me go!"

"Hold still!"

They both became numb, watching as the boulder began to move ever so slowly. Then it made a loud cracking sound and within seconds, tumbled down the mountain heading for the fjord, leaving behind a cloud of dust and a big black hole in the ground.

Iver released her, picked up a small packet from the ground and turned toward her. "What is this?"

"Seeds."

"You are planting seed - for what?

"Flowers."

He looked down on her. "Flowers, flowers are weeds...they destroy a pasture." He took the satchel from her and more seeds dropped to the ground...he stooped down, scooped up the seeds and shoved them into Jenny's hands, tossing the satchel at her feet. "Who gave you these seeds?"

She blinked in astonishment, wondering why he was so angry and turned away from him.

"Pick up every seed, do you understand? Every seed. Not even a pig could live on flowers!"

Her knees shook and she dropped to the ground to collect them, thankful to be alive so she could kill him. She mumbled, "I hate you."

Iver laughed. "I never asked to take care of you, a girl the likes of you with no sense. What use are you to me? This is my land, my home. After you have gone, my son and I cannot eat your damn flowers. When you are done picking up your seeds, burn them." He suddenly became quiet and listened, "What was that?"

"The moaning sound?"

Iver nodded, "You heard it before?"

"Several times."

"Never come here again. Now let's go."

As soon as they were back at the farm, Jenny rushed into her room and abruptly closed the door. She would make plans to return home; she would go home. She could not stay here another minute; she hated Iver, an insensitive oaf of a man. Moments later, she heard a soft knock on her door and Anna's voice, "Are you all right?"

"Yes, I'm just fine."

Jenny's clothes were strewn about the bed and shoved into her bags. "Iver's upset and wouldn't tell me what's happened." "Nothing happened except, except..." then Jenny burst into tears. "He saved me from falling into the fjord." "Were you near a ledge with an extraordinary nice view?" The tears were still flowing as Jenny nodded in agreement. "That explains why Iver is so upset. You are a very lucky woman. He lost his wife on that ledge."

The shock on Jenny's face surprised Anna. "I would have thought Mother would have told you about Iver's wife. Jenny, on this mountain we have places that appear to be heaven and others as hell, and that ledge is on the darker side. There is a dark ravine below where several people have died and if you hadn't noticed, there are no animals that step foot on that soil. It is too dangerous. The ledge may one day split off the side of the mountain and no one takes the chance of going with it. Iver is a man of few words - maybe too few - and sometimes I wish he would open up more. He keeps his thoughts to himself. It takes time to understand him. He was different once, before Father died."

"What happened to your father?"

"Iver was a man wanting his own land and had proposed a split of Holseth, taking the land further up the mountain. Father and Grandfather argued for days about the danger on the opposite side until Grandfather finally gave in and Iver began building his home. The first winter, while they were working on the final construction of the barn, an avalanche took the barn and our father with it."

"I'm so sorry!" Jenny wondered why anyone would want to stay on this mountain when there were safer places to live.

Anna moved forward and touched her shoulder. "Thank you. Our father was a good man, but the tragedy took a toll on everyone and I always had a feeling Iver blamed himself for the accident. He tried to get on with his life and with his grandfather's help, he continued building his home and a few months later, he moved his wife and their newborn son, Olaf, into the main house. Then tragedy struck that summer when she fell off the ledge where you were today. None of this excuses the way Iver acts; all it can do is explain that his sullen nature is not something he was born with."

For the first time since meeting Iver, Jenny felt like a heel. How cruel and unkind she had been to him! How it must have felt coming to the same spot and saving her! *Oh how thoughtless I've become.* "Anna, thank you. I've been so foolish. Where is Iver now?"

"I believe he's in the barn, cooling off,"

Jenny quickly went to the barn looking for Iver. She was near the door when she heard voices.

"She's young and spoiled and I did everything I could to change Mother's mind in allowing her to live with us."

Jenny stopped and through a crack in the door, she saw Iver pacing back and forth in front of Andreas.

"She's going to get herself killed or one of us."

Andreas raised his hand. "Iver, calm down. She's not that much of a bother. We'll have Marta talk to her and keep her closer to the house."

"She's in the way. We are not a boarding house for rich girls; she belongs in the city or the village. She can't cook, she can't help with chores. What does she do but wander the farm, sketching pictures while the rest of us are working for our livelihood."

Jenny's eyes blistered; of course she was everything he said she was, spoiled and inconsiderate. The family treated her as a guest; she'd offered to help but always felt in the way. She decided not to talk to Iver and walked back to the house.

"I think something else is stirring you up, Boy. Don't think I've ever seen you this fired up about anything." Iver ignored his grandfather's remark and returned to his own farm. He was confused, angry and frustrated. This young woman from Kristiania had stirred up emotions in him. She reminded him of what was missing in his life. He would try his best to avoid her. What a man doesn't see does him no harm.

He stayed at his farm for an entire week without visiting his mother and refusing to attend church on Sunday. Anna begged everyone to leave him alone, reminding all of them that this was the anniversary of his wife's death. Marta finally found her son heading down to the boathouse and hurried after him.

"For what are you in such a hurry?"

"I am off to the village."

"Village, without saying hello or asking if we need something?

"I need to get moving before Utroeno comes."

The seasonal afternoon wind that during the months of July and August blows from the ocean toward the mountains can get quite intense and many have been surprised in the middle of the fjord by its power forcing them to immediately seek harborage.

"Utroeno, this time of the year?" You can't be serious. Your grandfather would laugh his head off. That's not a good enough excuse for not stopping by five minutes to say hello to your mother. Let's get into the house. At least you can ask your grandfather if he needs something from the village or maybe Jenny can go with you? I think it would be good for both of you."

Defeated, Iver followed his mother into the house to find Jenny in work clothes, cleaning the kitchen. Their eyes met and Jenny smiled up at him. He was so taken by seeing her working that it took a moment to gain composure. It was agreed that Jenny and Andreas would accompany Iver to the village and Jenny would help pick up the few supplies Marta needed at the grocers. It would be hours before the two were able to be alone in the village outside the grocer's store and discuss the ledge incident.

"I want to apologize to you, Iver. Sometimes I am so headstrong that I don't see clearly. You saved my life. Thank you." Jenny extended her hand to him and just as he was about to take it, Andreas came running out of the grocers.

"Was it sugar your mother needed or flour?" he asked, surprised to find Jenny and Iver holding hands.

"Sugar," said Jenny quickly removing her hand.

"Mother gave you a list; it is in your shirt pocket," said Iver, wishing Andreas had stayed in the store.

"You're right, she did give me a list," said Andreas going back into the store.

Before meeting Jenny, Iver had decided he needed a strong woman from the village to live with him and raise Olaf. His sister, Anna, kept reminding him there weren't so many unmarried women within the village to choose from and if he waited much longer, he'd have to take whatever was available. Something had always held him back, even when he denied the need to live again with love. Was it the women he didn't understand or was it himself? There was at least one piece of his emotional understanding missing. The picture he had of Jenny now seemed altered and while rowing back to the farmhouse, listening to her conversation with his grandfather, he wondered if it was spring or love blossoming.

The Midsummer Visit

"Midsummer night is not long, but it sets many cradles rocking." Swedish Proverb

On June 23rd, two months after Jenny had the frightening experience on the mountain ledge and had settled into life on the mountain, she was invited to join the Holseth family in celebrating Midsummer. Summer solstice is incorporated into the Christian calendar as the feast day of St. John the Baptist and known as the day the sun stands still. The nights are as light as the days and it is believed to be when the earth's feminine energies peak. The women gathered healing herbs to throw on the bonfire to banish sickness and prevent bad luck, while the men drank beer and paced around like ornery ganders looking for a mate. It was a day in the middle, between the hectic spring farming and busy hay season, when everybody could take a short break and celebrate nature, a time when romances flourished like dandelions on a pasture.

Jenny woke up early in the morning and stood at the front door of the farmhouse to watch the moving shadows form cotton-white clouds, turning the valley, mountainside, and pasture into a bright and vibrant scene, accentuating the lush vegetation, shimmering in a symphonic blend of green. Buzzing bumblebees migrated from one colorful wildflower to the next and butterflies fluttered aimlessly, accompanied by an orchestra of grasshoppers and birds. Outside a fenced vegetable garden, a cow, tempted by the dark green leaves, reached out and stole a mouthful before pulling back and swatting flies to the hollow sound of her neck-bell. At Holseth as with other farms in the region, animal husbandry and agriculture were closely intermixed sources of livelihood and consequently the crop had to be protected from the animals. A dozen goats with brimming udders had surrounded the front of the house and taken strategic positions on boulders, the roof and stairs, waiting patiently to be milked.

That morning Jenny offered to help Marta with the milking, pulling weeds from the potato garden and baking the crisp flat bread they would take to the dairy farm. Andreas announced he would leave precisely at five in the afternoon and warned everyone to be ready for he would not wait. The truth was, everyone usually waited on him while Anna and Jon had offered to stay and do the evening and morning chores on both farms now that Anna was with child. The anticipation amongst the Holseth family was running high and everyone was in a lighter mood despite all the work that must get done before they left the farm. The feasting would go nonstop all night and it would be noon the next day before everyone returned.

By three o'clock in the afternoon, Jenny was exhausted and made herself a soft bed in the grass. She still wasn't used to such hard labor; her arms were hurting after rolling out dough and her back ached from pulling weeds. As she lay down, she wondered how the women could do such work, day after day. Lars had explained to her that their work schedule had been adopted based on horse capability. An early morning shift from five to eight, morning from nine to noon, the afternoon from two to five and in the evening from six to nine. Some days during the hectic hay season, the men would extend the evening a few more hours until dusk. With plenty of rest throughout the day to regain their strength, the schedule worked and would last until the last bit of grain and hay was harvested and stored for the winter.

"Jenny, Jenny, wake up. It's time to go!" Lars sat down next to her. *What a beautiful face she has,* he thought. He took a long piece of grass and began stroking her forehead. "Wake up Sleepy head; you've slept the hours away." Red curls framed her face; he wrapped one around his finger, brushed it against her nose and laughed when she sneezed. "Aren't you hungry?"

"Lars, what are you doing? Stop it!" she pulled the grass from his hand and pushed him back. Sadness came over her, awakening at the farmhouse and not where her dreams had taken her, walking in her mother's garden back home in Kristiania.

"You look so sad. Come, I can smell food. It will cheer you up and I am famished." Lars helped her up and as they walked up the field to the farmhouse, his lively chatter brightened her spirit. He would easily laugh at himself as his vivid imagination took him in several directions.

Walking beside him, it was difficult to not get caught up in his animated gestures and it was easy to see why so many women in the region had their eye on him. "If he'd just sit still long enough," remarked Marta, "maybe one day a woman could catch him."

After the light afternoon meal, Jenny retired to her room to change clothes. She hoped to have enough time to write her mother so she could mail it while in the village. She pushed the small, makeshift table against the tiny window to capture the daylight, dipped the pen and began:

June 23, 1880

Dear Mother

How would I ever believe just a few months ago that I would be sitting in this closet of room at a place almost unapproachable for wingless creatures, writing this letter?

I was shocked when my father revealed the story about Robert and I am sometimes still denying it in the hope it isn't true, but I guess sooner or later, the truth will prevail. I need to admit there were times when I wondered what was under his smooth, kind and charming surface. Could he possible be everything I had hoped for, including being accepted by you and my father or was he just too good to be true? Now, I have come to turn with the truth and accepted that Robert was not what he appeared, and I understand that the water was rougher under the surface then above and that a face doesn't always reveal what the mind is up to. And I guess my father was right when he said Robert is a thorn surrounded by roses.

Although I am learning to live with simple means that I never knew people could survive on, and wish I was home, the family here has been very nice to me. Marta's oldest daughter Anna is a true pleasure to be around and the first time I met her I wondered how can such a beauty be hidden away on a mountain? Marta's father, Andreas, is the family's storyteller, a role he performs with an enthusiasm that spellbinds the family just by the snap of his fingers. Lars, Marta's youngest son, seems to be the family's creative mind, always pondering either to improve something or just for the fun of it making the rest of the family walk on their toes. He's funny, speaks with an open mind and shares his feelings, in strong contrast to his brother, Iver, who's serious, angry and keeps his feelings to himself. It's obvious that Iver doesn't like me, but he has his own place so I don't run into him very often. His sister told me that his personality changed after losing both his father and wife to the mountain. Then there is Gusta, Andreas' youngest sister. I have never seen her, only heard her sneaking out of the house at night. She moves about like a spirit, but does no harm to anybody; she's Holseth's resident ghost.

A few weeks ago while climbing a part of this mountain, it dawned on me that we cannot tame, control and impose our will on nature the same way people struggle to do with each other in business and love. And instead of getting hostile, angry and deceitful, you learn to live on the mountain's premises. They can be your enemy or your friend, they may reveal you or protect you and it's crucial to acknowledge, respect and accept them to survive. While learning this essential lesson, something happened inside of me - somebody was knocking on the door of my heart. It was like a little child that wanted get out and play, to be free from what ifs, buts and maybes; to feel the blood rushing through my veins, to smell the mountain air, to touch the ancient bedrock, to hear the chirping birds and to admire the spectacular scenery. Now I know who that somebody was. It was me, Jenny, your only daughter who has many times felt like a caged bird. I am not saying this to hurt you; you did everything with the best intention to protect me, keep me amused, sending me to the best school and everything you thought I wanted, I could have. My financial future was secured; I would be sheltered from the rain and wouldn't have to do anything. Now I know how it feels like to be wet and cold, terrified and exhausted, hungry and thirsty and to have accomplished something.

I love you, Mother, even though there have been times I thought I hated you, especially when you did not accept Svein's family. But perhaps there was a reason for it and what would have happened if I married him? I will never know, but I want you to know that I have forgiven you. You had a reason for doing what you did. It's not always easy to have only one child. Now the bird is out of its cage and I feel free for the first time in my life and I want you to remember the looser the ties, the stronger the bond.

Your loving daughter
Jenny

Jenny folded the letter and carefully put it into an envelope. A rummage in the kitchen reminded her that she would have to hurry up if she was going with them to the village.

An hour later, a rowboat with the family onboard glided through the silent and clear water alongside the steep mountains that dived down through its surface and apparently disappeared into a bottomless pit. Jenny sat in the back and had already gotten out some fishing gear and was anxiously waiting for the big moment, to catch the first fish in her life. She had never seen a fish other than the ones that appeared on her dinner plate. Excited like a child, she pulled the line rhythmically as she was told. "The three most important things with fishing," Andreas said, "are patience, patience and patience." Jenny watched the shoreline where the seaweed made a brown line from the water to the bedrock thinking how amazing high and low tide was. How can so much water just rise and fall every day, year around? The smell from the seaweed tore her nose and was so distinctive that once you have smelled it, you will always recognize it. One of those smells that can't be explained by words, it has to be experienced. *But how can you ever explain any smell for that sake*? she wondered.

Marta sat in the front, watching the clouds drifting slowly to the west, a possible sign of continuing good weather, but according to Andreas, there would be rain because the cat had been eating grass. She had been up since four o'clock, preparing the dough for the flat bread she and Jenny had baked. All the women would bring food to share and the men made sure there was enough beer to fill a small pond. Marta didn't care so much for the frothy beverage but it made the men loosen up and more eager to dance and the women of the village loved to dance! She wondered if the Bailiff would stay and if this year she might get the courage to ask him to dance. Beyond childbearing age, Marta was still a prize for any man; several had come forward with gifts of proposals but she knew they wanted a woman who would cook and clean their houses. Her heart was still young, waiting for the right man to come forward. Her thoughts were disrupted by her father's voice.

"Did you get your herbs?" he asked

"Of course I did - not a Midsummer celebration without them," said Marta and shoved him a bouquet of various herbs she had picked.

"As long as you don't become like that Von Bingen lady."

"What are you talking about, Father?"

"Didn't your grandmother tell you about that woman? Don't you know that soon after she wrote about this herb healing stuff, the witch-hunt started and killed millions?"

"Are you talking about Sybil of the Rhine, the German writer from the twelfth century?" Marta was glad her father had mentioned the person she knew a lot about; this could be her unique opportunity to impress him. "..tenth child in the family who dedicated her to the church because they couldn't feed her? Who advised bishops, popes, and kings, used curative powers of natural objects for healing. Wrote thesis about natural history and medicinal uses of plants, animals, trees and stones and argued that the strength of love leads to a bitter daughter and lack of semen determines the child's sex. Is that the woman you're talking about?" she asked proudly.

"The other way around, Marta. The strength of the semen determines the child's sex, not the lack of it," corrected Andreas. "You did learn about her, I can tell."

Marta blushed and looked down in the boat a moment, but regained her posture quickly. "Of course I did. The problem is that you don't even remember after I got my first book from your mother and read about those things, I helped you get well from your ear inflammation, not once but three times. When you didn't send me off to continue my education, afraid of losing your only child, do you really think I stopped reading in between diaper changes, nursing, cooking, spinning, sawing and heavens knows what? Of course you don't remember that. I'll tell you one thing - if it wasn't for the books I could hide behind, wrapped in rags in the loft's room, I wouldn't be here talking to you today."

Andreas cleared his throat. "I do remember, though, that you have always had your speaking organ in the right place and maybe I have forgotten your knowledge about Von Bingen. I just want to make sure we don't threaten the Priest's power again. The likes of you would be among the first they throw on the bonfire."

"Come on, Father, that's hundred of years ago! People have gotten their senses back and don't succumb to a group of fanatic Catholic Priests anymore."

"They don't? Look at the obedient lambs in the church on Sundays and what enthralling effect the Priest has on the congregation."

"How would you know, you who hardly goes to church?"

"I have been there enough to see what's going on."

"You know it depends on the eyes that see and since we're not going to church today, let's instead find out how to get in to the valley or have you planned for us to walk the ten miles?"

"No, I have already thought about it."

Marta looked at the mountainside again and wondered how many times she had seen the same crevasses, waterfalls and weird-looking pine trees whose snow and rock avalanches had formed into troll-looking monsters. Some had their entire root system grabbing around large boulders like a gigantic octopus stretching its long fingers deep into every crack it could find. It had always amazed her how alive the mountain appeared to be, allowing her to discover something new every time.

Suddenly Jenny broke the silence and screamed out, "I have a fish, Andreas! Look! I have a fish."

Andreas took the line and as the fish reached the water's surface, Lars shouted, "A sea trout! Jenny, you've caught a trout! Wish it was larger; we could bake it on the bonfire tonight. This one isn't big enough to feed a bird." He swung the fish onboard.

"Give it here Boy. I have an idea," said Andreas, taking the fish and carefully releasing it from the hook. He held it up in front of him and spoke directly to the fish. "Calm down, calm down. I have something for you." Andreas pulled up a flask of cognac hidden in a side pocket, ripped the cork off with his teeth and poured a little bit of the liquid into the fish's mouth. He stroke the fish gently on his back, looked into his eyes and said, "Now go back and tell your grandfather there's more left in the bottle." He gently dropped the fish back into the fjord.

Lars looked at Jenny and smiled, "We can be glad it wasn't the water serpent's baby, otherwise we'd all be dropped into the water."

"Water serpent, are you serious?" Jenny had a worried look on her face.

"Years ago," Andreas began, "I and several boys from the neighboring farms decided to find the great Fjord Serpent. This was a mighty serpent the villagers believed lived in the deepest waters. At midnight on the day of the summer solstice, a night of the full moon, the boys secretly met at my parents' boathouse before rowing toward Skrenakken, a place where the fjord is more than fifteen hundred feet deep. An hour of heavy rowing tired the boys and they were no longer interested in finding the great monster; instead they turned back for home before their parents found them missing. As the boat began turning, they heard a mighty splash and a thud pushed the boat back. Terrified, they frantically rowed until they were a safe distance away. As they looked back at the fjord, the moonlight lit up the side of the mountain where the shadow of a giant, twisted snake-like creature appeared to weave in and out of the water. Then suddenly another splash and the shadow vanished. Afraid the serpent was coming after them, they rowed to save their lives." Andreas looked at Olaf who was swallowing every word. "The next morning," Andreas continued, "they shared the story of the shadowed creature with their families and only one old man believed them, one of the boys' grandfathers, for he, too, had seen the shadow of the Fjord Serpent when he was just a boy."

Jenny had heard tales of great monsters in the fresh and salt waters of Western Norway and knew many people believed they existed, but she had never been in waters where creatures might be. The beautiful fjord had just taken on a menacing look, making her feel a bit uncomfortable.

"It was a sign of good luck," said Andreas as he winked at Jenny.

Olaf looked up at his grandfather. "When I am older, I will go find the sea creature and slay him with my dagger if he tries to harm me," he said as he poked Kari in the back, pretending she was the sea monster.

Marta scolded Andreas. "Look what you've done now, filling the child's head with stories of sea creatures. You should be ashamed of yourself. All you boys saw was the shadow of a tree or a log against the mountain wall, and the thud could have been a floating tree or limb hitting the side of your boat. You're full of nonsense; I say no one has ever seen a sea monster except a group of old drunken men or over-imaginative boys."

"Don't listen to your grandmother boy; she wasn't born with a lick of imagination herself or an understanding about men and their adventures."

Throughout the entire trip, Iver remained quiet; all of his energy was spent rowing and keeping the slow rhythm of his grandfather and then a faster speed with Lars. Sometimes he listened to the conversations and other times his thoughts drifted away like the passing logs in the fjord or the birds flying overhead. Always he was aware of Jenny.

From her position back in the boat, Jenny had full control of what everybody was doing or looking at. She though about the little game she played with the man who had rowed them the very first day; he had been sitting in the same spot as Iver was sitting now and had been examining her a way only a man would do. She tried secretly to capture Iver's eyes without him noticing it, wondering if he would look at her the same way, but after a while she realized that he appeared oblivious to everyone else in the boat. He was completely in his own world. Not knowing what he was thinking made him even more interesting to her.

When they got the village Stranden in sight, Andreas brought up the story about how they believed the first settlers had inhabited the village. The tale suggest that in the year 1349, when the Black Death- the plague that killed so fast that you could be eating breakfast with your family and dinner with your ancestors in paradise - swept over the country, only two people survived in Stranden, a man and a woman. Neither of them knew about the other and both believed they were the only survivors. Then one night, the man had a dream that he saw a crying woman holding a dead child in a small house with a stone chimney. The images of the dream haunted him for several days until he decided to search for her. He left the remnants of his farm and headed across a mountain ridge. Having lost his wife, children, parents, friends and the rest of his community, he had nothing more to lose. He came to an adjacent valley where he began a relentless search from house to house, from farm to farm, but the only thing he ran into was the horror of death. He must have wanted to give up many times and wished he was dead too, but the voice inside of him said he must continue. Finally, after several more days, he saw smoke coming from a small house. The dream had come true and the rest is history, but the villagers are still thankful to the man who went after his dream and never gave up. This never giving up has ever since become a trademark of people in Stranden." Andreas ended the story with a solid slap on his chest in a proud gesture of his heritance.

At the village, they moored the boat to the wharf and carried their packs up the main street before stopping at the church. Andreas had made arrangements with a friend to pick them up and soon they found their places in the open wagon that would take them to the Seter, which is a small dairy farm or cheese farm away from the main farm. It's practical to have it where the cattle graze, instead of carrying the milk all the way down to the farm every day. The cheese farm is usually run by a young, unmarried maid; she stays in the Seter for the entire summer by herself.

Jenny had difficulties understanding that the girl would be alone the entire summer.

"Alone and alone," Lars commented. "The maids are not more alone than what they want to be; there are plenty of Sjyvjarar around."

"Sjyvjarar, what is that? You use so many strange words, Lars"

"The official meaning is a man who is proposing marriage," said Lars, smiling, "but we call practically every man who visits these lonely girls a Sjyvjarar."

"There are many stories about Sjyvrarar," said Andreas, "and how eager they have been in their search for a night in the hay."

Marta poked him in his side, reminding him the he didn't need to tell those stories now.

It was eight o'clock when they finally arrived at a meadow surrounded by three-thousand-foot tall mountains and a wide-open valley. Several turf-covered timber lodges and sheds surrounded the crystal clear brook flowing through the soft green pasture. Darker spots of grass and poison ivy were scattered around the pasture, reminding everybody where the cows had relieved themselves. The sun towering above the mountains would soon begin to descend and fill the valley with a two-mile long shadow. The east mountain ridges had another couple of hours with sunshine before twilight which would last until three o'clock in the morning when the sun rose again. Everyone had brought an extra sweater or coat with plans to remain throughout the night. The wagon had hardly stopped before Olaf and Kari jumped off and rushed to a group of children playing in the meadow. Everyone began walking towards men in the field dropping timber logs and dried bushes in a circle. This would be the center of the activity as the night wore on - the Midsummer bonfire to be lit at twilight.

About fifty people of all ages were spread around; some sat on the roof of the timber lodges, others on moss-covered rocks and tufts of grass, while some had gathered in small groups and a few others just strolled around. On top of an old rusty wood stove was a large kettle. "Smells like sour cream porridge," said Jenny as she and Marta passed by and placed their flat bread on the table next to the stove.

"You bet it is! It isn't a real Midsummer night without sour cream porridge," said Marta and sized up the other delicacies on the table. Different kind of biscuits, smoked cured ham, a coil of Mør, a special coarse sausage and of course, smoked leg of lamb, the real backbone for beer snack and most men's favorite meat.

Suddenly, the door to a lodge opened and two men waddled out with a huge cask between them and placed it on a flagstone. The mood among the men increased; some hooted, others cheered as their watering hole had been established and immediately they began to line up. Andreas was among the first and after getting his mug filled, he met the woman known only as The Widow, or "the old man's saving grace," as some called her.

Jenny and Marta had just sat down on a tree stump near the bonfire when a middle-aged, potbelly man, supporting an accordion, began to play. The louder music lifted the mood for the celebration and the villagers and farmers began to laugh and talk louder as dancers entered the area in front of the musician. Jenny had to smile. She had never seen people dancing on grass before and wondered how they managed to slide their feet on such a surface. While examining an older couple, she noticed that they did not slide their feet; they made small jumps from side to side, which explained their funny jerking motion. It was certainly different from the ballroom dance in Kristiania she was used too! She remembered the last time she went there with Robert when she felt like a queen on the top of her throne. But that was then, the time she believed she had found the man of her life.

She pushed the thought of Robert away and continued watching the locals.

Robert Blackstone and his bounty hunter, a giant of a man nicknamed Big, sat outside the two-roomed courthouse waiting for the Bailiff. Blackstone's men had finally traced Miss Mohr to several villages in this region and they'd narrowed it down to Stranden after Big had quietly been sitting in the local store, listening to the locals discussing their curiosity about the city woman. The day before Robert left Kristiania, he had received an untimely telegram from Queen Victoria expressly requesting his presence in England by November, which meant he had little time to waste in finding Jenny and persuading her to go with him. He planned to take her to England as his wife or lover; she had no choice in the matter once he abducted her or saved her from this poor village. And her father back in Kristiania could be as mad as he wanted. Robert's entire life had been spent making people angry and it didn't help that his appearance matched his temperament. His strong facial features resembled those of a sea hawk - dark, brooding, yet disturbingly handsome; men hated him on sight while it took women a little longer. Financially a success, he had secured his future long before by turning one ship into a fleet through every deceitful means made available to him, gaining him more enemies than a man needed in a lifetime. A successful, unpredictable shipbuilder, he held a prominent position at Queen Victoria's court; his successes procured him sanctions and under the guise of honest acts, he continued to commit crimes.

In the dead of winter, Robert Blackstone had come to Norway on business. For months he had suffered the frigid climate along with the cold, secretive Norwegians. Never had he met businessmen who showed so few emotions as the Norwegians before, or even after, money passed hands, making it impossible to see who was most satisfied with the deal. Now, with final negotiations under way, he would be purchasing enough wood from the Finnskog Forest to refurbish the Queen's aging ships as well as a few of his own. He had been anxious to return home to England until he met the beautiful young woman, Jenny Mohr.

When Bailiff Aslak Ospevik finally showed up and ushered them into a tiny room, he wasn't happy about being interrupted on Midsummer's eve.

"You said the woman you are looking for is your wife." He slowly walked around the table and sat down in an old worn office chair, well aware that according to the law, once a couple was married, the woman was regarded as the man's property and was not allowed to run away or oppose the man in any way.

Blackstone answered, having told Big to keep his mouth shut. "Yes. She has red hair, blue eyes and she left Kristiania in April. She told me she was going to visit a relative and never returned."

"And who was the relative?"

"Someone in Trondhjem, but when I contacted them, she had never shown up."

"Do you have a marriage certificate?"
Robert passed him a document.

The Bailiff grabbed it and held it up to the light a moment before dropping it on the table. "So what makes you believe she's in Stranden?"

"My man here heard a conversation at the grocer's discussing a woman from the city. He got the particulars and the woman fits the description of my wife."

The Bailiff sat back in his chair and said nothing, waiting for Robert to speak.

"I want you to take me to where this woman is staying so I can see for myself whether or not it is my wife."

"Alright, but there are papers you must sign."

After the third release, Blackstone had had enough, "Why do I have to sign so many releases? This does not make sense. I want to go now," he demanded.

The Bailiff took off his glasses and moved forward in the seat. "Mr. Blackstone, there are procedures you must follow. Finish signing the papers and then you can go."

Robert was annoyed at this stupid, methodical country Bailiff and exploded, "You don't know me, but I can buy this whole damn village if I wanted to."

Bailiff Ospevik scratched his head. "Buy the village? I didn't know it was for sale." He picked up the marriage certificate once more and held it in front of the oil lamp.

As Blackstone began tapping his fingers at the table again, the Bailiff looked over the document. "Please stop. It makes me nervous!"

Blackstone let out a deep sigh. "Do you always read documents upside down?"

"Yes always, that's how I read between the lines." The Bailiff suspected the document to be fraudulent.

"Give that back to me."

"No, I'll keep this until we speak with your wife," said the Bailiff and put it away in the drawer.

Robert checked his temper. He didn't want to cross this fool when he needed his help to find Jenny.

"You can go now and come back in two days," said the Bailiff.

"In two days! Hell no, I demand to be taken to her now!"

"That's impossible. I'm on my way to the village's Midsummer's Eve celebration and there is no one else that can help you. Come back in two days," ordered the Bailiff as he prepared to leave his office.

When Robert, with Big at his heels, followed the Bailiff out, it suddenly dawned on him that Jenny might be attending the same celebration. He remembered they were talking about it in the store as an all-village gathering and he managed to persuade the Bailiff for a lift. Standing outside, watching the Bailiff prepare to leave, Robert noticed he had one of the finest horses he had ever seen and wondered how it had been possible for the Bailiff to afford this prize. Throughout his entire life, Robert had learned to identify people's most cherished assets just in case blackmail would be necessary. Blackmail loses its effect if you don't strike where your victim is most vulnerable; the horse was obviously the Bailiff's most sensitive point. Using that horse, or threatening to kill or harm it, he could get this idiot of a Bailiff to do whatever he wanted.

Back at the celebration site, a tall, old man with snow-white hair came up to Jenny and tapped her shoulder. "Miss, would you dance with me?"

"I've never danced on grass!"

"Come on and give it a try, Miss. Nearer the night the grass will all be trampled by our feet and you won't know you're not on a solid floor."

"Go ahead," laughed Marta, "he's the slowest dancer in the region. Give it a whirl."

The old man took Jenny's hand and escorted her to the center of the field. "If you stumble or step on my feet, don't worry. Everybody steps on each other's feet here. Notice the solid shoes I have on; they have protective leather around the toes."

Jenny stared down at his feet.

He pointed to his shoes, "See, like armor, made them myself. I am the village's shoemaker."

Each time he stepped on her feet, Jenny wished she had her own armored shoes, but she would finish the dance just out of courtesy for the man, who appeared to be very nice. It's rude to interrupt a dance unless the man does some offensive advancement.

"You're the girl from Kristiania everyone talks about? And I hear tell you're hiding from an Englishman. Never liked them much; always so important. I traveled to England in my younger days. Almost married a woman from there but I escaped with my life; never understood their sense of humor."

Jenny stopped. "Did you ever marry?"

"See that woman over there at the head of the table? That's my wife."

Jenny saw a large woman busy laying out the food.

"She's a great cook," he said, patting his stomach, proud of the extra pounds around his middle.

"How about you? Are you a good cook?"

"Depends on whom I am cooking for, I guess," she answered, realizing that having someone else prepare food for you all the time doesn't make you a good cook. "You shouldn't bother with cooking Jenny; that's what cooks are for," her mother had told her once. "You will always have money to afford to employ a cook."

"I understand you stay at Holseth?"

Jenny nodded, realizing the gossip definitely reached everybody in this village.

“Then you probably know that Iver is proposing tonight?”

Jenny abruptly stopped dancing. That was news to her. Why hadn’t anybody told her? She didn’t even know that Iver was seeing anybody. She began dancing again. “No I don’t.” She looked about at the couples meeting one another and wondered if they met by chance. The few men she had met had been introduced to her, with the exception of Robert and Svein. Her mother would have never let her attend parties meeting strangers by chance.

After the dance was over, the shoemaker courteously ushered her back to her seat. He bowed in front of her. “Thanks for the first dance young lady and don’t worry about the Englishman. Most strangers who don’t know the lay of the land are lost before they have begun.”

He had hardly turned around before a tall, handsome, dark-haired man, who reminded her of a younger version of Robert, came forward. It appeared that he had been watching her and patiently waiting for his chance to dance. He impressed her with his fancy steps and began immediately to brag about himself, how he had bought a large piece of land and would one day become the largest landowner in the village. It was not his bragging that made her go with him to a nearby timber lodge; it must have been something else. Maybe it was just her curiosity to see the lodges from the inside, or maybe it was the man’s resemblance of a Robert without having his past.

The hinges squeaked as he opened the door and ushered Jenny into the one-room lodge. It had two square windows, one on each side, a cast iron wood-burning stove, a bed and a small table with two tree-stumps as chairs. Beside the stove was a neatly stacked pile of birch wood and right above hung kettles of various sizes. Jenny especially noticed a ten-gallon kettle of cast iron, its smoothed bottom witness of heavy use. “They use that for making cheese,” said the young man as he carefully bolted the door from the inside without Jenny noticing it. “Fill it up with milk and boil for God knows a long time.” He grabbed an iron rod with a hook at the end and lifted up one of the rings from the stove. "You see, you add or remove these rings to fit different sizes of kettles."

Jenny turned toward the bed that was nailed into wall and covered two-thirds of the room's length. The beautifully decorated nightstand was nothing more than an empty carton, covered with a piece of red and white striped fabric, a small crochet tablecloth and a vase of heather. She wondered what it would be like to live alone here all summer and understood why visitors would be highly welcome.

The young man put his arm around her shoulders and tried to pull her closer.

Jenny maneuvered elegantly out of his grip, walked across the room and began to examine a painting of a young woman sitting outside a lodge, milking a goat.

"A beautiful painting isn't it?" said the young man. He was so close behind her that Jenny could feel his warm breath on her neck.

He grabbed her shoulders, turned her around and tried to kiss her.

"What are you doing? Stop it!"

He laughed. "It's Midsummer's Eve. I asked you if you wanted to visit the lodge. What do you think I was talking about?"

Jenny pulled herself back and walked briskly to the door

While fiddling to open it, two hands suddenly grabbed around her breasts; at the same time, she felt his wet lips on her neck.

"Get your hands off me!" she yelled, wrenched herself loose and pushed the door open, rushed out and almost tripped as she ran down the steps. "It's only one thing you men are thinking about," she mumbled and walked briskly passed Lars who was standing by a pile of firewood

Lars caught up with her. "What's wrong, Jenny?"

"What's wrong, what's wrong," she turned on him. "Why didn't you warn me about what goes on in those lodges?"

He took her hand. "Come on. There's a beautiful walk by the edge of the water. You can let off steam there."

Jenny calmed down by holding his hand and somewhat reluctantly followed him. She would rather have been alone with no man around, but in spite of his straight forward character, Lars was indeed a gentleman.

The moss-covered path had purple wild flowers growing on either side and was lined by dwarf birches as it meandered alongside the silent lake. The late evening sun peeked through a pass between the snow-covered mountains, illuminating thousands of insects that swarmed over the water. Once in a while, a fish snatched one which had taken a rest on the surface, creating small circular lines on the water.

The soothing sound from the brook nearby blended in with the chirping birds and a distant roar from a waterfall softened Jenny's mood. "Will your parents ever let you marry?" asked Lars.

"My parents won't stand in my way of marrying."

"I'm confused. I thought that's what this is all about – you're hiding from the Englishman because of your parents' disapproval."

"Let's not discuss that Lars; it is too complicated." Jenny stopped and faced him.

"When the right one comes along, I might marry regardless of my parents' opinion."

Lars picked up a pebble and threw it across the brook. "How will you know you've met the right one?"

"I'll know. This time everything will feel right. I thought I loved Robert but everything became so messy. I think falling in love is like walking into a room with your eyes shut, and you know the person is there." Jenny wanted to change the subject and pointed at a little dam where a duck was graciously gliding around with five ducklings behind. "Look, aren't they pretty?"

Lars looked at where she pointed, and then a singing bird caught his attention.
"Listen to that bird, a yellow finch."

"Do you see it?"

"No, I just know by the sound. They all have their own unique chirp. My grandmother told me about the birds when I was a child and I have since enjoyed being able to distinguish them by their sounds."

"Do you think they talk to each other?"

"Of cause they do, like us, just a different language. Listen and you'll hear the response."

After a short silence, Jenny whispered enthusiastically, "Oh yes, I can hear it! Same tone and chirp, almost like an echo."

"You got it, Jenny. When you start to listen, you'll hear many different birds communicating with each other. At first it may just sound like disordered chatter, but soon you'll hear it is like a fine tuned orchestra. Sometimes I feel like the forest is alive and is talking to me. It was my grandfather who taught me how to listen and speak to the animals. I've never forgotten it."

It surprised Jenny that Lars was so in tuned with nature, a side of him she didn't know about. Her impression had been that he was a man just laughing, telling jokes and having fun without any regard for the soft and tender things in life, a man who would jump over the first woman he saw and then dump her. There was indeed a good heart behind the happy face. She began to like Lars more and more, but couldn't imagine anything else than friendship and would have to keep a safe distance no matter how much she wanted to hug and kiss him.

"You know Lars, I think what we learn as a child never goes away whether it's good or bad - it kind of stays with you. I remember my mother once told me about the plants and how you can talk to them to make them grow better. She would bustle around with her watering can and chatter, even giving them names. You should have seen them! They were absolutely beautiful. They loved her very much and I think they missed her when she died a few years ago."

"I guess most teachings are passed down from the elders to the young, but sometimes I wish the old could listen to us a little bit more. Look at my grandfather; can you ever imagine teaching him anything?"

"He's probably like many other older people. They don't take much in; it only goes out, but for your grandfather, that's great don't you think? Just leave him with his stories."

When the sun went down behind the mountain ridge, it became chilly and they decided to return to capture the moment they set a blaze to the bonfire.

The Bailiff finally arrived at the celebration with Robert and Big not far behind. Concerned about the uninvited guests, he headed for the circle of men around the beer barrels. After a few mugs, he found Marta and demanded she dance with him. She quit resisting and when his strong arms pulled her closer, he whispered in her ear, "Be calm, and keep dancing with me. We may have a bit of trouble on our hands." He twirled her quickly to the far end of the dancers.

"Take a look behind me and notice the two men who are standing near the horses."

"Don't recognize them," said Marta.

"It's Jenny's Mr. Blackstone."

The look on Marta's face prompted the Bailiff to kiss her cheek. "I said, don't panic. I've already talked to several men and he won't be allowed to lay a hand on her, even though he claims she's his husband."

"That's not true. He's lying."

"I know. We need to be ever watchful to see what he's planning. He hasn't broken the law but the moment he does, I can step in. Oh it feels good dancing with you!"

Marta blushed. Her face lit up and she pushed the Bailiff back. "Stop it! I'm not the maid of twenty years ago."

"Could have fooled me," said the Bailiff. "You are still a beautiful woman, Marta."

Both had been widowers for several years and although Marta had wondered what it might be like to have this man in her life, she usually kept her distance, fearing disappointment. He had been ever so despondent after his wife's death and just recently he had started noticing someone other than his horse.

"Do you know what Marta? You are beautiful." Marta hadn't expected this from the Bailiff and she immediately stopped dancing and began walking away. "Stop, Marta, please come back. What did I say? I promise not to talk. We'll just dance and enjoy the night." He took hold of her hand and wouldn't let go.

"You're causing a scene; people will notice."

"It's Midsummer's Eve; they'll forgive us. I'll leave you alone for now, since I need to find your father and Iver and make sure the Englishman doesn't ruin the party, but I'll be back and you will dance with me again."

Jorun, the woman who had been chasing Iver since he became a widower, had cornered him and demanded several dances. She was a strong, comely woman, just a few years younger than Iver and ready to be married. Since his wife died, she had taken it upon herself to tell everyone in the village that she was to be Iver's wife. After several lonely years watching Olaf grow up without a mother, Iver had almost proposed then thought the better of it. He didn't love Jorun. That day, as he watched Jenny from a distance and heard his brother's dreams of marrying her, he expected there would be a long line of suitors until she was safe within the vows of marriage. He hated knowing that a woman like her living on a mountain was preposterous. Jorun was maybe the best he could ever hope for. As she wrapped her arms around him and kissed his cheek, Iver noticed two strangers.

"Iver, Iver," she said, pulling his head towards her, "why aren't you paying attention to me?" She had decided that night she would give him what he wanted, what all men wanted, and she took his hand and put it over her breast. "Iver, let's have fun tonight. I know a place."

Iver was more concerned about the bonfire than this clinging woman; he paid his attention to a man who walked around the pile of timber logs and doused it with oil before igniting it with a match. The kindling began burning and in time the flames engulfed the dry wood. As the fire grew, several women came together with bundled sprigs of leaves and herbs, looking back at the Bailiff and the minister, waiting for a signal that all was safe for them to begin their yearly songs of celebration, old songs their grandmothers had taught them to bring good luck to their yearly harvest. This year as in the past, the young maids would wish for love; others would pray for safety or health, and the elders always remembered their loved ones. The sisterhood of Midsummer waited for the sign.

The Bailiff walked up to the minister to pay his respects. "I heard rumors you're going to baptize the Fuhrlie brothers tomorrow."

The minister nodded in stiff agreement as a man in the group with several beers under his belt laughed, "Fuhrlie brothers, those heathen dogs? They can't be baptized, not even with beer in the stoup!"

The minister turned to the drunken man. "Too much drink turns a man's tongue away from God."

The Bailiff motioned Andreas to quickly join them by the keg of beer. "Father, may we quench your thirst with a milder drink? I believe it is your favorite, mead?" said Andreas. Mead is an ancient Norse drink made by fermenting honey and water, which tastes like a sweet dry wine with very little alcohol.

"I always did have a taste for mead. Did I ever tell you about my family making it every hay season? I'd be glad to take a few swallows," said the minister.

Andreas reached out for the ladle and filled a large mug with one of the strongest beers made in the region. "Remember Father, this one has a different taste than the mead you remember. The honeybees around here are a lot wilder," he said, winking back at the group of men watching the minister take his first swallow.

"This is beer," said the minister.

"No, It's mead, just different hops," corrected Andreas as the minister took another swallow. Andreas was hoping that he could get him so drunk that he didn't even know his name.

"Now it's your turn," whispered Andreas to The Widow. "You keep talking to him about religion and I'll make sure his mug is never empty." Andreas knew how to get a man drunk; as soon as he had passed what he called the break-in point, where common sense and judgment began loosening their grip. At that point, most men were quite vulnerable and if you, in addition, had a seductive woman and a bunch of good stories, the victim was usually caught. It didn't take long for Andreas to realize he was in progress of getting the minister right where he wanted him and soon his elevated voice was getting the attention of people nearby. A few men who saw what was going on came forward and struck a friendly conversation with the minister and at the same time made sure they toasted frequently with him.

When he left the group, he staggered across the uneven pasture, heading toward the food table. As he approached the table bulging with food, Andreas tugged at the Bailiff's shirt sleeve. "Look at the minister, Aslak. I think he's hungry." Just as the Bailiff turned and looked where Andreas pointed, the minister tripped and nosedived forward and in a frantic attempt to prevent meeting the ground face to face, he instinctively reached out for whatever he could get a grip on.

The two women in charge with the food table had spent hours preparing and setting it. They realized in a fraction of a second their biggest nightmare had come true when the minister's hand grabbed onto the tablecloth and pulled everything with him into the ditch.

Andreas chuckled so hard he almost lost his breath, while a couple of strong women helped the minister up and ushered him into the nearest lodge. Stories would be told for years to come about the Midsummer night when the minister cleared the food table.

Lars and Jenny had just walked out of the grove of trees and were heading to the bonfire when Robert noticed her. It had been almost three months since he had seen her and his heart pounded. Unaware of Robert approaching her from behind, Jenny noticed a woman standing beside Iver and asked Lars if that was Jorun.

"Yes, she lives on another mountain farm with her parents and three younger siblings. She lost her husband to the sea; he drowned off the coast during the fishing season. Seems like Iver has been running after her the last couple of years. I would be surprised if he didn't propose tonight; this is indeed the night to do those kinds of things."

Jenny looked at the sky. It was one of those nights where thoughts and feelings seemed clearer and dreams might come true. Her thoughts were abruptly interrupted by a familiar voice.

"Jenny, at least we meet again. I have spent months looking for you," said Robert quickly coming up to her and holding out his hand.

Jenny's body stiffened. "Robert, how did you find me? What are you doing here?"

"I've come to talk, to find out why you left me," said Robert, irritated at the young man standing between him and Jenny.

Jenny motioned to Lars by her side. "It's alright Lars, let him talk."

Lars looked at the tall man standing next to Robert and didn't believe he would leave peacefully. It didn't look good.

"There's nothing to explain. We are over," said Jenny.

Lars put his arm around her waist.

"Take your bloody hands off her!"

"Lars, it's alright. Just leave me and let me speak with Robert."

Lars reluctantly moved away.

Jenny's heart quickened as she looked up at Robert and wondered what it was she felt for him.

Robert took her hands in his. "You are lovely, even in your pauper clothes. I've waited for this moment for two months. I've hardly lived, thinking of you every day and night and knowing that when we met again I must convince you of the passion I feel for you." He put his hand to her face.

"Stop it Robert, please stop this," said Jenny, moving away from him.

"Don't fool yourself, Jenny; you want to be with me as much as I want you. I can still see it in your eyes and nothing must ever come between us again."

"That may be true. I'm so confused but I will not go with you. I've promised my parents and I respect their wishes."

"Respect, respect their wishes, to keep you from marrying the man you love?"

"No Robert, to keep me from marrying the man my father remembers, Captain Blackstone." Jenny might as well have taken a dagger to his heart, but he managed to hide his distress very well and if one didn't know him, one could not tell what impact that word had on him.

Robert straightened himself up. "That was the past. It is not the Robert you know who stands before you." He took hold of her arm. "You are leaving with me. I've been called away by the Queen of England and you will travel with me as my wife. Whatever I've done, I'll fix it. Just have the decency to tell me how I've wronged you."

"You've done nothing wrong to me," Jenny remarked, underscoring the word "me". "I did care for you once. It seems like such a long time ago and if you cared for me as much as you say you do, you will leave me alone."

"I'm taking you away from this Jenny. You are coming with me," said Robert and motioned Big to come help him.

"Stop it! I'm not going anywhere with you. How can I convince you?"

"You can't. The look in your eyes tells me there's something still between us and I'll not let time take that away from me." He took hold of her arm and told Big to pick her up because they were leaving.

Jenny screamed as Lars quickly pushed her away from Robert.

Robert slugged him in the chest and knocked him into a bush.

Big moved forward and was just about to pick up Jenny when Iver suddenly showed up like an eagle and snapped her away, right in front of him. Iver had been watching the scene from a distance, just waiting for the right moment to act. He pulled Jenny away from the men and rushed through the dancers. A gaping Robert looked at Big, wondering what happened.

Jenny and Iver were already across the pasture and behind a shed when the Bailiff slowly moved up to Robert and asked if he could be of some help.

"Yes you can. My wife has gotten away and you did nothing to stop them."

"What exactly do you want me to do?" asked the Bailiff.

"I demand you help me bring my wife back! Is that so difficult to understand?" snapped Robert.

Behind the shed, Iver and Jenny tried to regain their breath. Iver needed to decide very quickly where to take her. He stared at her. "Now we have no time to argue; you just follow me. Do you understand?"

Jenny nodded. She would have to trust him, and at least he knew the lay of the land.

Iver scanned the area for a fraction of a second before pulling her with him across a pasture. He knew where to easily cross the river. Then he would take her to the neighboring cheese farm, hoping to find a horse. From there, he would have to cross a small bridge to get back on the main road. The trick was to get over the bridge before Robert got a chance to block their path; the bridge would then be the only way out. Since Iver and Jenny were taking a detour and considering whatever time Iver needed to find and saddle a horse, Robert would have plenty of time to get down to the bridge before them, so Iver would have to run the mile-long distance, well-hidden by trees and bushes. Now as they rushed to cross the river, Iver hoped that Robert would see them, tricking him into believing they would continue further in through the valley.

Sometime later, after stomping across a marsh, poking their way through a thicket and hobbling across a rock-fall, Iver and Jenny reached the neighboring cheese farm. Iver stormed into the first of the two lodges and shouted, "Anybody here? I need a horse," but no one answered. Finding both lodges abandoned, he saw a tail sticking out from behind a shed. He grabbed Jenny's arm. "Come on, there's one behind the shed."

An awestruck Jenny watched Iver harness the horse faster than she ever thought possible, and a moment later, a horse and a carriage took off for the bridge.

Robert had just discovered that Iver and Jenny had turned around and were heading back down the valley. He was now eagerly awaiting the Bailiff who was fiddling with the horse's harness. The Bailiff knew about the bridge and would make certain that Iver had enough time to cross it before he'd continue.

Impatient, Robert yelled, "What are you fiddling with?"

Then suddenly, in a stir of dust and horse hooves, Robert saw a carriage rush across the bridge at such speed that it rolled on its outer wheel, threatening to tilt any time. As the road straightened, the carriage settled back on both wheels before disappearing behind a cloud of dust.

"That must be them. Get the damn horse moving!" yelled Robert.

The Bailiff released his grip around the halter. "This is not a damn horse. I've had him for eight years and his name is Musse."

"I don't give a shit how long you have had him and I don't give a shit what his name is. Just get the bloody animal going! This is a chase, isn't it Bailiff or are you playing a game?"

"No games, Mr. Blackstone. Unless what you are telling me isn't true. If she's not your runaway wife then the tables may turn."

While the Bailiff was still fiddling with the harness, Robert jumped into the front seat and took hold of the reins yelling, "Yaah..haa!" The horse turned back to look at the driver and didn't budge.

The Bailiff shook his head. "What made you believe Musse would take orders from a stranger? Get in the back and don't pull any other stunts."

With the reins secured, the Bailiff set the horse in motion and followed the trail of the dust cloud down through the narrow and bumpy forest road.

"Could we at least go faster?" asked Robert.

"What?" shouted the Bailiff.

"Does the horse have only one speed?" yelled Robert.

"No, but if we go any faster, the potholes will crack the wheels and then we wouldn't move at all. If that's what you want, it's ok with me." He had already started to get this businessman deep down in his throat.

Robert realized it was futile to argue with the thick-skulled Bailiff. At a crossroad, he demanded they stop. He jumped out of the carriage and began immediately searching the ground.

"Looking for something? asked the Bailiff.

"What do you think? Searching for pebbles?"

"How would I know what a city careerist is looking for in the wilderness," said the Bailiff. "You're just wasting your time. They have gone to the right, away from the village. I can see it from here."

Blackstone didn't comment. He walked a few yards down the road and began poking into a blot of horse manure with a stick. "This is fresh, still warm; they have gone to the left," he exclaimed and jumped back into the carriage.

"How do you know it's from that specific horse? Did you smell the shit?" asked the Bailiff and reluctantly maneuvered the horse around.

"Just get to the village," said Blackstone and flung out his arms.

Further down the road, Iver was surprised the Bailiff hadn't caught up with them yet, not knowing his game, only that he had the fastest and most enduring horse in the region. He wondered if he'd had an accident. He halfway turned his head and yelled at Jenny, "Do you see them?"

"What?"

"Do you see the followers?" He shouted to drown the noise from the carriage.

Jenny looked back through the dust. "No. I think we have out-run them." She had already gotten enough from this wild ride and couldn't wait for it to be over. Her bottom ached from having only hardwood to sit on and it felt like Iver had tried to hit every pothole and rock on the road. She had tried to sit the way she had learned in her riding lessons, by putting more weight on her legs and less to her bottom, but soon found out the carriage didn't have any rhythms like a horse and it actually made it worse. The shaking and jarring made her wonder if her intestines were tearing loose. The horse's hoofs frequently kicked loose small pebbles, hitting her, and all the dust made it difficult to keep her eyes open.

When they finally reached the village, Jenny was completely exhausted and had difficulty stepping down from the carriage. She had heard women describing their first steps after a difficult labor, but this had to be worse. Iver, who had been sitting in the well-cushioned driver's seat, didn't seem to have any sympathy for how she felt as she waddled slowly away from the carriage.

He just grabbed her hand and said, "Hurry, let's go!" and dragged her alongside the shoreline and behind a shed. "Stay here and keep your head low while I get the boat ready." A moment later, he ushered her on board and began immediately to row away from shore, heading toward Holseth. The water was like a mirror and Iver was at his best. Maybe it was time to break the one hour and forty minute speed record Andreas had bragged about. He could use Jenny as a witness.

When the Bailiff reached the warehouse, he was surprised that the steamboat hadn't left yet. Usually the steamer would leave in the late afternoon. But when he noticed a half-dozen drunken crewmembers by the warehouse, he had his suspicions as to why the ship was still there. The carriage had hardly come to a complete stop before Blackstone jumped out. He had already noticed the rowboat pulling away and saw Jenny onboard. He looked at the Bailiff who didn't seem to have any intent to move.

"So what now? Aren't you going to get your ass out of that seat?"

"My territory ends here."

"Your what? Territory? What kind of nonsense is that?"

"Jurisdiction then, if that make more sense to you."

Blackstone flung out his arms. "Fine. I have had enough of you anyway."

"Good luck and thanks for the interesting company." The Bailiff turned his horse around while he muttered to himself, "You own me one for this, Marta."

Blackstone rushed toward the group of drunken men outside the warehouse. He needed to get the steamboat to go after them; the Bailiff he would deal with later. After a few words and money had changed hands, one man walked with Blackstone and his hunch man down to the shoreline where he pulled out a jolly boat. A short moment later, they climbed onboard the steamboat and after searching around for a moment, they approached the salon.

"Anybody here?" Robert yelled as he opened the door to a stench of booze and stale cigar smoke.

The small salon had benches on three sides with an oval-shaped table in the middle, decorated with a half-full bottle of whisky, empty beer bottles, a full ashtray and cockroaches fighting for breadcrumbs. On the floor lay a large butcher knife by a smoking pipe and a lidless can of chewing tobacco.

As Robert moved closer, he saw the body of a man dressed in oily overalls and a white shirt. Nearby, flies bounced against a dusty window where the early morning sun lit up the man's unshaven face. He snored with his inhale and whistled when he exhaled.

"Wake up!" hollered Robert as he clapped his hands by the man's ears causing his body to flinch.

The man opened his eyes, maneuvered himself up into a sitting position and placed a hand on his forehead. He obviously had a hang-over, thought Robert as he waited impatiently for him to respond.

"Am I blocking the way for anybody?" the man mumbled

"I need your help. You're dressed like the captain or did you just steal the clothes?"

"I'm the captain," said the man as he scratched his head, trying to figure out who had interrupted his sleep. "Who are you and what do you want?"

"I need you to follow a rowboat heading south on the fjord." Robert dropped a sizeable amount of money on the table.

"You can't buy a jolly for that," said the captain.

"There's more money on that table than you and your crew will make in a month; get this boat moving! We are following a rowboat."

The captain hesitated, then staggered toward the engine hatch and climbed down to the engine room while Robert took a step outside. He could barely see the rowboat in the distance. He turned to Big who was standing next to him. "Keep watching the boat." Robert headed back to the engine room and yelled at the captain, "What's the matter?"

The captain held onto a pipe wrench. "It's going to take at least an hour before we can get this baby started."

"An hour! Are you out of your mind?"

"If you know anything about steamboats, you'd know it takes time to heat the water," said the captain, pointing at the water temperature gauge. "You don't get steam out of lukewarm water."

"Where's your stoker?" demanded Robert.

The captain nodded towards a man sleeping on a straw rug. Robert rushed down the ladder, pulled the man up by the chest and shook him awake. "Start feeding the burner, or I'll throw your ass in with the coal!" The stoker opened his eyes, blinked several times and sat up.

"Wake up and attend the burner," yelled Robert.

The captain nodded at the stoker. "Go on, do as he says."

The stoker staggered to the boiler and grabbed hold of a shovel, missing his mark the first time, swearing all the while the coal rolled across the deck. It wasn't long before he was steady on his feet.

Robert looked at the gauges and found the water level high. He found the rusty valves and ordered, "Give me a wrench."

"For what?"

"I'm opening the valve."

"Why in the hell are you doing that?"

"To let out water."

"But that's the water from the boiler! Where will the steam come from if you let out all the water?" The captain muttered to himself, "Damn hangover. I always seem to run into idiots when I've been drinking."

"Old man, I don't appreciate being called an idiot and believe it or not, I know steam engines and by the time I have emptied out most of the water," Robert glanced at the stoker shuffling coal, "I'll have steam faster than you can get up that ladder." Robert knew if he let out too much water, he would run out of steam before catching up with Jenny and if he let out too little, it would take too long to get steam and he would lose track of them.

Jenny saw the concern on Iver's face the moment he realized smoke was pouring out from the steamboat. "Shall I help you row?" she asked.

Iver didn't mean to be rude when he simply said, "No." It would be better rowing alone than having someone who couldn't follow his rhythm. He had the weather on his side; this quiet morning was what the locals called the Black Silence. The expression came from the black image the fjord projected when it mirrored the dark portion of the mountains. He watched her as he always did, silently wondering what more excitement she might bring into his life. Small talk was impossible with her, almost painful because he didn't know where to begin. He wanted to reveal himself, but the invisible boundary between them made sharing his thoughts difficult, if not impossible.

Robert kept rushing up and down the ladder between the engine room and deck. He trusted neither the stoker nor the captain and noticed even though they were getting closer to the rowboat, the water level in the boiler had reached below the red line. The stoker kept an eye on the gauge while dropping coal. He stopped, leaned against the shovel, looked at Robert and said, "Mister, this boiler is about to burn up! We can't feed the fire anymore." The boiler had no more water to make steam.

Robert yelled at the stoker, "Fire up the second boiler."

"It would take hours," said the stoker.

"Just do it," demanded Robert. He knew the stoker was right, but he didn't have any other choice. He had gambled with the amount of water he had let out and now was the time to see if he had won or lost. He rushed up the ladder again and as he stormed out on the deck, he noticed the rowboat had just reached shore and Jenny and the mountain farmer were in progress of climbing up on a dock. As he looked at the dock getting closer, he felt comfortable he could make it, even if the steam ran out. The moving momentum of the ship in motion would do the rest.

When Iver and Jenny had gotten safely up on the dock, Iver grabbed her hand. "We must get to the ladder before them." The ladder was like any gate or door and the one who reached it first controlled the chase.

After the first few turns of the zigzagging path, Iver stopped and glanced down at the steamboat which was getting closer and closer to the dock. The captain had to be in the same condition as his crew by the warehouse, he thought, as the boat steered with undiminishing speed toward the dock. Iver couldn't believe what he saw and after telling Jenny to walk ahead of him, he remained still. This he had to watch.

Out of breath, Jenny stopped under a pine tree and threw herself down on the ground, cursing herself for not staying back at the farm. She remembered that she had sworn to never walk the path anymore, but it seemed like no matter how she wished and swore, she found herself in situations she had neither planned for, nor wanted to be in.

Iver noticed Robert was leaning over the ship's bow. He suddenly raised his hands and yelled, "Stop!" Nothing happened. The ship continued toward the dock at full speed. He turned toward the bridge and yelled, "Slow astern!" A second later, he waved both arms in the air shouting, "Full astern!" but not even the command of full speed in reverse seemed to help. Then the captain poked his head out from a peephole window which made it look like it was locked into a neckband before the guillotine blade would chop it off. "What?" he shouted.

Blackstone formed a spout with his hands, "Full astern, idiot!"

"I have no more power."

Blackstone signaled to the left in an attempt to get him to steer clear of the mountain, but the inevitable was about to happen. A few seconds later, the ship crashed into the dock, breaking the timber beams like matches and poking a huge dent in its bow.

Robert was thrown down on the dock and escaped with barely a scratch, while Big was screaming from an apparently broken arm. After Robert had composed himself, he realized Big would not be of much help and took off up the path by himself with only one thought on his mind - to bring Jenny back down the mountain. He checked his weapon in his side pocket and had no qualms about killing anyone getting in his way.

Jenny's body had gone past her mind and at the edge of exhaustion, she grabbed the ladder to support herself. She saw images of how she still struggled up the path. She looked up at the ladder and realized there was no way she could make it. She would just wait until Robert caught her and would willingly go back down with him and figure out a way to get away later. She had had enough of this place and promised herself again she would never walk this path anymore.

As Iver caught up with her, he noticed Robert was less than a hundred feet away. He didn't see his henchman and figured he had outrun him. In less than a minute, he could be face to face with him. Regardless of who it was, this wasn't the place to fight or argue with anybody. Just one uncontrolled side step, or losing concentration a second, could easy result in an involuntarily tumble down the mountainside. He noticed Jenny, hardly in this world, and realized that she would probably never manage to climb the ladder before she had rested, but damn it, this was not the time to rest! He shifted his attention from Robert, to the top of the ladder, and to Jenny, and to the abyss underneath and knew he had to make a move fast.

He grabbed Jenny around her waist, swiftly pulled her up like a rag doll and began climbing. Each step squeaked under their combined weight and threatened to crack the ladder. Halfway up, he noticed Robert less than ten yards away and knew once he touched the ladder, he could purposely or accidentally easily jerk them off. He had never felt so vulnerable and helpless before and silently prayed for a miracle. As he was about to yell at Robert not to touch the ladder and announce he would surrender, his inherited survival instinct surfaced. With his right arm still clutching around Jenny, he poked his knee in between two steps, released his left arm and scooped up a handful of dirt and pebbles and threw it down.

The dirt hit Robert straight in the face, catching him off guard just long enough for Iver to rush up the remaining steps where he rolled over on the pasture and released Jenny. With both hands free, he pulled up the ladder, peered down at Robert and let out a sigh of relief.

Jenny kept running as far away from Robert's voice as she could get. She didn't want to hear his pleading or his threats, and when Iver caught up to her, she was crying. "Fine mess I've gotten myself into," her tears flowed as she hurried away from him.

"Jenny, it's over. He can't get up without the ladder."

"You don't understand! No one understands. A part of me wants to be with him still, after all I know, after my parents..."

Iver spun her around a bit rougher than he had expected. "Then stop this madness! Go, go be with him. Just do us all a favor and make up your mind."

Robert had come too far to give up now. He wasn't leaving without Jenny and back down by the fjord, he broke into the Holseth's boathouse to find another ladder. After a few minutes of tearing through the old supplies, he decided to use the door and knocked it off the hinges and began busting it apart. Within minutes he would have had a reasonable ladder to help him up the mountain wall - if another boat hadn't hit the shore right there and then.

"What are you doing?" asked the Bailiff, climbing up on the damaged dock, with Andreas and Lars following close behind.

"I thought this was out of the way of your jurisdiction," quipped Robert.

"I was talking about the water, not the shore, and the dock where you are standing is above shore, so you are in my jurisdiction now, Mr. Blackstone."

Robert accepted that he had lost the first battle, knowing that any war has many battles and also that this war was by no means over. He paid Andreas for the damage to the boathouse and dock. Then he and Big were taken back to the village, kept under watch by the Bailiff and would be escorted out of Stranden the following morning with words of encouragement to never visit Stranden again while the Bailiff was still alive.

Robert knew he would never rest until Jenny was his wife or his mistress. The next time he returned he would be certain to have what he needed to take on the mountain. At least for now, he knew where she was and over the next few months until he returned from England, he would make sure that she didn't return to Kristiania by writing to her father and letting him know that he'd be back to the city to be with her. He'd shadow her every move. Christian would keep her on the mountain longer and what a miserable existence she would have living amongst the poorest people alive! By the time they met again, she would gladly accept his hand.

An hour before the ship pulled out, Robert slipped away and when he returned to the guesthouse to pick up his belongings, there was blood on his clothes. He cleaned up and with Big at his side, met the Bailiff who escorted them to the ship.

"You are a clever man, Bailiff; too clever for me I'm afraid. You never did believe the marriage certificate was real did you?"

The Bailiff kept quiet as Robert made several derogatory comments about country politics and local laws. By the time the ship left the dock, both men were glad to see the other fade away in the distance. It would be several hours before the Bailiff would find his horse lying in his stall in a pool of blood.

The Wedding

"After three days, both fish
and guest begin to smell."
Danish Proverb

In early August, the Holseth family was invited to a wedding. Jenny viewed the three days' feast as a perfect opportunity to be alone on the farm and had offered to care for the animals. Marta told her she wouldn't be able to enjoy the festivities while worrying about this Englishman coming back and asked her to please join them. Jenny agreed; going to the feast was indeed safer than remaining alone on the farm. As she trudged down the path with the family, she wondered if she'd ever be home again, especially when her parents had written explaining their position that she must remain on the mountain a few more months after they had received threats from Robert.

On that day, two couples were going to be married in the crowded Lutheran Church. Andreas' nephew and his bride were positioned to the right of the congregation and to the very front of the altar, symbolizing the girl's family's status; the young, beautiful woman wore with distinction a silver crown of virgins. The second couple stood to the left of the congregation and back from the altar. She, a plain middle-aged woman of simple means, wore a garland on her head symbolizing her non-virginal status.

After Andreas' nephew and his bride received the minister's loud and pompous blessing, the dark robed, mean-spirited, balding minister walked to the back and greeted the second couple, stopping just inches away from the bride. "You, Susanne Marie Jorgenson, Satan's daughter, will be punished by the Holy Spirit for not abstaining from carnal lust." His last word rolled off his tongue as if he enjoyed the pleasure of it. He returned to the front and his fist hit the pulpit; the congregation jumped while he leaned toward the source of his anger. "Sinner, you shame your kind!" His face looked like a serpent; the blood vessels in the whites of his eyes turning bright red and flashed at the shocked congregation. He then looked down again on poor Susanne. "I will perform the marriage ceremony only to save your child's soul, but you will not have my blessing or God's."

Susanne was shaken and downcast by the minister's unexpected behavior and disclosures. Just a few months with child, she was now convinced the congregation could see her swollen belly underneath her bridal dress, her sin exposed to everybody. That the man next to her had taken her by force was not a subject to be discussed. Unshaken by the minister, the bridegroom, a tall somber man, stood next to his unlucky bride, thinking about his farm. Susanne was a hard worker and he would either get the best out of her and her nine-year-old lazy son, or he would beat it out of them. After the ceremony there would be no party for Susanne.

On hearing the minister's words, Jenny's fingers dug into the wooden pew as her emotions moved from disgust to outrage. She wanted to scream out and tell the entire congregation about his conduct during Midsummer's Eve, but then realized they all knew, of course, and so she kept quiet. As he quickly and without grace stood over Susanne while she repeated her vows, Jenny stood up from her seat, silently left the church and started running. Out of breath, she stopped at the top of a hill overlooking the countryside and paced back and forth. How dare that disgusting man in God's name refuse to bless both marriages? She could still see the minister standing over Susanne, thick-lipped monster, cursing a marriage before it had even started. She kicked into the ground and muttered, "How dare he strip her in front of the entire congregation!"

"So you walked out?" Jenny jumped and faced Iver. "Do you always walk out of church whenever you don't agree with something?"

"I do, I mean I have before," replied Jenny, surprised to see him.

Iver shook his head and looked out over the scenery. "I'm sure the Elders will take care of his outbursts, at least quiet him for a while. I'm sorry you were offended."

"I wasn't offended. I never said I was offended. You make me sound like an immature schoolgirl," snapped Jenny.

"Well if you weren't an immature school girl, why did you run out of church?"

"I left your church because your minister does not represent God; you don't give blessings to the rich and not to the poor. Why did you leave the church? Shouldn't you be with your family?"

"True, but it is such a beautiful day and you gave me an excuse to get some fresh air." Iver sat down and leaned against a tree.

"Why? Why does it seem that there is not enough room in this forsaken part of the country for the two of us?" Jenny walked back to the church as quickly as she had left it.

Iver didn't watch her; instead he looked at a few colored leaves from a large oak tree, the very first sign of fall and mumbled, "I've wondered the same thing myself, Jenny girl, since the day I met you."

The congregation poured out of the small church and assembled near the front door as families eagerly congratulated one another. The unfortunate bride was leaving with her husband, followed by just a handful of people when Jenny noticed she had dropped her handkerchief. Jenny picked it up and by the time she caught up with her, she was already in the buggy. "Hello, hello, wait; you've dropped your handkerchief."

The bride popped her head out of the carriage. "Oh, thank you! It was a gift from my mother. I would have missed it."

"You're welcome and congratulations; my name

is Jenny."

"I am Susanne; thank you again," the sad-looking woman's face lit up speaking with Jenny. "Maybe we will meet again."

"I'd like that," said Jenny and waved at the bride as the buggy pulled away. She walked back and mingled with the others who were getting ready to go to the wedding party a few miles away from the village. More than twenty horses with buggies, carriages and wagons were lined up outside the church to bring all the guests to the bride's home. The bride and groom would ride in the fist buggy, followed by their closest relatives. Jenny tried to stay away from Iver, hoping she would not be placed in a buggy with him and was glad when she found herself with Andreas and Marta. They were in the middle of the procession and as the horse trotted up Main Street, Jenny said, "I felt so sad for Susanne. It was so cruel of the minister."

Andreas nodded, "He's known to especially throw his wrath over unmarried mothers. He believes himself to be a powerful man and can say whatever he wants; his words are law and no one dares question him."

"What about the elders of your church? Isn't he made accountable for his actions?"

"No, they believe as he does and if they don't disagree, they won't speak up."

As the cortege made a sharp turn, Jenny had a better view of the young bride. The couple seemed so happy and totally absorbed by themselves and the moment she wondered if this was a marriage of pure love. "We don't marry for love; we marry for necessity," Marta had told her. "A man without a wife can never run a farm and a woman without a man is subject to being frozen out by society. If this marriage doesn't hold water, you can blame it on my father." She continued, "It was he who started the whole thing."

"What do you mean, Marta?"

"Andreas was the honorary spokesperson for the groom. A close family member shall assist the groom and give him the best recommendation when he officially proposes marriage."

That would certainly be another event when Jenny would want to be alone with her lover - the time he proposed. How unromantic could you possible be, taking with you a spokesperson to propose marriage? "So what happened when your nephew proposed, Andreas? Was the bride aware of his intentions?"

"I think she had a suspicion. You know gossip travels faster than man, but when she saw how we were dressed, in knee shorts, with braided ribbons around our legs, white shirts, and tall black hats topping our heads like stovepipes, she must have known for sure. Anyone who doesn't get an idea from that is not fit to get married. When I knocked on the door, I could almost hear her knees rattle. The bride's father welcomed us and once inside, I realized our visit was indeed not unexpected; the table had already been set with their best dishes. We remained mute about our intentions until after the meal, where I did my best to reflect only the best light on my nephew and complemented the bride's father and family as much as I could. After the meal, I asked for permission to tell a story. I wanted them to loosen up and laugh, so I could get to the point of our visit."

"And did they laugh?"

"Yes. I told them the story about a woman living on a remote farm with only her husband and cat who were all visited by a minister."

"Was this a true story?"

Andreas nodded, "Yes, this story happened many years ago. The old woman knew it was not acceptable for a woman to wear pants, but her day-to-day life on the mountain farm made it impractical to always be wearing dresses. The winter came, covering the paths with ice and snow, and she found it difficult to get safely to church on Sundays. Instead, to keep in the graces of God, she read a few verses from the bible and sang a few hymns until the weather would let her return to church. When the minister heard she had difficulty getting to his sermons, he offered to visit her twice a month to bring the word of God into her house. His first visit came unexpectedly; she had miscalculated the days, but after opening the door, she smiled and ushered him into the living room. As they sat down at the table, it dawned on her - she was still in her pants! She looked at him, blushed and said, 'I apologize for my appearance today and if I had remembered you were coming, I would surely have taken off my pants.'

"The bride's father exploded in a big belly laugh and I knew I had won the first round. Soon it became easier and easier to get her father laughing and then, feeling braver, I formally declared my nephew's intentions."

Jenny could clearly see the scene with old woman and the minister. Andreas made it so alive. "Did you get yes right away?"

"Certainly I did."

"So then it was just to announce the wedding?"

"It doesn't go that fast, my dear," Marta said. "It takes at least two years from the proposal to the wedding. During this time, two essential family meetings take place at Christmas time. The first would be held at the bride's family where the grounds for marriage will be discussed."

"Grounds for marriage?"

"Bloodline and sufficient goods would have to be looked at."

It surprised Jenny that they were so concerned about bloodline. She thought that was an issue only among royal families and the high society class. *Why would people up here care about bloodline? Seems like the entire bunch inbreed from one end to the next. Isn't it difficult enough to find a spouse you like among the few available when you also should be concern about the bloodline?* she wondered.

Marta told her that it was not so much about like or dislike. "You search for a suitable wife through the bloodline first, so when a man officially proposes, he has already gotten a suggestion from his family. Everybody knows everybody and what they stand for. A lifelong commitment is such an important thing that we consider the young ones to be too immature to make that decision. Therefore the practical comes first and the feelings that were supposed to be kept a bay anyway will have to wait."

What if feelings and love never came? Jenny wondered. *What would it be like to live all your life with a man you don't love? And what is love anyway? Is it true that you can't define love because it is an experience?* She turned toward Marta. "What if a woman gets proposals from two men from the same bloodline? How does she decide which one to pick?"

"In cooperation with her parents, she would add the assets from the two suitors' farms and then make her choice."

"So the richest will win her, then."

"Yes, that's fair to say."

On top of a hill, the cortege came to stop to give the horses a few minutes rest while the guests got a chance to stretch their legs and get a nice view of the village. Jenny and Marta walked together the few yards to the lookout point while continuing their conversation. Jenny turned to Marta. "So then the wedding plans can be set, I assume."

"Almost, but first there have to be two family meetings to make the final decision. If the outcome from the first meeting was yes, the second meeting, or engagement party, held at the groom's family would announce where the financial details, party and other practical things would be discussed. When the wedding date has been set and announced, the bride can no longer accept other suitors and the bridegroom could hardly look at another girl."

"So then the preparations begin."

"Yes, the bride's and the groom's families are from that point in a frenzy of activities, preparing food and reserving key people to manage the wedding feast and like a slow-moving mudslide, the process rolls on until this very special day." Marta paused and took a deep breath. "Not even the death of the bride's aunt last week could postpone it. Her funeral has been rescheduled and will be held this coming Tuesday."

Andreas, who had been coming up behind them, chipped in, "Her coffin has been temporarily put away on the loft, right above where we soon will eat, drink, and dance. Maybe she will join us." He winked and poked Jenny in her side.

"How do you know where they placed her coffin, Father?"

"I helped them carry it up the stairs; as you might know by now my dear daughter, I have accepted to be the Governor of the feast and have taken part in the planning. I know every corner in that house."

Jenny said she wasn't comfortable about having

a feast with a dead person in the same house, but Andreas told her that was not uncommon.

"From time to time, death and party goes hand in hand," he said, emphasizing that practical issues were most often considered before the preference.

The lead coachman announced the continuation and all the guests scrambled to get back into their carriages. Andreas took the seat facing Jenny and continued talking about death and celebration. "Too many people take death too seriously," he began. "Surely it's always sad to lose someone, but we need to look at the one leaving and going home after many years of hard work. We celebrate what that person has accomplished; therefore, we brew beer for a funeral as well as for a birth or a wedding."

Jenny nodded, hoping the more she knew the more she would be able to understand and accept the strange norms and customs of these people, but thinking about Robert, she would never be able to understand how he could do what he did. Killing a person in self defense is one thing; planning to execute hundreds, like cockroaches, is quite another. She pushed her thoughts of Robert out of her head and faced Andreas.

"But sometimes things just get out of hand."

Andreas continued and told the story of where an older man had taken his last breath, been put in a coffin and was stowed away, waiting for burial a few days later. Preparing for the funeral feast was already in the works and in the kitchen, a group of women were busy preparing food while his two sons and two other men were more concerned about tasting the beer, wondering if it had become too strong or had the right amount of hops. There was only one way to find out and a couple of hours later, the men were busy playing cards on the coffin's lid, unaware that the distressed widow had been watching them. "I see the beer was strong this time. Shame on you! Don't you have any respect for my dear husband?" she had yelled. One of the men excused himself by saying that her husband had been a devoted card player so he would not mind. Hours later, the women joined the men and once the beer had worked with them too, the coffin was moved and raised up against the wall to give room for dancing.

Jenny was stunned. How could they be so disrespectful of the dead? It seemed like they treated birth, marriage and death the same way, with a lot of food and beer. *How can you celebrate that a person is dead*? she wondered. Even though a get-together after a funeral was not new to her, she certainly didn't get drunk and begin dancing around the coffin! She hoped for the people's own sake that this was an exception, an event that had indeed gotten out of control.

Upon arrival, the hosts greeted them and Jenny had hardly stepped down from the buggy before a man with a gray apron handed her a colorful bowl of newly-brewed beer. After accepting the bowl, she turned to Andreas, frowning.

"Beer is always served first and is more important than the church ceremony; it's the ultimate symbol of recognizing the young couple as legally married. You must drink it or the family will be offended," he said.

"Don't listen to him, Jenny. All men think the beer is the most important," said Marta. She reached out for the crisp bread and honey cakes; true to the marriage day customs, all the women had baked and brought food in a fierce competition to show off to the relatives who was the best cook. She had used only well-proven recipes and had overseen the baking during the growth phase of the moon to make sure nothing went wrong. She had learned from her grandfather, also a devoted beer brewer, that the moon phases had great impact on fermentation.

More buggies arrived and people began stepping out. Men and women immediately separated and gathered into small groups where they began to chatter. It was like every move they made was a struggle, as if their bodies were dressed-up bronze sculptures. One women's wide black and dark-gray frieze skirts swayed only an inch from the ground, stirring up dust when she moved. People greeted each other by a stiff bow made with their entire upper body; their tight neckbands must have made it difficult to bow their heads, or perhaps they were afraid of losing their large hats which were decorated with different kinds of garlands and feathers. It appeared that everybody was examining each other's dresses and hats to find out from which kind of family they came from.

Jenny though it all looked like a fashion show and to a certain degree it was; a wedding gave people a unique opportunity to show off.

A few hours later, Andreas called the guests for dinner. In addition to directing the cooks, the cellar man, and all the helpers, Andreas would give the first speech and entertain the organized seating around the four long dinner tables. Only close relatives had the honor of sitting by the bride and groom's table. The other two long tables had women at one end and men at the other, and the children and adolescents would eat in the hay barn.

It surprised Jenny how bashful some of the guests seemed to be. In contrast to their Viking ancestors, they kept their heads low and clustered together as far away from the table as they could, while Andreas had to take them by the shirtsleeves, one at a time, and escort them across the floor to their assigned seats. "What's wrong with those people?"

"Wrong, what do you mean, Jenny?"

"Why are they so bashful?"

"They're not as bashful as they appear; it's just the custom. Old custom dictates you keep a very low profile during the seating of weddings and other large festivities. This won't last long. A few beers from now and everything changes."

Jenny looked around and was amazed at how many people they had managed to fit into the small living room. Small tables had been put together to form the long ones and were covered up with white plain table cloths. On one side, the benches were placed up against the wall, making a perfect back support. On the other side, the benches were so close that the people from the two adjacent tables could almost lean against each other's backs. Every inch of the room had been utilized to the fullest. Back home in Kristiania, Jenny's mother would need four times as much space to fit so many people. Suddenly, a loud discussion erupted between two men and caught her attention. It seemed like they were upset about the seating arrangement.

Marta smiled at Jenny. "It happens at every wedding. Just like children fighting for their seat at a birthday party. The seating has to do with family pride and reputation. They take it as a personal insult and are afraid of unfavorable judgments from the villagers."

It didn't make sense to Jenny that anybody would judge you because of your seating, but she had seen so many other strange behaviors of these people that nothing seemed to surprise her anymore. As she understood, the closer you were related to the bride or groom, the closer you may sit to them during the wedding dinner. And since everybody knew everybody, people would soon notice if a relative was sitting too far away and conclude that he or she was not regarded as good enough to hold their place in the family's pecking order.

Andreas went over and stopped the argument between the bride's two cousins. The older would get the preferred seat. Andreas took the younger by the collar and pulled him to his seat where the sulking man immediately bowed his head to avoid eye contact of the other guests around the table. When Andreas had completed the seating, everyone turned to the fiddler marching in, playing a wedding tune, leading the happy bride and groom to the dinner table. For those involved in setting up the party, this was the first time to see the couple. The bride wore a one hundred-year-old silver crown, twelve inches high with sixteen small ball-pointed spears, marked with an evil spirit protective, Angesti, the emblem of Christ, shaped like small Viking shields, hanging from both sides of the crown touching past her shoulders. Many other brides had used the same crown. The shiny polished silver made a sharp contrast to the bride's black dress with its hem embroidered to protect her from evil spirits sneaking under her skirt. On the wall behind the couple hung a light gray hand-woven rug, braided with a red heart-shaped garland with the first letters of the bride's and the groom's names inside.

While a servant served the newlyweds the sour cream porridge, the symbol to protect them from starving, Jenny noticed several young men had slightly repositioned their chairs to face her. Through the crowded tables she found Iver and as soon as their eyes met, he looked away. After the servers brought out the food, some of the men, and especially a couple of older women, slurped like starved animals as they downed the hot milk soup by drinking directly out of the bowl.

Marta noticed Jenny was watching them and whispered, "Some people starve themselves for days. Now they will eat as much as they can to save their own food."

Jenny wondered what would happen if she married a man from the village whose mother was eating like that? Wow, her mother would get a heart attack and die during the wedding dinner! Somehow she now understood her mother's resistance concerning her marrying a person from a lower class. It wasn't all about money and wealth; poorer people did indeed behave differently. Instead of using fine silverware, they used spoons made of buckhorn making a fine milk soup taste like rancid goat milk. "You have to use the spoon several times to get rid of the rancid taste," Marta had told her. Well, that didn't help much for the wedding guests who had gotten a new spoon to use only one time. But for the host, the importance of showing that they did indeed have plenty of new spoons seemed to be more important than causing some guests to be dissatisfied with the soup. After all, they could easy claim the soup had been made by someone else and brought to the feast. The men had one good solution - they downed the soup with beer, but the ones who didn't worship the beer so much would be leaving the table with a rancid taste. Next time, if there ever would be a next time, Jenny would do as Marta had done - bring her own spoon.

A couple of hours later, when most had finishing eating, Andreas tapped his spoon against his cup, asking for attention. "It's a big honor for me to welcome this beautiful bride and handsome groom to the world of marriage. Both have made an important decision that will affect the rest of their lives and may this marriage solve any disputes among your families."

Marta whispered to Jenny, "These two families have a long and ugly past. It's a miracle the elders have accepted the marriage in the first place."

Andreas looked at the newlyweds. "May you, young woman, be blessed with many healthy children and serve your man the best you can. And you, Mister, treat the soil with love and it will feed a large herd of animals, and cherish your wife with the same love and she will remain strong."

After the groom gave his thank-you speech to the bride's family, Andreas cleared his voice and said, "I would like to tell the story about when the bride's great grandfather wanted to buy a piece of land from the groom's family."

Marta leaned toward Jenny. "He is brave; this story is offensive to some of them. Watch the bride's family's reaction."

"The old man had a reputation of being as smart as a fox and almost always got what he wanted," Andreas began, "but in case he should face unexpected difficulties, he brought with him a bottle of whisky to the mountain farm. When he arrived, the farmer ushered him into his finest living room and offered him food. After hearing about the visitor's mission, he expressed a sincere interest in selling the land at the offered price; he just needed to clarify a few details about its use. As the small talk continued, the old man thought he could get a better deal by loosening up the farmer, so he put the bottle of whiskey on the table. The farmer rolled his eyes; it wasn't every day he saw a bottle of fine whiskey or much less tasted the noble liquid. The old man got excited and hoped to get the price even lower. He would wait for the right moment and pull up the papers for him to sign. Like hunting - wait for the prey, aim and shoot at the right moment. But the more the farmer drank, the more problems he saw with the deal and with only a quarter left of the bottle, he became so difficult to talk with that the old man began to doubt they would be able to strike a deal that day. After the bottle was empty, the farmer became so obstinate he chased the old man out of the house and told him to never set his foot on his property again."

As Marta had suspected, the groom's family laughed, but many of the bride's family remained quiet. Andreas had to tell another story, putting the groom's family in the brunt's role, before proceeding with the dinner closure. After the dinner, the guests who didn't like to dance went into rooms to continue talking. Soon the chatter reached the noise level known as Wedding Buzz - a condition where everybody talks so loudly nobody hears anything.

Jenny was watching the women and a few men, trying to figure out what they were talking about, but it was impossible and she doubted that any of them could either. These were definitely not people who courteously asked for attention before speaking, as she was used to in her own family's gatherings; they just spurted out, rambling about nothing and every thing. It appeared that they had either not seen each other for a long time or had been totally isolated. And now, everything that had happened to every person in the village during the last year was trying to be exchanged in a matter of minutes.

The dance began shortly after dinner and true to the customs, the bride and groom were the first on the floor. At the second song, men of all ages lined up to get the honor of dancing with the bride. While watching the bride, Jenny heard a familiar voice.

"Miss, do you want to dance?"

There, standing before her, was the handsome man from the Midsummer feast again, the one who reminded her of Robert. He was tall, with large brown eyes and jet-black hair neatly combed and a row of white, flawless teeth under his mustache. His bloodline had to be from other parts of the world.

"I am, that is, I was going ..." Jenny was flustered, remembering him to be an excellent dancer. Even on the grassy pasture he had impressed her and if it wasn't for his conduct, she wouldn't mind dancing with him.

"Better dance floor than the one we had in the valley," he said with a grin.

Jenny nodded, "I see they have dropped flour on it."

"They don't seem to be stingy with anything today, flour on the floor, beer in the casks, food on the table and I'd call myself lucky standing before such a beautiful woman. I promise to behave myself if you grant me one dance."

Jenny grabbed his reached-out hand; his dancing was superb and she almost felt like she was home dancing at a ball. It didn't take long before the guests noticed both of them. Several men approached Jenny and after an hour of dancing, she excused herself. She had already danced with Andreas and

Lars and wondered why Iver hadn't come forward. She had watched him from a distance and he spent all his time talking to an old man near the doorway. For some reason tonight she wanted him to come forward and ask her to dance, to notice she was alive. She declined several offers to dance, thinking he might ask her. Then, as she was about to give up waiting, he headed directly towards her. Anxiously she wondered what to say to him. When he passed her and asked a woman next to her to dance, Jenny became irritated, wondering why her feelings had been hurt. He hadn't even noticed her - not a nod or a simple hello. She watched every step he took as he led his partner about the makeshift dance floor with sure steps and the dignified air of an accomplished dancer.

Furious with Iver for slighting her, Jenny broke all rules of prudent conduct and after downing a large mug of beer, poked her way into the crowd and asked the first single man she met to dance with her. It didn't take long before a long line of men stood waiting to have a chance to dance with the beautiful woman from Kristiania. One more beer and one last dance and she had to be carried to her sleeping quarters where she fell down on the mattress with an empty look at the ceiling. At the moment the two men who had carried her in closed the door behind them, the ceiling began to move from side to side, back and forth. It was like the entire room started to weave. Jenny had never been so drunk before and was glad nobody from her family had seen her. Not even her aunt would have taking lightly to her getting so drunk. She couldn't even think about what her mother would do; probably try to convince her father to disinherit her, claiming that a person who can't handle herself better would not be fit to be the heir of the estate. Images from the day's activities flushed through her mind, fighting for her attention. Then she began to drift off and suddenly she was out like a light.

The mountain rims had turned orange and the golden gleam was signaling a new day when the other guests began looking for their prearranged sleeping spots. Soon they would be asleep while the sun would break through and ignite activities in the dew-wet grass.

Jenny woke up with the sun shining on her face; at the moment she sat up, she realized how much she had drunk. So this was what it was like to have a hangover - definitely not a feeling one would strive after! Although she had a few drinks now and then before, she had never been drunk. Her head ached and she felt as if she wanted to throw up. She got on her feet and tiptoed over snoring bodies and slowly opened the door, hoping no one would wake up and notice her. She just wanted to be alone without answering questions and explaining herself. After finding a suitable rock to sit on, she took a few deep breaths, filling her lungs with the crisp morning air before exhaling slowly. A masterpiece of a cobweb nearby took her attention away from herself. The light from the sun made the dew-wet web shine as a tracery of white gold. The easy recognizable net would warn any insect; only a bumblebee didn't seem to care. It almost got caught before it landed safely on the edge of a purple orchid and disappeared into the cloves of the flower.

While gradually getting better and enjoying the beautiful morning, Jenny noticed Lars stumble out of the hay-barn and head for a grove nearby, carrying a blanket. *He must have been one of the men sleeping in the barn* she thought as she watched him pacing around and wondered what he was looking for. Suddenly, he spread the blanket out on the ground. Maybe he wanted to get away from sleeping drunks and sleep outside now that it had gotten warmer, but when she saw him taking off his coat and throwing it on the ground; she knew there had to be something else going on. Nothing that Lars did ever surprise her; he always had a reason for doing what he did, no matter how strange it looked.

"Lars, what were you doing up there?" she asked as he was heading back toward the barn.

Lars turned and headed in her direction as soon as he saw her. "Good morning, Jenny. How are YOU feeling today? I noticed that you had plenty of drink last night."

Jenny blushed; she couldn't think about anything more embarrassing than to be reminded of being drunk. "I am ok. I think the beer was just too strong for me; you know, I am not used to drinking any alcohol."

Lars laughed. "That's ok. Even old ladies who rarely touch the stuff got drunk last night. You should have seen one of them - she lost her balance and almost tore down the desert table!"

Jenny smiled. Lars did indeed see the humor in most things. "So what were you doing in the woods? It seemed like you danced."

"Yes, I danced with the devil to get the booze out of my body." He smiled, "No, no. I am just joking. I found an army of lice on my coat and blanket."

"Lice?" Jenny felt something begin to crawl down her neck just by the word of it. She had heard about lice in certain schools in Kristiania, schools on the eastside where the poor people lived, and among dirty traders who lived on the road and walked from house to house. She instinctively backed off.

"It's ok Jenny. I am clean and in a few hours, my coat will be too."

"Would they just walk off then? I figure that was your intention instead of picking them one by one."

"No. I have others for the job; they eat them."

"Eat them, who?"

"Ants. I left my blanket and coat on an ant hill."

Jenny shook her head. "Do you know, Lars, if everybody thought like you, a lot of things would be much easier everywhere?"

Lars nodded, "Yep, maybe."

At exactly four o'clock in the afternoon, the women started clucking like hens in a barnyard pen, knowing their men would soon be inebriated as the moonshine surfaced and the punch drinking began. The cellar man had the greatest honor at the wedding and the most difficult; he needed to make sure the beer flowed and the punch bowl never emptied while at the same time not allowing any guest to become drunk - an almost impossible task. On this second wedding day, quarrels began, unresolved disputes erupted with fervor exploding into fistfights and name-calling. The common notion was that a man could get three fistfights out of every bottle of moonshine consumed. Carefully planned, this was also the time when the guests were passed the giving bowl, dolling out money or gifts to the newlyweds. Only a few guests carried money, so the majority would sign a pledge with many regretting it the following day. Andreas supervised as the guests lined up and came forward, either placing their contribution in a bowl, or whispering into his ear their pledge. Even though it happened at every wedding, it always came as a surprise when the Governor of the Feast yelled out the name of the giver and the amount. Most gave more then they could afford, showing off wealth they didn't have. Instead of coming forward in line, everyone would try to be the last to give, so they could hear what others had given and then surpass it. The importance of looking good in the eyes of others usually overruled all common sense.

When the third day neared its end, Andreas called all the guests into the main living room for an announcement. He stepped on a chair and looked down on the tired celebrants saying, "This wedding has come to its end. We have consumed two sheep, one of the largest halibut pulled up from the fjord, eaten all the crushed grain and emptied all the beer casks. On behalf of both families and myself, bless all of you and everything you have consumed, but now, as you have eaten the hosts out of the house, it's time to go home."

Immediately a muttering began among the guests; not everybody seemed to agree with this announcement. A three-day's wedding was coming to an end, but while some of the guests began to gather their coats and hats, others lifted their glasses in a cheer, ready to continue.

Jenny felt quite different from the day she came, but didn't know exactly what it was. It was something inside of her that had changed. Maybe it was just because a whole new and unfamiliar experience had grabbed her more than a regular wedding back home would do. Here she had met new people, listened to an unbelievable minister, tasted different food, seen amazing table manners and even gotten drunk for the first time. She had to admit, it had been quite interesting. She had accepted the people for the way they were, except Iver. She didn't understand why he didn't ask her to dance. She had actually hoped that this wedding would be a time when he would loosen up, a time when they could sit and talk and talk, a time when he could open up his closed heart, a time when she could learn to know him. But instead, he had completely ignored her.

As Andreas was about to step down from the chair, a man staggered out from the crowd yelling, "No, ich ich it's not over y-y-yet." He turned around and was met by cheering.

"No it's not!"

The man walked slowly toward Andreas and began to tie his hands together with a rope while yelling at the crowd, "We need a new Governor of the Feast. Who will volunteer?"

Jenny poked Marta in her side and whispered," What are they doing to Andreas?"

"Just watch, Jenny. He knows what's going on and is in on it. This happens almost every time at the end of the feast."

A bear of a man came forward. "I do."

"Any objections?" asked the leader as he finished up with Andreas.

After a short silence, he grabbed the volunteer's hand and lifted it in the air. "Do you swear that this feast isn't over yet?"

"I swear," said the man.

"You are hereby elected to be our new Governor of the Feast."

After the cheering had settled down, they heard footsteps on the roof and a moment later, a rope came down through the smoke vent. The new leader took it and tied it around Andreas' waist.

"Make a good knot so he doesn't fall and hurt himself," yelled a woman in the crowd. More laughter followed. When the leader was finished, he faced the ceiling and shouted, "Heave."

The rope tightened and Andreas dangled two feet off the floor. The new Governor of the Feast looked at him. "It's not over yet." When Andreas didn't respond, the man flipped his fingers and Andreas ascended a foot higher.

"I agree, the feast isn't over yet," answered Andreas.

When they dropped him to the floor, a round of applause broke out. Most of the guests honored the first request to end the feast and prepared to go home, while a small number would remain cheerful for one more night. For the wedding hosts, as with many others, the outrageous amount of food consumed would lead to poverty for months to come. That was the reason the Danish King Christian VII, ruler of Denmark and Norway, had decreed in 1793 explicit wedding laws to be enforced by the local bailiff and minister, limiting the number of guests to thirty-two people, including the bride, groom and relatives. Nothing more than a four-course dinner could be served without wine or coffee. The wedding could last only one day, with the exception that sixteen of the guests could, on the second day, dance from six o'clock in the evening until midnight if they did not sit down to eat. Only home-woven clothes could be worn. In truth, a little village in Norway, far away from the king of Denmark, had never paid attention to the edict, especially since the rules were seldom enforced, and now, almost a hundred years later in a union with Sweden, those rules were just a cold blast from the past.

When the Holseth family was ready to leave, Jenny stopped in front of Iver just before entering the buggy, wanting to tell him how disappointed she was that he hadn't asked her to dance, then thought the better of it. There was nothing between the two of them that mattered and she remained quiet the entire trip back to Holseth. The wedding had turned out to be a grand success and Marta was proud of her father who had handled his responsibilities well.

The Tidal Wave

"What breaks in a moment may
take years to mend."
Swedish Proverb

Jenny's dancing with every eligible bachelor at the wedding kept the wagging tongues busy until the end of October when the villagers' lives abruptly would change for decades to come. The peaceful village of Stranden was about to be forever transformed when a shoulder of the mountain across the fjord that had been cut deeply by an eroding stream felt a shift in the earth which dropped it into the fjord. The villagers immediately felt the aftermath, awaking to a portal of change where ties were strengthened among family, friends and enemies and lives were lost. A year from then, when autumn stretched its colors and sounds upon the land, a large engraved marker would be set in the village square to remember the lost ones.

Power transcends the mountain across the fjord from Stranden. Its size resembles a magnificent cathedral, but no cathedral can actually compare to the mountain's natural splendor with contrasting paths spiraling up to hanging valleys and onto colored forests. At timberline, small rocks appear, then boulders, until the rock becomes large sheets of insurmountable granite, collecting snow and ice - the mountain's last adornment. A bird glides along the side of the mountain and makes man envious of its wings. The grounded man must walk for hours, slowly moving up the mountain, stopping only to look back from where he came to glimpse his insignificance. The scenery clears man's thoughts for retrospection, his ascension cleansed, his descent calmed. One never leaves the mountain unchanged. For millions of years, this mountain has known snow and rain. The water forms white foamy streams that trickle down their favored paths and by sheer volume, gain momentum and disappear into gorges partly hidden by fir trees and dwarf birches.

This breathtaking quiet October morning, Jenny prepared to spend the entire day and night with Anna at Iver's farm. Anna's husband, Jon, and the rest of the men of Holseth would be in Stranden for Traders Day. She had packed just a few items in a bag and took her time walking to the farm. Near the farm, she stopped at a ledge of the mountain to catch a glimpse of the fjord; she noticed a boat appearing like a small dot passing by. She sat close to the edge of the rock, took her hat off, and unpinned her hair, allowing it to cascade down her shoulders. Enjoying this time alone, she lay back on the rock and closed her eyes to the sun.

Nothing on the two farms at Holseth ever went unnoticed by Iver, and now as Olaf, Jon, and the dog walked with him to his mother's farm, he recognized Jenny's pack. He told them to go on without him, that he would catch up later and then commanded the dog to follow Olaf. Reluctantly, the dog turned back several times, then obeyed and moved on down the path. Iver found Jenny rocking back and forth singing and was touched by the beauty of her voice, the sadness in her song and the tears.

"Jenny, Jenny, it's me."

She opened her eyes as he stood above her. "How did you know I was here?" She quickly sat up, straightened her dress and pulled her hair back away from her face.

"Why are you here?"

"To be with Anna; Marta suggested it."

She moved away as he sat down on the rock. The summer had changed his appearance so that he was almost handsome but still disagreeable. He looked out over the fjord, wanting to ask her why she had been crying and pointed out several rowboats. Traders Day was the most important day for the farmers. That day their crops would be sold along with bartering for winter supplies. "I'd best be off. I'll walk you to the farm to make sure you get there safely."

"I can make it to the farm by myself," Jenny snapped. "You don't always have to take care of me."

He extended his hand and she turned away. "I didn't mean to upset you; it just seems you find ways to get in trouble."

She glared back at him.

"All right, all right, I'm off. I'm sure you will be fine but promise me you'll stay on the path. Before I leave, is there anything you need from Stranden?"

"No!" she said hotly and headed up the path, then stopped, turned around and found him standing where she had left him by the boulders, watching her walk away. She came back to him. "There is something you can do for me. I ordered a pair of cape-skinned gloves from the store. I forgot to pack mine when I left home. Would you please pick them up? I've already paid for them."

"Cape-skinned gloves? I hope you were smart enough to have them lined with fleece, otherwise they'll be useless. Our winters are harsh."

"Iver, you are so practical it is nauseating. I don't plan to be here throughout your winter. You asked me if there's something you could get me. I told you my gloves."

"You'll have them tomorrow."

She couldn't hear him since she was already out of sight. Disgusted with himself, he headed to his mother's. Without trying he always seemed to make her angry.

At Holseth, the wind moved through the large aspen making its bright yellow leaves tremor, a soft rattling - the sound of the passing season. The sheer push of the wind caused the leaves to lose their grip and take a final flight across the pasture, drifting and settling on the ground. Iver's dog chasing a squirrel up a tree stirred up the pasture which was aflame with the bright yellow leaves. The squirrel spread its tail and with its prominent front teeth, chattered a reprimand at the dog while moving further up a branch.

A moment later, Andreas walked across the pasture, waving a cane behind a half-dozen sheep. He ushered them into the barn, bolted the door, and headed back to the house where he met Olaf. "Where is your father?"

Olaf pointed, "Over there."

"Over where?"

"He comes later."

"Come on boy! Let's go find your grandmother." Andreas took off his wet coat, hung it over the rod behind the wood stove, sat down at the kitchen table and began to rub his cold hands while Olaf was already stuffing himself with bread and butter.

"Did you find all of them?" asked Marta as she covered the bread bowl and wiped the flour off her hands.

"Every single one, even the black-faced ewe. The snow forced them down to the valley."

Marta handed her father a bowl of Brennsnut soup made from lamb, rutabagas, potatoes and carrots. He tore a piece of bread and dipped it into the hot liquid, tasting the broth. "Sometimes I think your dear Mother is still in the kitchen. This soup tastes like hers."

Marta smiled and sat down next to her father as he asked, "Where is Jenny?"

"With Anna. Remember I told you since Anna is with child, I would feel better if someone stayed and Jenny offered. They both get on so well with one another."

"I've noticed this morning something is odd about the animals...I can't put my finger on it but they seem to be acting out of sorts, fidgety."

"What's odd about that? They always act strange this time of the year; the weather is getting ready to change."

"The weather, it's not the weather this time. Something else has them riled. I've been with animals all my life and don't tell me it's just snow. Early this morning I saw fish jumping out of the water. The fish don't jump after insects in October." He waved the spoon in front of her nose. "I tell you something is about to happen and I have a feeling it has to do with the fjord."

"Whatever it is, you don't have time to worry. I thought you had plans to go with the boys to Stranden today?"

"That's tomorrow."

"You're mistaken; today is Trading Day. You haven't heard a word I've said all morning."

He slowly got up from the chair and headed to his room.

"Sit down." Marta pointed to a pack on the floor. "Everything you need is ready."

Two hours later, Andreas sat in the rowboat with his grandson and Jon, still feeling uneasy about the day.

The coastal steamboat docked at two o'clock in the afternoon and brought curious and nosy villagers to the shoreline. Today might be the last time of the year for some distant farmers to visit the village. Everyone would be stockpiling food and supplies for the winter. It was also the refueling day for gossip and with so many people gathered, new stories were launched and old ones improved. After docking by their church shed, the Holseth men walked to the Old Trading House to make the arrangements to transport their cheese and butter to Aalesund. After delivering the last churn, they headed up the main street to the store amidst the hustle and bustle of activity. Friends and relatives greeted them as they passed, but it was Lars who enjoyed the walk the most because of all the attention he received from the women in the village.

Just before they reached the store, an uneasy feeling came over Iver. Maybe his grandfather was right - something felt wrong about the day. He wanted to suggest they buy their supplies and head right back to the mountain until he glanced over at his brother and grandfather and decided against it. They had all worked hard the past month and it wasn't often they could spend time drinking with friends. They would be home in the morning. As the Holseth men walked into the general store, the owner, a short stubby man with a round belly in his mid-fifties, leaned against the counter and said, "Lars Holseth, if I ever catch you within ten feet of my niece, I'll hang you like a fish to dry by the dock."

Lars smiled back at the old grocer and held up his hands. Andreas came to his defense. "Leave the boy alone. It still surprises me a man as ugly as you would have such a beautiful niece." Everyone in the store laughed, including the grocer, who was one of the three most powerful men in the village, along with the Bailiff and the minister. The grocer was an honest man; he knew all of his customers by name and treated them as family and would allow credit to run longer than he should. He kept the store stocked with a variety of food and merchandise with the slogan written on the wall: "I have everything and will order the rest." His personal power came from the success of the store and gossip. The store had long been the locals' meeting place and if you wanted to know anything about the villagers, you asked the grocer. Only a few people didn't care for him because of his passion for playing tricks, but being the only grocer in the village, they didn't hold it against him for too long. Today he was in an excellent mood since he would sell most of his stock. The steamer had brought him two kinds of fruit never before seen in the village - limes and oranges. When he saw the Holseth men walk in, he quickly hid the oranges, leaving the limes on the counter.

"So what can I get the Holseth men today?"

"Ten mark of salt, a bag of flour, and everything else on my daughter's list," said Andreas, handing him Marta's list.

The grocer looked at the list, turned around and began to place the items on the counter when he suddenly stopped and looked at Andreas over his glasses. "I got a new tropical wonder fruit in today. It's called orange and it comes all the way from Spain," he boasted and pushed a basket of limes in front of him.

"Is this it?" asked Andreas and picked up a lime from the basket.

"Yes go ahead and eat it; it's on me. Free of charge."

Andreas took a big bite. Instantly his entire face changed into several pained expressions and as he choked on the last bite, he whispered, "You call this a tropical wonder? Your oranges are too sour."

The grocer let out a howl, laughing so hard his eyes watered. He pulled out the basket from below the counter and handed Andreas an orange. "Try this. It's riper than the green one." While Andreas soothed his palate with the orange, a bell above the door chimed, signaling another customer. The store was already crowded when a tall, muscular man in his mid-thirties, with reddish-brown curly hair under his hat and a waxed mustache, wearing overalls walked in. He nodded to the grocer and loudly greeted Lars, his drinking buddy, before taking a seat next to Iver.

"It's been a few months. Heard about the woman from Kristiania," he said, jabbing Iver in the ribs.

The bachelor farmer, known to everyone as the Stud, was Iver's former schoolmate. He came by his nickname somewhat seedily for his successful maneuvers with women. He was known to check out every new woman who came to the village and would hound the newcomer until they met, then use all his masculine wiles to spirit her away to his bed. Not particularly handsome, it had never stopped him from pursuing beautiful women. He had powerful, penetrating eyes that could make a women blush. The joke ran among the men that he could ignite an old frigid maid from the Royal House just by looking through the keyhole. After joking about the woman from Kristiania where he tried to find out which of the two Holseth brothers had slept with her, he invited them to his house for oppskøkje, a local expression for an event where home brewed beer is tasted and judged. The Stud was famous for the best beer in the village.

The grocer looked over at Jon who had been standing quietly at the end of the counter. He had heard rumors that his wife was expecting. "Is it true your Anna's with child?"

Jon's face lit up, pleased that someone had asked him about Anna. "Four more months."

"So what do you think it's going to be?"

"A boy," he answered without hesitation.

"What makes you so sure it's a boy?"

Everybody in the store looked at Jon. He wasn't

among those who talked too much, but when he did, people usually listened.

"Frequency, just frequency," he answered.

The grocer frowned. "Never heard of that one. Frequency? Explain it."

Jon leaned over the counter, "You know, if you hover over your woman daily during her critical period, it becomes a boy; if less than twice a week, it becomes a girl."

The grocer grinned and gave Jon a slap on the back. "Well done young man, well done!"

After leaving the store, the Holseth men secured their purchases in the church shed and hurried to Jon's parents for supper. At six o'clock the three men prepared to take off for their beer date. Jon had declined and wished them a joyful night and said that he would meet them in the morning. The Stud lived a couple of miles away from the center of the village; his ancestors had been some of the early settlers and had taken the best land above the village.

A whiff of yeast and the bitter smell of hops hit them as they entered the Stud's home and were greeted by their host. The furniture, decorations and stuffed animals spoke to men. Taxidermy was Stud's hobby and he could make any taxidermist envious of his abilities. Bored with the four-legged creatures, he had moved on to birds and had several sitting above the fireplace, but it was the crow that caught Iver's attention. Its glossy feathers and black eyes had taken on an amber color by the fireplace and it appeared it would take flight any moment. A dozen men who were already seated, greeted the latecomers and resumed telling their sultry jokes.

The ever-circulating drinking bowl had been passed on to a man with a big head in his late forties who came from a distant farm in one of the village's side valleys and was known to not to ride the same day as he saddled. He was a nice and considerate man with a speaking impairment making him finishing each sentence with a long hum. With his elbows planted firmly on the table, he tilted his head forward over the bowl, took a deep breath, rolled his eyes and took a big gulp of the brew, swished it around in his mouth for a long time, loudly swallowed and then belched. Still holding the bowl close to his nose as if he wanted to reaffirm its taste with the smell, he moved the bowl in such a way its content began to roll around, threatening to go over the rim.

The Stud walked over and bumped him on his head with his knuckles. "It's bad luck to slow down the bowl; you can hold the brew in your mouth all night if you want, but always pass the bowl. The man nicknamed The Head was so slow that gossip tongues said he couldn't work outside in the fields because the vultures would take him for being dead. The Stud looked at him and shook his head. "Do you know why you haven't been eaten by a vulture yet?"

The Head passed the bowl, wiped his mouth, belched again and thought for a long time before responding, "No I don't hummm."

Stud looked at the men across the table, "I don't either."

After the bowl had passed by several men, The Head raised his voice. "I know why the vultures haven't gotten me yet hummm. There are no vultures in the valley hummm." He chuckled so hard his upper body shook.

The sacred beer bowl being passed came from the Stud's ancestors. Peasant farmers from Otta Valley had carved the bowl in 1604 out of birch wood and decorated it with a floral design in red, white and blue. On the outside, just under the rim, they had carved the rhyme, "Drikk av mig med Lempe, thi jeg kan Tørsten dempe, paa noksaa stor en kæmpe", "You may drink of me with ease, for I can suppress the thirst on quite a big giant." The antique bowl would be passed from one man to another, never touching the table. It was believed the bowl should never rest but continue being handed from one man to another to prevent the next brew from becoming sour. One of the problems by having everybody drinking from the same bowl was that some of the men used chewing tobacco, so each would have to find a clean spot. But usually after the bowl had made a few rounds, nobody seemed to care. "The brown spots are more hygienic than the clean ones," the users claimed, arguing that the tobacco killed possible germs.

After several beers, stories, jokes and a few national hymns, the men were beyond being quarrelsome and the noise level had increased to a point only the ones who yelled got anybody's attention. The Stud pumped Andreas for news about Jenny and finally gave up with the old man and turned to Lars and Iver thinking the beer had surely made their tongues loose enough to answer his questions.

"Let's get the truth. What is going on with you boys and the girl on your farm?"

With clenched jaw, Iver responded, "Stud, get off it! As I told you in the store and I tell you now, she is a friend of our mother's and will be leaving soon. It was her aunt that treated our mother at the hospital.

The Stud noticed Iver clench his fists and changed the subject; no need to start a fight in his own house. Since none of these men were interested, he'd find a way to meet her.

The drinking continued and soon reached the level where intimate discussions and confessions flowed like the beer. Just after midnight some of the men had returned to their homes; others had either passed out or were still reminiscing and drinking. Iver went outside to freshen up and was met by large snowflakes mixed with rain; the season's first snow was under way. He thought about his inability to act normal around Jenny. Why had she caused such a stir in him? He could still see her lying on the ledge above the fjord with her hair loose, remembering her sad expression. Why the tears? Did she miss her family or was it Blackstone? No one in his life had ever made him ask so many questions. As he stood there and pondered about his feelings, he felt the ground suddenly begin to shake. He wondered if he had been drinking that much or maybe the beer had been extraordinary strong this time; he had heard numerous stories about strange feelings men had after drinking, but that was usually after they had been going at it for several days or weeks - not after just one night. No, this had to be real. The earth was indeed moving, the oil lamp outside the barn flared more than normal and a rattling sound came from the wall behind the kitchen, a hanging spot for large pots and pans. Iver had never experienced an earthquake before; they were not common in the region. Then, just as the earth became silent again, a deep roaring and rumbling sound came rolling from somewhere out in the dark. Iver rushed inside to wake up the others, suspecting a huge avalanche.

A moment later, one after the other came staggering out looking into the darkness and seeing nothing, wondering why Iver had demanded them out. Then the noise of breaking timber and the woeful sound of a steamboat whistle that wouldn't stop sobered up a few of them enough to believe something extraordinary indeed had happened.

It didn't take long before the group of men was rushing toward the village. Soon they would all be sobered up even more by the horrific devastation. The moon had just broken through the clouds and its light allowed them to see across the fjord. In the haunting moonlight, they saw a gray portion of the mountainside across the fjord gradually appearing from behind a fading cloud of dust, exposing a large, empty wound.

"God almighty! A block of the Rammerfjell Mountain has plunged into the fjord!" said Andreas.

As they continued as fast as their feet could take them, stumbling, tripping and expecting the worst, they were met by a cacophony of sounds, the flushing of birds out of bushes, screams from men and women, shrill retreating sounds from animals and the unfamiliar haunting sound of a broken village.

Earlier the same day, when Anna had watched Jenny approaching the house, she knew by the look on her face that Iver must have crossed her path. Over the past few months, she had looked at Jenny as a new-found sister and would miss her terribly when she returned to Kristiania. Life on the mountain can be lonely and Jenny had filled the need Anna had for a woman's company. She loved her husband, appreciated the help Iver had given them, looked forward to the birth of her first child - so many new events were happening in her life for she and Jon would be moving to their own farm in the spring.

When Jenny approached the house, she noticed how beautiful Anna looked, in spite of having a six-month-old fetus growing inside of her, as she sat on the front steps apparently waiting for her. She was thankful to have a woman her age on this mountain.

"So you met Iver?"

"How did you guess?"

"By the look on your face. No one at Holseth can make you as mad as he can."

Jenny rolled her eyes. "Your brother is impossible."

"Maybe he's in love with you?"

Jenny backed off as if she was stung by an electric eel. "In love with me! You've got to be joking, Anna. People in love with one another don't behave like that. He hates me; it's quite obvious."

"I don't think it's you he hates. He hates his own feelings and you're the one who brings them up and the only way he knows how to suppress them is to attack you."

"Why does he want to suppress his feelings?" Jenny couldn't imagine that Iver cared for her at all. He had clearly demonstrated his resentment and was always making her feel bad about herself.

"I don't know Jenny, but some people do. Maybe they are afraid of themselves, afraid of where those feelings may take them."

"Well then, they can't get their heart's desire if they are afraid of getting it."

"Certainly. I know it may not make sense for people like us, Jenny. When we feel something good for someone, especially if we think its love, we let them know; don't you think so?"

"Yes, somehow, I guess. Although we might not always get our message across, we certainly don't behave hostilely toward the person we want to entice. But still, don't you think that all people dream about the perfect love to come around?"

"Yes I do, except me."

"What do you mean Anna?"

"I don't dream about what I have."

Jenny pushed Anna on her shoulder. "Oh lucky you."

Anna smiled; her face lit up. "Yes I am lucky. Jon is more to me than I had ever dreamed about. I can't imagine the pain of losing him. We have known each other since childhood and I have always felt that I wanted to marry him, even though neither of us had much land and goods."

"I thought you married only if certain assets were compatible? Didn't your family resist your marriage on those grounds?"

"Grandfather tried, but my mother understood me and persuaded him. You know my father was already gone by then. I think one of the reasons my mother wanted me to go ahead and marry Jon was that she saw that I could have what she never had. Jon brings out the child in me, the part of me that wants to play and not worry about what tomorrow brings."

"Reminds me of your brother, Lars."

"The difference with Lars is that he doesn't see when to stop playing. Jon does."

Jenny envied Anna; it was easy to see that she was very much in love with Jon. After helping her with the farm chores, they continued talking about the subject of love and feelings until late into the night.

Jenny didn't know how long she had been sleeping when she suddenly woke up by the windows rattling and the house shaking. After getting on her feet, she found Anna already up and looking out the window. "Did you hear the rumble?"

Anna nodded. "I've been up for the longest time. I was dreaming about Jon coming home early; then I woke up to a rattling house.

"A snow avalanche?"

"I don't think so. Not enough snow to cause an avalanche. Could be boulders."

She looked at Jenny, clearly worried. "Jenny, I have a terrible feeling something bad has happened somewhere and I would like to check if my mother is all right, but I don't feel like it." She gently stroked her stomach. "I think the baby wants me to stay inside today. Do you mind?" Then she looked toward the door, gasping.

"What is it Anna?"

"Look at the dog!"

"The dog, what about him?"

"Look at his tail!"

"Seems quite normal to me."

"No it's not normal! When a dog lies lengthwise on the floorboards like that and bangs his tail against the wood, death is imminent within the household. The myth says he is hammering the lid of a casket."

Jenny put her arm around her friend's shoulders. "Oh come on, Anna, that's only an old myth. Nothing to take seriously."

"Let's hope that! I don't know if I can take any more deaths now."

"As soon as the day breaks, I'll be happy to see about your mother."

A couple of hours later, Jenny headed down the path toward her house and saw nothing out of the ordinary - no fallen trees or signs of avalanches anywhere. She entered the house and found Marta pacing back and forth in the living room.

"I am going to the village, Jenny. Do you want to go with me? I need someone to help me row." Like most mountain farmers, Marta always hesitated before asking someone for help; instead, she would push herself almost to exhaustion. It was the concern of being a burden and an attempt to free themselves from relying on others that made them so hesitant to ask for help. There would always come a day when help would not be available, no matter how much you asked, so instead, they had learned to notice when someone needed help and would without being asked, step in.

That was the case with the mountain farmer who during the busy hay season, saw someone was struggling up against the wind down on the fjord. He immediately threw his tools on the ground and began the twenty-minute-long decent down to the fjord just in time to catch the struggling person. Without any form of expected compensation, he offered to help the man to get to the village to get some medicine that his sick wife needed, even though he knew the day would go by and some of his hay could get wet by the predicted rain. It was late when they came back and the farmer got his compensation for the trip, the knowing that the man's wife would suffer less by getting the medicine faster.

Jenny was grateful that Marta finally had asked for her help and it was obvious it was her company she wanted, not help with the rowing. Jenny had never rowed a boat before and Marta knew it. "I'll be happy to join you Marta, but what shall we do about Anna? She'll be worried when I don't come back."

"I'm going to make sure she is alright and then I'll come down and get you. You could help Kari with the animals until I return."

An hour later, Marta and Jenny got the rowboat on the water and as they pushed it away from shore, it dawned on Marta how silent the fjord was, like a huge polished slate of ice reflecting the black portions of the mountains. She wondered how the surface could possibly have returned to such a silence if something had plunged into it only hours before. Or maybe the last night's rumble could have come from a mudslide in a valley that had not reached the water at all. She could only speculate what had happened, making it all just more mysterious. She grabbed the oars and began to row, making the boat glide like a black swan in between the massive mountains, so quiet and yet so frightening. Rowing long distances during the winter months required more than just dipping the oars into the water and pulling; you needed to find a rhythm that caused as little energy as possible, but at the same time kept the body warm without getting sweaty. Rowing slow and steady was always more effective and gentler to the arms and back than hard rowing with frequent breaks. A sweaty body gets cold and cold muscles get tired faster.

Jenny had positioned herself all the way in the back of the boat, her favorite place. Marta had brought a pillow for her to sit on and some extra clothes; for the person sitting still it could get quite chilly after a while. She wrapped her shawl around her shoulders and watched the cotton ball-sized snowflakes instantly disappearing as they hit the water. Interesting how the snowflakes suddenly died and were transformed into water. She wondered what lay ahead, what would she see and feel and how mysterious this not knowing or the unknown really is. Mountains disappearing into the clouds seem to create more images of what you don't see than what you do see. A story with no closure puts the mind into a frenzy of figuring out what the mystery was. Sailing on an open ocean by letting go of the sight of shore creates anxiousness about what to find on the other side. No wonder the old sailors who thought the earth was flat were afraid of continuing! Jenny thought about how strange it was that a room can become instantly mysterious the moment the light goes off and why some people fear the unknown, like Iver, while others cherish it, like Lars. It seemed like Lars, who was like an open book and hid nothing about himself, was drawn to the unknown, while Iver who was closed, would strive to avoid it; could that be because Lars was actually afraid of himself? Or was it that what one doesn't have, one wants, and therefore we avoid what we do have. The more questions she asked herself about Iver, the more mysterious he seemed to get. Could it all have to do with losing his father and wife so close to each other? She remembered Anna had said that his sullen nature was not something he had been born with. Maybe he was different as a child. *But he is not in love with me. Anna has to be wrong there.* Jenny wanted to ask Marta about him and get her perspective, but then she thought it would have to wait to another time; maybe she wanted to keep the secret a little longer and in the mean time, have the unknown entice her.

Marta had decided that this time, she would seek out the bad news rather than waiting for it to be delivered. Too many times had she been waiting for her boys and husband to come back when boulders had tumbled down the mountainside and she knew all too well what it felt like to have someone knocking on her door, starting the sentence with... "I am sorry, but..." The moment the news about her husband's accident was delivered on her front steps would always haunt her. She had had this hunch that something terrible had happened and when she saw the neighboring farmer walking up to her house, she knew he had bad news, very bad news. It was like his slow, hesitating steps told her there was nothing more anybody could do. And when she opened the door, she had just asked, "Who was it?" The only comfort she seemed to find now was that the hunch she had that time was stronger than what she was feeling now - or was it?

As they reached the tongue of land called Uksneset, the fjord made a ninety-degree turn toward the village and as Marta turned the boat, she saw a large, uprooted aspen floating in the water. She rested the oars and looked around for more when she noticed several small pine trees floating close to the shoreline. The shoreline clearly showed signs of huge waves; moss and bushes had been ripped off from the bedrock and the water was brown from dirt. Her eyes were searching the mountainside for possible avalanche tracks when Jenny suddenly exclaimed, "Oh my God! Look at that!"

Marta turned around and saw a huge white wound in the mountain. They both became numb and just stared motionless for a long time. Marta didn't doubt the magnitude; such a huge portion of the mountain couldn't have fallen into the fjord without creating a huge wave and devastating damage. And the more she looked, the more debris she noticed ahead of them. She picked up the oars again and began to row harder and faster then ever before, dreading what she would find.

Jenny clutched her hands around the boat's rim, as if she was afraid of falling into the water. She began to feel nauseous. At once her-own issues of hiding from Robert seemed so minor and insignificant. Even before seeing anything of the devastation, she began to feel a strong belonging to these people, as if she was one of them, and a strong desire to help someone in need. Maybe she should have studied to become a nurse instead of taking her mother's advice to study to be a psychologist when she said, "You don't need education for work, Jenny. You will never have to work; you need education only for being presentable for the family."

As they got closer they noticed broken pieces of furniture, parts of mattresses, planks of all kinds of shapes and sizes, and bails of hay floating in the water, leaving no doubt that the tidal wave had done its ravage on populated grounds. But however large the wave must have been, the fjord had now become almost silent again, only a few swells, long waves moving back and forth without breaking, causing the debris to slowly bounce up and down in the muddy water.

Suddenly Jenny covered up a scream and stared at what looked like a dead horse. As she got closer, she saw the animal's legs had somehow become tangled in a wood grid, keeping it afloat. The panic must have driven him to break down his bin's gate, trying to get out. Now she began to really understand that people had most likely perished too. The sight of the horse made her want to throw up. She had always loved horses and had got her own when she was only twelve, an animal she groomed every day and which became her best friend. She felt a deep sadness and a tear rolled down her cheek when she thought that maybe a twelve-year-old girl had just lost her best friend.

A little light came in the way of a kitten, apparently unharmed, sitting on what appeared to be a rooftop of a house, soaking wet and shivering with cold. As soon as the boat came within reach, Jenny grabbed the frightened animal and put it under her coat with only his head visible. Soon she could feel its comfortable purr. Jenny had found a new friend in the middle of death and devastation.

Why? Marta wondered. Why did she have to face this again? She tried to figure out where her sons and father could have been when the wave hit. For the first time, she really hoped they had gone to the Stud and gotten so drunk that they had passed out and stayed the night. She knew he lived too far away from the shoreline to be taken by the wave. If they didn't stay there, they would most likely be at Jon's family, who lived by the water. Even a strong easterly gale on high tide was enough to spurt water up against their house, so it must have been gone for sure. Her question was quite simple, yet so frightening. *Who had been staying in the house?* Again she was faced with this dreadful feeling of not knowing. When her husband was killed, she knew someone had died when the neighbor walked up to her house, but didn't know who.

Jenny interrupted Marta's thoughts by motioning her to row toward a piece of furniture dipping in the water. After getting there, she turned the boat so Jenny could reach it.

When Jenny hauled it into the boat, she saw it was a bed's headboard. A chill and sadness run through her when she saw the inscription in the wood: Synnøve May 23 1879. They both looked around, hoping to see the baby, but soon realized it could be anywhere, most likely dead. If anybody survived the tidal wave itself, the cold water would kill them within minutes. Jenny sent a silent prayer that the baby had not suffered and dropped the headboard back into the water, wondering if the baby's parents had perished too. It shouldn't take too much thinking to figure out if an entire house had been flushed into the fjord during the middle of the night, most likely the whole family was gone. Soon it would be revealed to her that not only one house had been taken, but many.

Suddenly Marta began a frenzy row backwards; she had obviously discovered something. Jenny froze in her seat at the sight of what appeared to be a body and as they got closer, they saw it was a person holding on to a milking stool. Facing down, the back of its head almost broke the surface while a hand seemed to be locked into the stool's handle.

Marta slowed down and gently maneuvered the boat alongside the body. She knew everybody in the village and wondered who it was. It was a man, still in his pajamas, but he had one shoe on. It must have happened very fast. Marta grabbed the body and turned it around, letting out a scream at the sight of the pale-looking face glaring at her just under the water's surface. "Oh my God." She instinctively closed her eyes and turned away. Her entire body shivered and as she opened her eyes again, they were motionless and stared into a void. A tear rolled down her cheek.

"Do you know him, Marta?"

It took a long time before Marta realized Jenny had asked her a question. She took a deep breath, exhaled slowly, nodded and said, "It's the village's Bailiff."

Jenny didn't know how much he meant to her, but he was obviously a good friend or maybe more because she had never seen Marta so heavyhearted before.

Marta struggled a long time to release the milking stool from the body's hand and had to almost break its fingers from the stool's handle. They would take the body with them to the village for a proper burial, but during their effort to haul it into the boat, they suddenly lost their grip. The heavy body fell back into the water and without anything keeping it afloat anymore, it began immediately to sink toward its watery grave. Marta leaned over the boat's rim and saw the mirror image of her own face blending in with the fading silhouette of the disappearing body. She took off a garland from her neck, threw it on the water and said, "Sometimes dreams come true, sometimes not. Rest in peace."

She wiped a tear off her face, turned the boat and headed toward the village. One more time had she sent a dear one to the grave. The last time she saw Aslak happy and alive was at the Midsummer party. He had come up to her and asked her to dance and one of the first things he said was, "Do you remember it was here we first met 35 years ago?" She had stepped back, surprised that a man remembered such romantic events. Back then, he was the love of her life and she became heartbroken beyond repair when a beautiful woman swept him away. It was like he had torn open her chest, ripped out her heart and taken it with him. From then on, she became cold, like if her feelings too had disappeared and she began to believe again in the old tradition of "marry only for necessity", a tradition she had originally never believed in, causing many arguments with her father.

Now, 35 years later, she hadn't resisted when his strong arms pulled her closer and looked at her with the same blue eyes, on the same face, just sprinkled with a few wrinkles that only enhanced his manhood. Suddenly he had kissed her gently on her cheek. An impulse of excitement had bounced from her cheek down through her spine, tickled her stomach and turned into a warm sensation between her legs. Could there possibly be anything between them now that they had both become widowers? Would there ever be an opportunity for her to have what she had once wanted the most in this world?

"Do you know what Marta? Back then I never saw the beauty behind your glasses, the beauty that shines from the depth of your soul, but I see it now and I know there is much more about you I didn't know then. I had the perfect gem stone, but I didn't see how it shone." She remembered that his words had grabbed her with such a force she thought she would faint and she paid her full attention as he continued, "I guess I was taken by another kind of beauty then, maybe to prove myself. I remember how proud I was when my friends made remarks about my beautiful wife, but I know now what I really wanted was a woman shining from the inside."

Marta looked at the havoc around them, realizing her most secret dreams hadn't come true and so far hers had been a life of hardship, death and devastation.

As they reached shore about the same place as the wharf used to be, they saw that the general store, the old trading house, the Bailiff's and doctor's offices were gone and the church sheds had been flushed away with all of their winter supplies. The church bell lay on its side, filled with mud. The pulpit seemed to be in one piece and had been dragged down to the shoreline and the church's tower was floating nearby with a crow sitting on top of the spire. It was hard to remember what the village had looked like.

Marta had no time to dwell on the material damage; she had to find out if her sons and father were alive and she rushed up what used to be the main street. The haunting sound of the steamboat's whistle underscored the woeful atmosphere. The wave had thrown the boat on land approximately thirty yards from the shoreline. The boat lay side down with its bow pointing at the remaining foundation of the church, as if it were showing her the way to her father who stood beside several dead bodies. Marta screamed out, "No, no, no!" and ran toward him.

Andreas took her immediately into his arms and comforted her. "Lars and Iver are alive and all right, but..."

Marta released herself and looked straight at him. "But, but what Father, what? Tell me!"

Andreas nodded at one of the dead bodies. "Jon was the first we found."

"Oh no, not Jon!" Immediately Marta leaned down, grabbed the cold and lifeless body's hand and looked at his apathetic face that just a day earlier had been so full of life. One more light was gone. How many more would have to be switched off from her life before she would walk in endless darkness? She wiped off a tear and remembered how happy he was when Anna told him she was with child. She clutched his dead hand. "I'll make sure your baby will be taken very good care of and when it gets old enough to understand, I will tell it how great a father it had." Slowly she stood up, took a last look at him before turning away, dreading the moment when she had to tell Anna.

Jenny had passed both Andreas and Marta in her confusion about the devastation and had forgotten the cat she rescued and to ask about Lars and Iver. Her mind must have blocked them out completely. In a daze she stopped wondering where to begin, when everything around her was destruction, death and chaos and people screaming from everywhere. It was when she saw the graveyard that she realized that not only did the wave strike rich and poor, young and old, it didn't even leave the dead unharmed. The wave had tilted tombstones, opened graves, shattered and tossed around caskets and pieces of skeletons like sticks and stones, and washed several gravesites all the way down to bedrock, flushing the heart of Stranden right into the fjord.

She ran away from the horrific sight and headed toward a group of people a little bit further away from the shoreline. It was only when she saw Lars and two other men digging in the mud that it dawned on her that she had forgotten them the moment she stepped ashore - a reminder of what such havoc might do to one's mind. As she looked frantically around in the hope of spotting Iver, she saw whole sections of houses, sheds and barns had been tossed into the muddy fjord among broken trees and debris. Half of the village was gone except on the north side where the wave had bounced up against a hill, protecting everything above. Streams of water and mud were still retreating back into the fjord. Jenny rushed toward Lars; she had to find out if Iver was alive. No matter how badly he had been treating her, she didn't want him dead. Somehow, she would like to know if the thing Anna was talking about was true and if Iver was dead now, he would have taken it with him and she would never ever know if he cared for her. "Please be alive Iver," she muttered as she grabbed Lars and stammered out the words, "Whe.. where is Iver? Is he alive?"

Lars looked at her a bit surprised at how eager she seemed to know. "Yes Jenny, he's all right."

Jenny let out a sigh of relief and looked around, wondering where to begin.

The villagers still alive were either speechless or in tears, trying to understand. Moments before, they were in a quiet village, sleeping and they awoke to devastation. Some paced in frenzy, trying to grab onto bits and pieces of debris and to make sense of their injuries; others screamed out for help from all directions and those who had not sustained an injury were trying to follow sounds. Broken trees, splintered timber logs, twisted cows, mangled, desperate animals and people struggling to get loose, dead sheep tossed about mixed with the screams and moans of people and personal belonging scattered around the muddy ground. It was all tangled and distorted - unreal.

Suddenly a hysterical scream rose above the other noise. “My baby, my baby! Where is my baby?”

Jenny rushed toward a woman who was stomping the ground. Her knees buckled and she knelt in the mud, beating her chest. A man approached her and gently lifted her up, “It’s alright Clara, I’ve found our baby,” he said as he carried her off.

Another woman looked up at the moon and shouted, “Is this doomsday? Is this the final hour? Where is my husband, Oh God! Where is my husband, my grandchild, my little one? Where is she?” She remained talking to her God while a man was digging feverishly beside her.

Jenny grabbed a piece of broken wood and jumped in with him, helping him dig and almost choked when she saw something that looked like the leg of a small child. She threw away the piece of wood, fell down on her knees and began to scoop out the mud with her bare hands, not even noticing how dirty she was getting and how cold the mud was. Jenny’s long, well-groomed nails soon became history as she carefully continued with her relentless scooping. It was indeed a child’s leg she had seen and deep sadness rushed through her as they exposed more and more of the body. *This child couldn’t possible have survived,* she thought, and she was dreadfully right. The moment she pulled the body of the little girl out of the mud, her little arms and legs dangled like rubber straps and her lifeless head tilted backwards. Her hair was so smeared with mud it was impossible to see its original color, but it appeared that it had been blond. Jenny wiped the child's cheeks and forehead clean and handed the body to the man.

The man clutched it close to his chest and began sobbing uncontrollably.

Jenny touched his shoulder, trying to comfort him. It was the only thing she could do. What else can one do to show compassion to a father who has just lost his little girl?

Through all the frantic activity, Jenny caught the eye of Susanne, the bride whom the minister had refused to bless a couple of months earlier. With his head tilted, bible opened, reading a verse over a dead man's body, Susanne stood next to the minister without any expression and nodded at Jenny. The two women had met several times in the village and enjoyed each other's company. Now Susanne stood over the remains of her husband, the man who had beat her because of her difficulty with cooking and he never noticed that she did not grieve. But it was the body next to him which made Jenny's heart jump. Recognizing Jon, Jenny felt a deep sadness for Anna and the unborn child who would never see its father and she wondered if Iver would be the man to help her now. Maybe that was good for him, having a sister to care for. Although she would not replace his wife, she could help him open up more and talk about his feelings.

A crying young boy Olaf's age got Jenny's attention. She moved over to the boy who looked at her with a face anguished by fear. "My father, where is my father?"

Jenny tried to reassure him that everything was all right and started to take him to safety when he cried out, "No, no, we have to find my father!"

"Is this your home?" she asked, looking at the remains of a house.

The boy nodded.

A voice from the rubble yelled out, "I need help over here!"

Jenny set the boy back on the ground and as she got closer to the mud-covered person wanting help, she saw it was Iver, struggling to move a large beam. At first she wanted to back out and help someone else - there was enough to grab on to everywhere, but then she heard a moaning sound under the rubble. Why would she even care who it was she was helping when she could help save a life? How could she even think that would matter?

At the moment Iver saw her, he flung his arms in a resigned gesture. "I need a man for this, not a woman." He turned away from her, grabbed the beam once more when Jenny suddenly did something she never thought was possible. Without any regard of her own physical limitations, she went down on her knees, crawled under the beam and lifted it with her shoulder so much that Iver was able to push it aside. Jenny had no idea how she did it; somehow she felt an incredible power and based on Iver's facial expression, he seemed to be as surprised as she was.

Iver suspected the sight underneath the layer of mud might be disturbing, so he told Jenny to keep the boy at bay. As he managed to uncover the unfortunate soul under the rubble, Iver saw his eyes were glossy and frightened. His speech was slurred when he said, "I heard my son, where is he, please let me see my boy, I need to tell him, I need to tell him..."

"It's alright, everything is alright," said Iver. He held the man's hand as his life started to fade.

"Boy, boy, you're a good boy...take care, take care, take care of your mother," he whispered as his eyes closed and his soul left his body.

Upon hearing his father's voice, the boy wrenched himself loose from Jenny and ran toward him where he dropped onto his father's chest and sobbed loudly.

It was too much for Iver; he struggled to stay on his feet. How much more of this could he take? Suddenly he felt that the ground they were standing on was sliding down the hill. He swiftly grabbed the boy and moved away.

The boy kicked his legs trying to get loose. "My mother! Help me find my mother!"

Jenny was watching the scene. *Oh my poor little boy! Not his mother too!* She looked into the rubble, thinking that it would be an impossible task to find anyone alive under the heavy debris.

Iver handed the boy to Jenny. "Alright, let's look for your mother." It didn't take long before they found her, alive, underneath a portion of a roof. Concerned about causing her more injury from the sharp edges of broken wood, Iver called out for help and together several men lifted the entire piece. Lucky to have escaped with apparently only minor cuts and bruises, she reached out for her boy and he clutched onto her hand as one of the men carried her away to safer ground.

When Jenny noticed that the minister was still reading from the bible over the dead, anger and an immediate need for action brewed up inside of her and she couldn't stop herself from yelling as loud as everybody around could hear, "Minister, wouldn't it be better to use your effort toward the wounded instead of dwelling with the dead?"

Iver's jaw dropped and he looked amazedly at Jenny, before continuing to dig in the rubble.

Jenny didn't wait for the Minister's or anybody else's reaction; she just hurried up a hill toward the nearest untouched farm. She needed a place to set up a makeshift hospital.

When she walked in to the living room, she was met by the eyes of a dozen women and children. An oil lamp lit up their apathetic-looking faces, with the exception of one young woman who had her face buried in the palms of her hands.

At first Jenny wondered why they just sat there without doing anything to help, but then she realized a catastrophe of this magnitude can do a lot of things to one's mind.

Suddenly, the young woman took her hands away from her face and broke out in a wail, gasping frequently for air. An older woman sitting next to her put her hand around her shoulders and began to talk to her.

Jenny spoke. "Who's the owner?"

A middle-aged woman raised her hand.

Jenny realized this was not a time to ask - it was a time to tell. "We need this room for the wounded; the furniture must be replaced with whatever you have of mattresses."

A minute later they were working like ants. It is amazing how immobilized people become during a catastrophe until someone takes the lead and tells them what to do. Jenny continued organizing the rescue and getting the wounded brought into the house where deep bleeding cuts and bruises appeared to be the most common injuries. Since the doctor was reported missing and his office with all medical supplies had been washed away, she announced that she needed fine fabric to use as bandages. Never in her whole life had Jenny felt as needed as she did then! No slap on her back or good grades in school could ever compare with this. Now she understood what her aunt meant when she insisted that she learned first aid. "You never know when you are needed, and it usually comes when you are least expecting it."

Soon it became known among the other survivors where to bring the wounded and that the woman from Kristiania had taken the lead. No one questioned her abilities; they were all glad that someone had taken the initiative.

It didn't take long before the first victim was carried in; a small child wrapped in a blanket was rushed to Jenny. "We found him in the water," a man said. Jenny grabbed the cold body. She couldn't find any pulse and there was no sign of injuries. *He must have drowned,* she thought. She instantly began with artificial resuscitation. For minutes which felt like hours, she determinedly continued until the little body began to move and started coughing. At that moment, the midwife came to her assistance and to everybody's surprise, the boy survived. "How could he," a woman asked, "after hours in the water?" The two men who had found him came to the conclusion that he must have been trapped in an air pocket from the rubble that recently collapsed. Jenny knew a small child could survive a long time under water, but it was still a mystery why he had not frozen to death. As she tuned toward the door, she noticed Iver had been watching it all. Their eyes met a moment before he had to give way to one more person to be carried in.

"He fell into rubble trying to save a horse," a person said.

Jenny froze when she saw the piece of wood impaled into his lower abdominal region. He must have suffered a lot, but it was obvious that he didn't have much time left; she was actually surprised that he was still alive. Somehow the wood must have prevented him from bleeding to death. There was nothing anybody could do other than to be with him in the last minutes of his life. Jenny began to feel nausea. She rushed out of the shed and threw up; this was just getting to be too much for her. When she came back in, she saw Iver was kneeling beside the dying man, holding his hand. *He must have been a friend of his*, she thought.

"Stud, what's this about?" Iver asked. "You can't leave us now; who else in this village will take care of all the lonely women?"

The Stud smiled and clutched Iver's hand. "I guess you're right. I better stay."

Jenny took a cloth and wiped the blood off his face.

The Stud opened his eyes one more time and smiled up at Jenny. "It's angels I'm seeing." He coughed up blood and pulled Iver's face close to his as he continued to look into Jenny's eyes. "I must have been good." Then his eyes became lifeless and his body fell back down. One more great character had left the village, just in his effort to save others.

It was obvious to Jenny that Iver hadn't expected her to take the lead in the rescuing effort, even though he didn't say anything. The way he looked at her showed a clear sign of respect. Surely a catastrophe does a lot to people, bringing them together - enemies become friends and family disputes become obsolete. She wondered if this could make Iver open himself up again. Could one disaster mend what another broke?

Clothes began to arrive and were passed out since many of the victims had managed to escape the wave wearing only their sleeping garments. A group of women had turned the kitchen and nearby room into a field kitchen and now kettles of hot soup were passed around. Many hadn't had anything to eat or drink since the tragedy struck, but it wouldn't be long before more food, housing, clothes and medicine would be needed.

To get the attention from other villages, a group of men had rushed to the tongue of land Usenet and lit a fire on a cairn. The Vikings had used that place as one link in a chain of communication points throughout the fjord that started at the coastal town Aalesund and went about 60 miles in through the entire fjord to the village of Geiranger. A fire or smoke at one of those cairns indicated war or that immediate help was needed. The Norwegian coast, with its inlets and fjords, has more than seven hundred such cairns or landmarks, usually a pile of rocks located on a mountaintop or on a tongue of land by the water. The old Viking signal had been observed by a fisherman outside the village of Stordal who knew instantly something had happened in Stranden. Nobody had ever lit a fire on that place since the Vikings roamed the area.

A couple of hours later, a dozen boats were searching among the debris, but it was only corpses they brought to shore, which were placed among the others previously found. The rain turned into snow and within the hour, it covered the scars in the landscape like a white bandage. In the fjord, parts of houses, barns, hay bails and debris had also gotten into the layer of snow and looked like miniature icebergs floating around.

Iver stood motionless looking out over the fjord as more boats appeared bringing supplies and offering help. It had been hours since he and the Stud had been standing outside, looking up at the stars and now Stud was dead. Jenny didn't realize that Iver had noticed her until he put his arm on her shoulder. To Iver, this was the most comforting moment since the earth shook. Soon his grandfather and brother came to stand by his side, villagers got closer, and all around him were now faces of lifeless men, women and children, cut, bruised and covered in dirt, overlooking the ghostly remains of their village. The village would be rebuilt and in a few years there would be nothing other than the scar in the mountain reminding future generations of what had happened. For the survivors, however, the emotional havoc would hunt them to the grave; personalities would change - some to the better, some to the worse. In a few hours, the darkness would again enfold them and a new sleepless night could begin, one of many to come.

The next day, Jenny and the rest of the Holseth family returned to the farm, exhausted. There wasn't much more they could do; the survivors' immediate physical needs had been taken care of. Now, for them as for the rest of the villagers, the long road to mental healing had just begun.

Anna watched them coming up the path, anxious to know what had happened. Then she noticed there were only five of them - or was it all six? Her heart started to beat faster; never had it been so difficult to count to six! She waited until all had passed the trees down by the edge of the pasture so she could see them clearer, but still there were only five of them. It took another couple of agonizing minutes until she had it confirmed - Jon was not among them. Why didn't he return? Had he stopped by the boathouse for a while or maybe he had just stayed with his mother one more night? Of course he had! Nothing had happened to him. When Jenny and her mother stepped into the house, Anna opened her mouth to ask about Jon, but not a word came out. She just stood, looking at them. Neither Jenny nor Marta needed to say anything; their faces could not hide the bad news. Anna's eyes watered, a tear rolled down her cheek before she dropped down and wailed uncontrollably. Marta leaned down beside her and gently stroked her stomach. "I know how you feel Anna, but you need to be strong. You have another Jon who needs you now."

Anna looked up, first at her mother, then at Jenny, her face covered in tears. "Why? Why did God do this to me?"

Jenny touched her shoulder. "I don't know, Anna. Life is not fair, never been and never will be and even though an old scripture says that when God closes a door, he will open a window, I don't expect you to see that now. Maybe later." She didn't know what say - what could she say?

The Christmas Present

"God gives every bird its food, but does not drop it into the nest." Danish Proverb

Two months had passed since the tidal wave changed the face of the village and altered the spirits of its inhabitants. In spite of the wounds, Christmas would be observed with joyous celebration. When Iver asked Lars to take Olaf to the village for the children's Santa Lucia Day, Lars pestered Jenny into joining them and on December 13th, the foursome headed down the path with Olaf in the lead, next to Kari carrying the lantern. December is a dark month in Norway, except for a few hours of light during the day and the occasional display from the Aurora Borealis. The other source of light was Santa Lucia herself, who had been a symbol of hope ever since she was burned at the stake in Sicily in the year 304 AD. She reappeared every December 13 to shed light in this darkest period of the year.

As they began to take off on their journey, Andreas hurried from the house to join them.

"Your mother thought this over and to ease her mind, sent me to accompany you to the village." Lars began to protest until Andreas held up his hand to quiet him. "You know the gossips and there will be several at the schoolhouse today."

While rowing, Lars suddenly pointed to the sky and exclaimed, "Look, the Northern lights!"

Kari chimed in, "I think the light looks like hundreds of glistening yellow birds flapping their wings."

"Grandmother always says the lights look like curtains blowing in the wind," interrupted Olaf, eager to get turned round in the boat.

"Well I know the truth," said Andreas. "It's the breath from the flying dragon."

"Sure Grandpa," Kari rolled her eyes and flapped her arms in the air; then Olaf copied her antics.

"Stop it," said Lars. "You're both making the boat wobble. Enough about dragons; let's quiet down and get safely to the village."

Thousands of beaming stars competed with the light display and everyone felt a sense of wonder and awe. Lars was sure Jenny thought of him as a possible suitor since he had noticed several times how she would look at him. It was obvious she favored him over Iver and it was about time he settled down to one woman. He figured this Blackstone mess would soon be over. Not being fond of farming, without money or property, he'd have to get work and he had been making plans that would surprise the entire family.

For Jenny, the Christmas preparations, rituals and listening to the tales had been a learning experience. She didn't know so much had to be done so long in advance. Even the candles they made themselves. Clothes had been cut and sewed and shoes had been made. Andreas had insisted on showing her the preparation for brewing beer where he first put a sack of barley grain in water and let it soak for three days before spreading it out in the barn's hayloft to sprout. Then it was ground into coarse flour and poured back into the sack again; all this had to be completed by a certain date. From then on, no one could spin, grind grain or do any other heavy Christmas-preparation work and the children were not allowed to be outside after dark because the Wood Nymph, the light-giving Santa Lucia's dark rival, would be lurking around.

Jenny though about the preparations back home in Kristiania. There wasn't much she saw or was involved with - food, clothes, decorations and even presents just appeared, brought by the maid, servants or families. She realized now that back home, she had just been aware of the duck gliding graciously in the water and didn't see the busy feet under the surface.

After several errands in the village, they spent a few hours with Andreas' cousin, then headed to the schoolhouse. As the villagers were still rebuilding the church after the tidal wave, for the time being all religious activity had been moved to the schoolhouse. Jenny noticed clouds thickening around the mountains and by the time they arrived to the gathering, large snowflakes had begun to fall. In the absence of wind, Jenny could hear the small puffs as the flakes fell softly to the ground. She closed her eyes and lifted her head to the sky, letting the flakes gently kiss her face before they melted away. Then she heard the faint sound of children and remembered her childhood and a Santa Lucia Day celebration in Kristiania when she had been the Lucia queen.

Every year the village chooses a young girl to represent the Saint of Light and this year the lucky one had curly blonde hair and wore a long white dress with a red sash around her waist. Her crown of green leaves and lighted candles symbolized the shedding of light in December, the darkest period of the year. The decorated carriage and small horse lit the way for the children, who were all carefully carrying candles, parading in two rows. The snow was dense and the light from the candles created an orange halo around the children's heads. Jenny spotted Olaf in the procession and as he passed by, he slipped on a patch of ice and knocked into the boy ahead of him. Embarrassed, both boys scrambled to their feet, picked up their candles and caught up to the procession. Both Lars and Jenny tried their best not to laugh at Olaf as they walked behind the villagers. Before Jenny knew what was happening, Lars had gently taken her hand. She smiled and thought he was being kind so she wouldn't make the same mistake as Olaf, slipping on the ice.

The minister welcomed everyone as the families congregated into the schoolhouse. Soon after the congregation was settled, the children began to read Christmas poems while ginger cookies and saffron bread were passed around. After the service, the adults were laughing and joking about their chores, braiding candlewicks, spinning thread, grinding grain and baking cookies and not the least, preparing for brewing the Christmas beer. Jenny joined the women clustered in small groups and found her self comfortable with their conversations since she had been a part of the chores on the Holseth farm and understood just how much work it had taken to get everything done. Lars had gone to the back of the room with the men who were talking about their favorite subject, beer. The old Christian rights dictated that every household must brew its own beer; otherwise, they would be called "Heathen Dogs." The men had now been waiting anxiously for a few days of milder weather to take the chill out of the frigid cellars so the brewing could begin. About two weeks before Christmas, the last taste of fall usually came as a strong south east wind, hovering across the mountains, causing a warming effect on the leeward side. This year the wind seemed to be late and the men were starting to worry.

While the men continued to boast about their brewing, the women either talked to Jenny or about her. Several of them had noticed Lars had been holding Jenny's hand and stirred the pot - didn't they make a handsome couple? Did you see him smile at her? And did you notice how she looked at him? By the time the rumors would make it back to Holseth, several young ladies in the area would have broken hearts. Andreas would be asked about their betrothal and Marta would fret and when she finally cornered Lars, he would laugh, wishing the stories were true, while Andreas would never hear the end of his worthlessness as a chaperone.

A week after Santa Lucia Day, the mild weather arrived and Andreas declared it Holseth brewing day. Brewing beer was done as a religious rite and Andreas was strict with the rituals. Today he would just clean out the kettle and the jil, the fifty-gallon hand-crafted barrel-shaped wood container, and collect all the ingredients to make them ready for the following day. The actually brewing could not take place before he had completed a part of the ritual in the village. He cleaned himself up, anticipating a night with The Widow, which he called "the sacrament" to ensure flawless fertilization; the boys called it, "Grandfather getting laid." Andreas paced like a gander waiting for Iver to take him to the village.

Marta knew exactly what he was up to and cornered him. "Father, I don't think you should go today; you complained about your limbs hurting just the other day."

At first the old man didn't answer. He had been looking forward to this day for an entire year, and no one could stop him from seeing The Widow. When Iver arrived, he put on his coat, strapped his pack on his back, walked to the door and grinned at his daughter. "Which limbs were you talking about?"

Marta blushed and threw a piece of bread at him. He caught it and thanked her for her kindness. He put the piece of bread in his mouth and headed down the path.

The next day, Iver and Lars had already started the brewing process by heating up the first kettle of water. They held the boiling hot kettle between them, ready to pour the liquid over the malted barley, when Andreas stormed down the stairs. His sudden intrusion scared the dog and caused Lars to loosen his grip. As the kettle dropped to the floor, Lars cursed, "Damn it! It took us hours to heat that water."

"What in the world is going on down there?" Marta yelled from the kitchen. Every year someone always spilled a kettle of water until they got the hang of it. Andreas heard her and shouted, "Nosey woman!"

"Watch out old man, that's our mother," said Lars.

"I know and I've always felt sorry for you."

Four kettles of boiling water later, Andreas prepared to add the hops. "What do you have in there this year?" asked Lars as Andreas dropped a brown fabric sack of hops and other mysterious items into the jil.

"I'll tell you when it's finished."

With a wooden stick, he started to stir the pot. Andreas knew the art of hopping beer, where the timing and temperature was as important as the contents in the sack. Always mysterious about his brewing, if the beer turned out good, he'd share his secret with his grandson. When the brew cooled off, he brought out the yeast. He held the same strain of yeast the family had used for over a hundred years in his hand and he started to chant to remove the evil spirits and prevent rancidity. He poured the yeast evenly on top of the brew, stuck his head into the jil and howled.

Lars laughed. "I think The Widow did the trick."

Within ten minutes, a brown bubbly froth began to develop on the top of the liquid and Andreas looked down on it again and enthusiastically exclaimed, "Come look men at these devils." He blew them a kiss and covered the jil with a piece of heavy cloth before tip-toeing up the stairs. For the next two sacred days, no one was allowed to come near the brew and Andreas instructed the women to tip-toe if they had to cross the floor and only whisper if they needed to talk; the yeast needed quietness to work. The beer turned out to be one of the best they had ever made and the boys credited The Widow for most of its success and toasted her with the first round.

The hectic Christmas preparations reached their peak the last Sunday before Christmas Eve, called Black Sunday or Washing Day when everyone in the region scrubbed their houses and their bodies. Walls, ceilings, benches, shelves and floors would be cleaned with a mixture of water, lye and sand. In a cleaning frenzy, Marta brought in a large wooden tub from the barn, placed it in the middle of the living room and wiped off the year-long accumulation of dust to make it ready for the annual bath.

While eating breakfast and waiting for the water kettles to heat, Marta picked up her mother's wooden spoon with the carved symbol of the cross and waved it back and forth in front of her father's face, grinning like a cat. "Today is Washing Day. And you, my dear father, will not go down to the boathouse. We have a lot to do and I need your help." She brought the wooden spoon closer to his face. "Now, about your bath. If I cannot find you when it is your turn, I swear on my mother's grave that I will drop salt in your beer!"

"You horrid daughter! Touch my beer and I'll throw you out of the house and leave you to the two-headed trolls."

"Just try me old man! When I call your name, you better come or it's down in the cellar I go." Marta pushed the spoon into the salt bowl. Everyone tried not to laugh except Jenny, who became disgusted that they fought about taking a bath, until Lars whispered in her ear, "They do this every year. Sometimes Grandfather wins, but this year, I think she's got him."

With all the work done, Marta gave her final approval. She threatened the men with bodily harm and forced them to stay in the loft until they were called. No one was ever allowed to enter the kitchen when the women took a bath.

They honored Jenny with the first bath and alone in the kitchen, the steam from the hot water permeated the room, fogging the windows and tempting Jenny into the old wooden tub. She carefully laid her clothes on the table, unwound her hair, allowing it to freely cascade down her back. She stepped into the tub and her nipples turned hard, taking on a deep pink color, jutting out of the warm water. In this humble kitchen, the fairest of Norwegian maids took on a soft, vulnerable glow. Her callused hands softened and her long, beautiful body relaxed. She closed her eyes and drifted back to Kristiania and her own room, remembering how excited she was as a little girl when the maid announced bath time. She had always liked the water and bath time was one of her favorite moments. After, she would lie in a warm, safe bed with her mother reading stories. Later in her childhood and adolescence, a warm bath meant party and a nice family dinner. Now, the sensation from the water flowed through her making every cell alive. She took several deep breaths and exhaled slowly, making her body relax even more. She rubbed the soap between her hands and put the foam on her neck from where she began a downward massaging movement. As she reached her breasts, she made small circles with her fingers around the nipples without touching them. Then she cupped her breasts gently and began to stroke her hands slowly down toward her abdominal area and on the outside of her thighs before stopping on her knees. She moved her body back and slipped down to let both knees touch the sides of the tub, opening up her vulnerability while the waterline tickled her nipples. The warm sensation increased and at once she had forgotten all the cold days of exhaustion and despair; this was only a moment of pleasure. She moved her hands slowly from her knees to the inside of her thighs, stroking them with a rotating gentleness only she knew about - her private secret to ignite every cell. Heat began brewing between her legs exceeding the lukewarm water. As her hands met each other, a jolt of tingling pleasure shot through her spine. Her breath became short and shallow and her body started to vibrate. She looked around and listened for possible intruders, then quickly grabbed the towel and laid it over the tub in front of her. Then she slipped back to her position with one hand on her breast and the other on the inside of her thigh, which she continued moving slowly toward her crotch. Now she couldn't resist anymore and began to massage the part of her that had now become hard as rubber. In spite of her nervousness of someone walking in on her, she continued to bring herself higher and higher toward levels she hadn't been in for several months. She moved her hand from her breast and covered her mouth; now there was no way back. She drifted away, far into space, just as her entire body tightened and exploded in pleasure. She put a finger into her mouth and almost bit it to bleeding. She wanted to scream, but managed to control it, letting out only a low hoarse moan. A few seconds later, her tense body slipped back into the water, relaxed. Embarrassed that someone could have watched her, she instinctively looked nervously around. Then she suddenly remembered the bath needed to be shared by others. She stood up, wringing water out of her hair, just as Iver walked in. Their eyes locked as he took in every part of her before she could drop back into the water.

His body stiffened and became heated as he stumbled with an apology and retreated outside. He looked about the farm and in his mind's eye, could still see the water dripping down Jenny's breasts and along her legs. He started running. He ran so hard he no longer felt his breathing or the heat rising from his body. What a fool he had been thinking he didn't yearn to be with a beautiful woman! Arriving at his farm, his body crashed against the door and once inside, he paced and pounded his hands together until they were numb. Desperately, he fought against a fierce desire for her. "Damn it, this too painful! I can't live like this. I don't ever want to see her again."

Jenny had hurried out of the tub and had rushed to her bedroom. *I have never met such a stupid, rude, inconsiderate oaf in all my life!* she told her bedroom walls. *Every time I turn around he embarrasses me. If I never saw him again, I would be the luckiest woman alive.* She dropped onto the bed, wondering how much longer she could put up with living in these small quarters on this lost mountain. She couldn't stand the thought of being undressed in front of Iver and she wanted to scream. Whether Robert was in England or Norway, it didn't matter to her; all that mattered was that she leave the farm, so she wrote her parents explaining her plans to return home after Christmas. She would explain to her parents that she was over her infatuation with Blackstone and that they had nothing to worry about. This was how Marta found her, asleep, sprawled out on the bed, with pen and paper lying next to her, but regardless of what she wrote, the weather would make it impossible for her letter to be mailed for some time.

Three days later, in the early morning of Christmas Eve, Jenny came out of her bedroom to find everyone scurrying about, talking about a large crate having been left at the boathouse.

"A crate? What could it be? Who could have sent it? It must be a mistake," said Marta.

Lars shook his head. "I have no idea who sent it. I've asked Iver to help me carry it up."

Andreas remarked, "This is very odd; no one ever delivers anything. We always have to go to the village to get mail and packages."

The decision was made to take time out from the extra Christmas work to bring up the crate. This meant everyone would have to work a little harder to have everything done by five o'clock when the Holseth family, like all the other families in the region, would be inside their homes, commemorating Christmas Eve.

With all the Christmas excitement, Marta asked Jenny, "Dear, you seem to be the only one patient enough to stir the porridge. Do you mind?" Glad to get warmed by the stove, Jenny put on an apron and chuckled as she thought of how different today would be if she were at home with her parents. She certainly would not be standing by a hot stove, stirring puddings in a plain country dress! Every now and then, she looked across the room at the women as they decorated the table and she found herself enjoying their Christmas stories. As always, the source of their laughter was Lars' mishaps and odd inventions he had given as gifts. She felt a deep longing to be home, to be with her own family and clumsily dropped the spoon into the hot liquid, tried to retrieve it and burned her hand. "I'm sorry Marta. I was thinking about my mother," Jenny explained as the older woman rubbed butter and cream on her hand and retrieved the spoon.

"I know how hard this must be for you, but we are all glad you're with us this Christmas. I know it will not be what you are used to, but we will have a fine celebration just the same." Marta glanced over at her daughters. "Enough dallying girls! Come, there is so much to do before the clock strikes five."

Jenny was comforted by Marta's words, but she knew one person on the mountain had never accepted her. How a mother like Marta could have two sons so different in looks and nature was beyond her.

Marta went back to decorating the table with Anna, thinking how much she would miss Jenny when she returned to Kristiania. So many changes, events and faces had passed by this mountain farm! Her memory of the farm stretched back to when she was a small child...but no one had brought such charm and gaiety to it as this young woman from Kristiania. Jenny's ability to brighten up a room by only stepping into it would sober all of them when the time came for her to leave. Over the next few hours, the women could not contain their curiosity about the mysterious crate, and every now and then, one or the other would look out the window to see if the men had returned.

Finally Olaf stuck his head in from outside. "It's here, it's here," he called and the door shut abruptly behind him.

It took some time for Iver to open the crate and by the way he pried open the planks, it became obvious to everybody that he was angry. He and Jenny hadn't spoken to one another since the bath. When he finally pried the last plank from the top, the mystery was over.

He and Lars picked up the hand-carved cherry wood wardrobe trunk and carried it into the house. They set it down at Jenny's feet and waited for her response. Surprised and embarrassed by the elaborate gift, she bent down, touching the most delicate carving of her name encircled by birds and flowers and she quickly asked if they would carry it to her room. Marta and Anna looked a bit disappointed when Jenny shut the door to her room.

Just past noon on Christmas Eve, the time of year when sunrise is only an hour from sunset, the winter sun, low on the horizon, peeked through a pass in the mountains and sent a ribbon of red light to the mountainside. The newly fallen snow reflected the sun's rays into thousands of tiny light beams.

Glad the snowfall had been light, Andreas waded across the pasture, heading for a little grove behind the barn. He had plans to surprise Jenny with a Christmas tree. She had shared with the family her Christmas customs in Kristiania and how many families decorated a pine tree, symbolizing belief in renewed life. He thought it was an odd custom - why anyone would bring a tree into the house didn't make much sense to him. Marta always hung evergreen boughs over the doors and windows to keep away witches, ghosts, evil spirits and illness, but a tree in the house would be a first for everyone on the mountain! If he were a younger man, he would have asked for Jenny's hand months ago. He was a man who appreciated a fine woman and had never understood Iver's apparent dislike for the girl, for if he could be young once again and fancy free...his thoughts trailed off until he reached the boundary of the grove.

His heart lightened at the scene ahead. He was a man's man, with a poet's heart, and he never took the beauty of his homeland for granted. For before him, his eyes took in the glittering of snow-covered pines limbs hanging down, forming arches. As he moved forward, he felt like a king upon entering his throne room. Memories of his boyhood surfaced and he thought he saw the shadow of his father up ahead, and as a gentle puff of wind brushed the limbs of the trees, he thought he could hear his father call out to him.

Hurry Andreas, hurry. He stopped for a moment and looked around; what tricks nature can pull on an old sentimental fool! A chirp from a bird broke the silence, and then he heard a whiff from the swaying limbs when portions of snow fell off the trees transforming into a white mist falling softly to the ground. He found several small trees clustered near a tall, motherly pine and after deciding on one, he took the axe and with just a few sweeps, the tree broke away from its base. When he bent over to pick it up, his arm and hand were numb. A feeling of nausea came over him and before he knew it, he was lying flat on his back.

His eyes opened and he wasn't sure how long he'd been out in the snow. After checking the sun in progress of going down behind a mountain, he figured probably a half an hour. His breathing had become a bit labored and when a rush of energy came over him, he knew it was fear. He had never been afraid of dying, so why now? Was it the death or leaving this beautiful scenery behind? After picking up the tree, he headed back to the house, glad that no one had found him in such a state. His daughter worried about him enough as it was and this would just give her another excuse to take him to a doctor. He had never been to a doctor and he planned to die without seeing one. At the beginning of the year, Andreas had had a feeling something might happen to him and as he walked away from the grove, he turned back for just a moment to look at what, he wasn't sure. The pines - they did seem more beautiful than before. He thought of himself as a man at the end of his life, seeing the world through his heart and not his head. He felt an odd sensation as if his heart cried out, for surely he would miss this mountain and his home and a lump grew in his throat and tears began to swell.

Marta had Andreas place the tree in the front room by the window. She and Kari decorated it with the few things they had made and Olaf ran to get Jenny. He pulled her into the room and she was very surprised to find the small pine covered in homemade stars.

"This is such a surprise!" Marta pointed at Andreas and he pointed back at Marta, neither one wanting to take the credit. Jenny thanked them both and gave Andreas a kiss on the cheek. His blush was so red it appeared he had drunk several beers too many. Little did they know, this small group gathered around the first Christmas tree at Holseth, that every household in the entire region would one day make this a Christmas tradition.

Lars interrupted them. "Well now I've seen everything! A tree in the house!" He laughed and turned to his grandfather. "If you're feeling up to it Old Man, I put the lamb ribs on the spit and need your help."

"Old man, old man! I'd beat you up the path any day," barked Andreas as he got up from his chair and followed his grandson out the door, pleased that the tree had made Jenny happy.

Marta noticed that her father's unsure step had a tired gait. Was it the holiday? All the extra chores? Or was his age finally catching up to him? She decided to get busy so she wouldn't think about it now and would save her concerns for a quieter day. She said a quick prayer of thanks over the cooking and then spoke to her deceased mother as she had every Christmas since her death. "Mother, the family's together. Bless you for helping watch over us and keeping us safe. I miss you and as I promised you, I am taking good care of Father, although he does try me at times. May you continue to be in the light of the Lord and in the safety of his home."

An hour later, when Iver carried wood from the barn, he noticed Jenny's bedroom window reflected a sparkling golden color; the flashing flecks of gold lured him to the window. He saw her standing in front of a small mirror, dressed in a gown of gold covered with soft, rose-colored embroidery. Her hair was pulled up with an ivory comb and her earrings and necklace glistened by the candlelight. Numb, he couldn't look away from the most exquisite woman reflected in the mirror. Tears flowed down her cheeks as she crumbled a parchment paper and threw it at the mirror. The trunk was open. Robert Blackstone had struck again. She laid her head down on the dressing table and wept. Helpless and embarrassed, Iver backed away from the window.

Since finding Jenny in the open tub, Iver's manhood had been in a fever pitch. His memory of her in the bath had kept him restless at night like a pacing caged wolf and now this - beauty beyond his wildest imagination. The sick feeling he had every time he thought about her was now back in full force. Iver Holseth, the poor mountain farmer, desired a woman from far away, whose position in society did not match his own. In a daze, he stumbled back to the barn where he dumped a bucket of cold water over his head. His body shook, releasing pellets of water into the air, and then the saddest sound resonated throughout the barn - the sound of a breaking heart.

This is how Andreas found him, wet and cold, sitting in the hay with a blanket wrapped around him and his dog by his side. Andreas didn't talk, but left and returned from the house with dry clothes. He would not intrude. This was a turning point in their relationship, which over the years had been somewhat strained by the grandson's dire outlook on life and the grandfather's bouts of foolery. Andreas sat down next to his grandson and did what came naturally to him - he told a story.

At the stroke of five, with all the chores completed, the Holseth family, except Jenny, walked outside to hear the distant church bells from Stranden. In perfect weather, the sound could be heard several miles from the village. The hint of a single bell tolled, followed by an echo, then more chiming. Gaining momentum, the sounds traveled quickly in through the fjord, bouncing between the mountains. When the night returned to stillness, the family returned to the house to begin their celebration and from then until the dark of Christmas day, no one would be caught outside showing disrespect for the holy day.

Iver was the last one to come into the house; he walked over to the wood burner and toyed with the fire. The warmth gave him comfort and when he finally allowed his body to relax, he found that he was tired. After his grandfather had left him in the barn, he decided to stay away from the farm after Christmas. He needed to get through this holiday for his mother's sake and then he would disappear. He told himself he cared nothing for this woman and until she returned to

Kristiania, he would keep to himself. He looked around at his family, dressed up in their finest clothes, and wondered how they would all feel when Jenny walked into the room dressed in her finery. She would make them all feel like poor peasants, mocking them.

When the door to her room opened, Marta said, "Jenny, how beautiful you look this Christmas Eve. The collar I crocheted looks beautiful on your dress! I'm so glad you like it."

Iver poked the fire so hard one log fell out and landed at his feet. He retrieved it with his hands, burned his fingers and wiped the soot on his shirtsleeve. Just a few hours ago Jenny was dressed like a princess attending the finest ball and now here she stood in front of his family in a plain brown dress with the white collar his mother had given her as a gift. All her trimmings of gold and jewels were hidden back in the wooden chest and she had no idea of the impact her actions played on Iver. What she did see for the first time since she had arrived at Holseth was his face soften as he smiled at her.

"And the comb in you hair," exclaimed Marta, "I have never seen anything like it. Was that your mother's?"

"No, just a gift." Jenny had found the ivory comb engraved with the same design as the trunk and wondered if this was something from Robert's past. It was the only item from the trunk she would ever wear.

After Iver returned from changing his shirt, Andreas gladly said grace and Marta read a few lines from the bible.

Their finest food had been brought out and placed on a beautifully decorated table with a white crocheted cloth and a row of candles. As with any wedding, they could eat as much as the wanted. The main dish was what they called "Pinnekjott", meaning stick meat made from ribs of lamb. It was the Vikings who invented the name from piercing long thin sticks of birch wood into the meat before holding it over the fire. Now, cooks usually steamed it to make the meat tender before frying it over open fire as a touch up.

Making the main dish on Christmas Eve was the house master's responsibility. It was the only meal he was in charge of and was considered an art the same as brewing beer. The first phase had taken place a couple of months earlier when Andreas picked the finest rib from a "Jimbre," which is a lamb that has been grazing out two summers. The rib was soaked in brine for a few days, and then put in a little wood cage covered with a net to protect it from birds, and hung up under the roof at the most southerly facing part of the house. Although some people hung the rib under the ceiling inside the food-storing shed together with other food, Andreas had always insisted that it hung outside to catch the season's last southerly mild winds and at the same time, was protected from rain during the several weeks' long drying period. About twenty-four hours before the Christmas dinner, Andreas cut the rib and soaked it in cold water. If it was too salty, he would have to change the water during the night and the art was to get it as perfect as possible, not too salty and not too bland.

Around two o'clock in the afternoon on Christmas Eve, he would put a two-inch thick layer of barkless pieces of birch wood in a kettle and fill it with water until it just covered the wood. Then he would put in the previously cut pieces of ribs and steam them. If there happened to be any blunt individual in the house, or around, who hadn't realized Christmas was approaching, the next few hours of distinctive sweet-and-rancid smell of lamb would salivate their palates, reminding them of the big event.

In addition to the meat, they had boiled potatoes, crisp bread, mashed rutabagas, a little bowl of pure fat from the ribs known just as Christmas Eve Fat and, of course, the beer. Although the men brewed the beer, it was the women's responsibility to take the chill out of it and to serve it. By taking the chill out of the beer, you enhanced its taste. It was done by heat-shocking it - heating up an empty iron kettle and pouring the cold beer into the glowing hot kettle for a just couple of seconds before pouring it back to its original container. It should then have a two-inch thick layer of foam.

Suddenly a stamping noise from outside startled everyone; a knocking sound like snow off boots sent Andreas to investigate. Marta froze. "Oh Holy Night! A visitor on Christmas Eve?"

Jenny's face flushed, praying it wasn't Robert, but nothing would ever surprise her regarding that man, although she doubted he would come in this weather. She leaned forward to get a better look at the door, anxiously waiting to see who it was. Iver and Lars jumped up and followed Andreas to the door. Then, slowly, the door handle moved. Lars turned back at Olaf and whispered, "Olaf, Olaf, come here with us...it may be the Christmas Elf coming to get the youngest grandson since we forgot to leave the Christmas porridge on the front step!" A frightened Olaf scooted down as far as he could in his chair.

"Stop that Lars! It isn't funny." Marta held up her wooden spoon with the symbol of the cross.

"Or did you forget to paint the holy cross on the door, Mother?"

"That's it, Lars! Now you are scaring all of us."

Suddenly the door gave out a loud wham and sagged at the hinges and everybody held their breaths as a creature wrapped in a huge blanket covered with snow stumbled in. The men instinctively backed off while the others screamed at the moment the creature exposed its face and brushed the snow off the hood. Then a sigh of relief could be heard as they realized it was Gusta.

"Gusta, what in God's name are you doing here?" asked Andreas and helped her in.

"I am hungry, and I've come to Christmas dinner," she said as she glanced at all the startled faces.

Marta glared at her father and went to welcome her aunt, wrapping both arms around her while praying that Gusta would behave herself. She felt cold to the touch and much thinner, *close to the bones,* thought Marta, much like her mother before she died.

Gusta hugged her niece so hard she almost choked, and then whispered in her ear, "I came to help. I came to help."

"Help me with what Gusta?"

"Time will tell, it will, it will."

No, thought Marta as she drew back from her aunt. *How dare she come and spoil their Christmas!* She escorted her to the bedroom to help her get presentable for dinner, while Andreas poured another round of Christmas beer and told Jenny the story about when Gusta went missing. Andreas had told this tale many times and still the family sat spellbound, listening to every word. They could hear Marta and

Gusta talking from the bedroom and Jenny was afraid Andreas wouldn't be able to finish his story before they returned.

"So what happened? Who found her?" she asked.

"Her husband. Gusta was sixteen and I think I told you she was beautiful."

"Yes Grandfather," said Olaf, "you told us already."

"We searched for days, fearing she had dropped into a gorge or drown in the fjord. Somehow she had traveled across the water and ended up miles from home. A young man found her and took her to his family's farm where she lay ill for several weeks. The young man, taken with her beauty, soon became her husband. Our parents were relieved that something wonderful had finally happened to their daughter. But fate had never been kind to Gusta, for her husband drowned a week after their marriage and poor Gusta watched it happen from shore."

Jenny shook her head, "The poor dear."

"The real tragedy," said Anna, "was that she never seemed to recover. And she's different in the head. She continues to wander as she did as a child, from place to place, but now she brings people her visions."

Lars looked at Jenny,

"She sees the future."

After finishing eating, the men complimented the woman for perfect de-chilling of the beer and beautiful table decorating; they would always do that regardless whether they meant it or not. This was not the time to get on the women's bad side!

The food would be left on the table to welcome all their dead ancestors to come back and eat. No one in the house would sneak into the kitchen that night for fear they might see a ghost - except Gusta, who later could be found talking to the empty chairs. Everyone had their own opinion about Gusta; her family kept it to themselves. The villagers were divided. Some thought she brought good luck, while others were certain she led the way for the fairy folk and trolls with bad luck following close behind. In either case, just to be safe, if she asked for food, they always fed her.

Early on Christmas Day, an excited Olaf rushed into the kitchen. “Grandma, Grandma come look!”

“Oh my,” said Marta when she noticed the beautifully wrapped presents under the tree. Where could these have come from? She knew some people gave each other presents on Christmas Eve, but on Christmas day? Soon everybody faced Jenny.

“Now I can share with you the secret of the trunk. My parents sent it to me as my Christmas gift with all these presents inside for each of you. I do hope you like them.”

Olaf couldn’t contain himself and Jenny urged him to open his gift. He tore off the wrapping and cradled a replica of a ship in his hands. Wide-eyed, he turned to his father who had been watching from the hall. He lifted the toy in the air. “Isn’t she a beauty?”

Iver’s dark eyes met Jenny’s. *She is a beauty*, he thought, *and she is lying.* Just as he suspected, the mysterious crate was indeed from Robert. Jenny had an odd feeling that Iver knew she had lied. How was that possible when no one had seen the contents of the trunk? The small packages she had asked her mother to send and the items she had bought surely hadn’t interested him; he barely noticed she was alive.

Marta had everyone’s attention as she unwrapped a tea set with a lacy pattern of rose-hued pink flowers on exquisite white Bavarian china. She carefully cradled a translucent teacup in her hands while trying to find the right words of thanks, but it was Jenny who spoke next.

“I wanted to thank you for giving me a safe place to live these past months.”

Marta’s eyes watered; never had she received such an extravagant gift!

All the gifts were opened except one and Jenny turned to find Iver had left the house with the excuse of a forgotten chore. When Marta realized her son was gone, she threw up her hands and said a quick prayer to the gods. No one dared to venture outside on Christmas day and now her son was beating a path home and Gusta was probably out talking to the trees. Thank goodness the holiday would soon be over!

Later in the day, Jenny picked up Iver's gift and put it away in her trunk, thinking how rude he was just to walk out on her. She pulled out a letter from her mother and the familiar handwriting for a few moments took her home to Kristiania. When she finished re-reading it, she knew that when the weather permitted, her family was also ready for her to return home. By now, society's interest in her scandalous behavior with Robert must have faded and moved on to others. The extravagant gifts had upset her, but not as he would have expected. When she looked at her reflection in the mirror, she wanted to walk up to Iver Holseth in the Paris gown and say, "Look at me! I am a beautiful woman worthy of your interest."

January 13th, the last day of Christmas, finally arrived, a day of closure, reflection and wrapping up. To most people it was a relief; now they could be free to do whatever they pleased without having to adhere to strict norms and rituals. Life could get back to normal again.

Jenny was helping Marta with cleaning and putting away decorations and everything else related to Christmas. She thought about all the customs and norms that were so different from the ones she was used too, like the custom of going to church on Christmas Eve - it was expected that you showed up and you couldn't hide your absence either - an empty pew would tell. Fortunately for the Holseth's, they could always excuse their absence on inaccessible paths or rough seas. The norms continued to dictate what you could do on the second day of Christmas, which was devoted to family and as with Christmas Day, it was strictly forbidden to appear in public in any way, or visit someone outside your closest family or in-laws.

The first time both young and old could get a fresh breath from all family-related chatter was the third day when the real festivities could begin. On this day, they didn't use any excuses of inaccessible or dangerous paths; instead, some would take huge risks to get to visit neighbors and friends to eat, drink and resolve disputes. It was crucial to work out any unresolved issues and it was extremely important that nobody had any grudge against each other when the New

Year arrived. The neighbors changed roles from being a host one year to a guest the next. But even at these apparently casual gatherings, many activities were dictated by norms. Like the mandatory sermon after food had been consumed and beer drunken, to scientific comments about its taste, appearance and alcohol content. The housewife would hand out a collection of sermons and hymnbooks while the master placed himself at the end table to prepare for the devotion. Anybody who was not present at this time was called upon; nobody could snick away from this holy moment. For the children, this was sometimes the hardest moment during the entire Christmas season. The reading was done with a great deal of pathos and after singing a hymn, it was time for silence so the words had time to manifest. Any comment about the scripture could be done with only a simple question; discussing it was not appropriate. That would expose the individual as one who doubted the bible and even if you did, nobody dared to let the others know that you were a non-believer.

After this holy moment, it was time for the host to show his food supply. It was a way of showing off that they had an ample amount of food by letting their guests peek into the grain bins, flour containers, cheese boxes and butter churns, the same way as Jenny's family would show off an exclusive collection of paintings, china ware and crystal chandeliers. When it came to the smoked cured ham and other meat products, the amount itself wasn't enough; the quality had to be judged by its appearance and smell. Any criticism had to appear favorable to the host, regardless of the individual's opinion, but at the same time, one shouldn't appear too agreeable either, which would indicate disrespect; therefore, one had to select one's words very carefully.

When the last bit of Christmas was put away, Marta started muttering that turned into chanting as she picked up a broom and started sweeping away imaginary cobwebs in the air.

Jenny couldn't understand a word she was saying and wondered what was wrong with her. She had heard tales about people who had almost instantly become insane, especially after intense emotional or physical hardship. A chill flew through her; could Christmas have been too much for Marta? She thought about Gusta who apparently had become insane after watching a horrible event.

In a crazed frenzy, Marta twirled around the room, flung open the front door and with a last big sweep of the broom screamed, "Out! Get out of my house!"

Concerned, Jenny asked Marta, "What is wrong? Who do you want to get out? Do you want me to leave?"

Marta leaned over the broom. "Nothing is wrong, my dear, and of course, I don't want you to leave. I just chased Christmas out of the house." Then she slammed the door. "Christmas has a tendency to get stuck in certain places." She put away the broom and gave Jenny a warm hug. "I am ok, Jenny. I am fine."

The Midwife

"Odin, the Norse god of death, hung himself from Yggdrasill, the ash-tree of knowledge, to obtain magical powers. He became a celebrant of violent death, at times taking the form of a wolf to linger near the victim. The Vikings understood their god and when the lone wolf appeared, they knew death was imminent and that Odin would greet them at the entry of Valhalla."

Compiled from Norse Mythology

Jenny awoke to the sound of Anna's cry, "Jon, Jon, I need you now! Mother somebody please help me!" and rushed into her room.

"What's wrong Anna? Is it...?" Before she could say another word, Anna moaned again as the next wave of pain swept through her.

Jenny picked up the blanket from the floor and laid it over her body. "Anna is it the baby? It's too early..."

Anna nodded and asked for her mother again. The last few days Jenny had offered to stay with Anna since Iver would be spending a few days with Marta, helping his grandfather with some refurbishing work on one of the loft rooms. It would be easier to just spend the night instead of running back and forth and crossing the sometimes dangerous ravine that separated the two farms. Jenny dressed quickly and prepared to go out in the dark winter morning to tell Marta; then she returned to Anna's room.

"Anna, listen. I will send your mother to stay with you and somebody will get the midwife. Listen carefully," she laid a wet cloth on her friend's forehead. "Within the hour, your mother will be with you. Did you hear me? Your Mother will be here. Until then do not leave this room. I've set food and fresh water on this stand so you won't need to go into the kitchen."

"Jenny, don't leave me alone! Oh how I miss Jon! Why did he have to die?"

"No more talk about dying. You have a baby coming. Now listen to me. It will be sometime before the baby will show up and you need the midwife." She held Anna's hands. "Anna, there's nothing to worry about. I'll have the midwife here before you know it."

"I need your strength, Jenny! Don't go."

The word "strength" buzzed in Jenny's mind; no one had said anything to her like that before. "You have it Anna. You are strong and I promise I will be back." Anna's soft cries bothered Jenny as she shut the door.

In the morning darkness, heavy clouds crashed into one another and when Jenny stepped down off the steps, she had to fight to stay upright against the wind. She wrapped her woolen scarf tightly around her neck and walked as fast as she could while trying not to slip on the ice. Whoever would go, a journey to fetch the midwife would not be an easy one, for Anna's baby had decided to be born on the day the western region of Norway would be hit with a record-breaking snowstorm.

As she approached the thirty-foot wide and fifteen-foot deep riverbed of a ravine, Jenny had no idea of how dangerous it really was. She had only one thought in mind - get to Marta and tell her the baby was coming. The ravine where snow avalanches and rocks had carved out formations and throughout the years torn off every bush, tree and bit of dirt down to bedrock now had a thick layer of ice covered up with the newly fallen snow. She should have been cautious, testing every step as she moved forward, but instead she crossed the ravine as if it was a beautiful spring day, not knowing that one wrong move could be fatal. Sometimes ignorance aids you; sometimes it kills you and the mountains seem to give, take or protect randomly without any specific pattern - or do they?

Does nature have any agenda of deciding when and whom to strike?
Inside the farmhouse, Andreas looked up from his paper. "Marta, stop it. You've been fidgeting about getting up and down to look out that window for the past half-hour and I can't read my paper." He dropped the back issues of the regional trading paper on the table. "You've seen snow before, so I gather you must be expecting company in this snowstorm?" He got up and looked out the window. "Yep, looks like snow. Now will you go sit down or find something to....."

A roaring noise interrupted him. He looked at the mountainside across the fjord, then back at his daughter. He had no doubt what that kind of noise was. His face had suddenly turned serious. "I wonder where it came from."

No one spoke for several minutes; they just looked out the window and listened intensively. Only the clock on the wall broke the silence.

Suddenly Andreas pointed at a figure by the barn and exclaimed, "Well I'll be! It's Jenny. What brings her out in this weather?"
"I knew it! Anna's having the baby."

A moment later, a pale and frosty looking Jenny stepped into the room, took off her coat, hung it over a chair and headed to the wood stove. Andreas looked at her.

"Have you seen a ghost, Jenny?"

"No, but....."

Marta broke in. "Father, I told you this morning I thought the baby was coming early. Didn't I tell you?" She quickly disappeared into her bedroom.
Jenny squeezed her hands over the stove.

"I was lucky! An avalanche came right behind me." Her entire body was still shaking.
Marta returned with her bag on one arm and her coat on the other. "I need to get over to Anna."

Andreas shook his head. "I don't think that's a good idea." He nodded at Jenny who told her about the avalanche that had nearly hit her.

Marta moved toward the door. "I can't let Anna stay there alone!"

"Come back here Daughter! You're not going anywhere," said Andreas.

"God will help me cross the ravine."

Andreas jerked the bag out of her hands. "God has already told you not go, but if you are eager to meet him right now, I won't stop you." He knew that a second, bigger avalanche always came down the same ravine; the one nearly hitting Jenny was just a taste of what was coming.

Marta looked at him a long time without saying a word; she knew her father was right. She slowly took her coat off, pulled her sweater tight around her shoulders and sat down at the table. "Anna needs me." She looked at Jenny and then at Andreas for some sign she was right and after all, she could go, but they both shook their heads. She took a deep breath and looked at the candle in front of her as she tried to explain the dread. It was the same feeling that had enveloped her the day the boys had dug her husband out from his snow-packed grave. She grabbed a broom from behind the wood stove and knocked on the ceiling with its shaft. "Iver, the baby is coming!"

Andreas moved to get his clothes.

"Where are you going?"

"To get the Midwife, where else?"

"No Father, you're not going!"

"It's not the path down to the fjord that is blocked; it's the trail to Iver's house."

"I know. I also know that you can't make it to the fjord in your condition."

"I feel as young as ever before and by the way, I don't think Iver can row the big boat alone. You know Lars took the dinghy."

Marta knew it was difficult for anybody to row the big boat alone, but she just couldn't bear the strain of having her father going to the village in this weather. And as always, when she needed Lars for something, he was nurturing some of his projects in the village.

"Ok go ahead, and then we might meet with God in heaven."

Andreas knew his daughter had him. If he took off with Iver, she would be heading toward Anna as soon as he was out of her sight. She had always had a tendency to get the last trick on him.

Jenny stood up, walked to the window and looked out. "I'll go with Iver." She knew it would be tough to be so close to him for so long, but for Anna, she would be willing to do whatever it took to help get her the midwife. Now, after she lost her husband, Jenny didn't even dare to think about the possibilities of Anna losing her baby too.

"Are you sure Jenny?" Marta asked.

"Yes I am. I know how to row now. Lars has taught me and by the way, there is something inside of me telling me to go, too. I just need some extra clothes and food."

"That's the easy part, but..."

"I have made up my mind, Marta. You know I have never felt that I have made any difference to anybody and I owe it the Anna to do whatever I can to help her."

Marta looked at her a long time. "But you have always been a good help to all of us, and have you forgotten what you did in the village? People are still talking about how you organized the whole thing; the woman from Kristiania who took the lead will be talked about for years to come."

"After I came to Holseth, maybe I have, but back in Kristiania, I got every thing served on a silver plate; even the things I wanted to do by myself were done for me."

"Here you have been wonderful, Jenny, absolutely wonderful."

"Call it whatever, but if I can make that boat move a little bit faster, I insist that I go."

Marta knew that two would row faster than one.

When Iver learned about Jenny's suggestion to go with him, he immediately resisted, but gave in to the fact that even though Jenny would not be of much help, little bit was better than nothing. And since this was an emergency, he agreed to let her go.

Half an hour later they were ready and as they headed toward the door, Iver walked up to his mother. "Do you remember the speaking machine Lars was talking about a few moths ago?"

Marta nodded, "Yes, what about it?"

"You know, I don't think he was as stupid as some of us thought when we suggested it would never have a practical use. I tell you one thing Mother, if we had one now, none of us would have to go to the village in this weather." He then wrapped both arms around her and kissed her on the cheek. "We'll be fine, and don't you worry."

Marta was stunned. He had never kissed her like that! Then he squeezed his grandfather on the shoulder. "Goodbye Old Man," and walked out. Outside, he turned to his dog and ordered him back to the house. "Stay. You watch over them." Reluctantly the dog turned back and headed for the top step, standing guard.

Andreas shook his head and in a muffled voice said, "I wonder what's gotten into Iver this morning?" He looked at Marta for a possible answer, but she was silent as the grave, already deep in her own thoughts.

All her life Marta had been waiting for something or someone - wait, wait, wait...*Oh dear, please God help me, this is so hard.* She prayed for a safe journey for Iver and Jenny and for Anna's baby to wait. Maybe there was some truth in the saying that, "Nothing is so bad that it's not good for something." Emergencies and a common threat do bring people together. Could there possibly be another tone between Jenny and Iver after this? Then she decided to spend the day cooking to keep sane - pray and cook seemed to be all she could do.

As Iver and Jenny reached the boathouse, Iver noticed the wind was much calmer down by the fjord than in higher elevations, but he knew that could change quickly. The current north westerly wouldn't pose any problem, but he feared it would soon turn to a north wind. He had learned from Andreas that when a storm system comes in from the coast, the wind usually begins from the south and turns clockwise to the west and north, so the issue was not if, but when. They would have to make the two-hour trip to Uksvik Bay and back with the midwife before the wind changed direction, which could transform the fjord from a calm pond to a boiling hell in a matter of minutes.

The fourteen-foot boat had three rows of seats called thwarts and on a good day could seat eight to ten people. Rather than one sitting up front and the other behind, Iver and Jenny would take the center seat, sitting next to each other, managing one oar each. This was the hardest part for Iver, but if Jenny ever was going to be of some help, that seemed to be the only way and if it didn't work out, he would just place her in the back and grab both oars himself.

They pulled the boat out and lowered it slowly down the makeshift slide of seaweed-covered timber logs so it didn't drop too fast into the water. Halfway down, Iver jumped on board, and with an oar, steered it clear of the hidden rocks under the water's surface. It was always a challenge to set out a boat during low tide. Certain to be clear of the sharp rocks, Jenny jumped onboard and pushed the boat away from shore.

At Holseth, no one heard Gusta as she tip-toed down the stairs. The howling wind covered up the sound of the squeaking hinges as she opened the door and walked out into the storm. The wind tugged at her long brown wool scarf wrapped around her head and tucked underneath the collar of her heavy coat. With both hands holding tight to the collar, she leaned forward and waded through the soft, deep layer of powdered snow with the hem of her coat sweeping it like a broom between her legs. As she passed the barn, she moved behind the drifts of snow and looked back to see if anyone had seen her. The wind and falling snow swept her footprints away almost as quickly as she moved her feet. She headed toward the ravine.

Many years ago, on the day her husband died, she had been standing at the edge of a cliff overlooking the fjord, screaming bitterly at the gods. Almost stepping into a void and falling to her death, invisible hands had yanked her back and pushed her into the bushes. Shocked into silence, she lay for hours, tears flowing, turning into soft whimpers, and there she had slept, her heart utterly broken. Hours later, she awoke to wet licks below her chin. Nestled against her neck she found herself eye-to-eye with a starving male pup. Believing the gods had touched her and delivered this dog into her care, she kept the helpless animal close and months later, both could be seen walking the mountains together. The dog had the appearance of a wolf, the cunning of a fox and a brownish red and white spotted coat that was like no other dog in the region. So when his body finally grew to match his giant paws, Gusta christened him the Spotted Wolf. He protected her until the day he died and by that time, Gusta and her dog were known by the villagers and country folks alike as being from the spirits. No one dared bother her. The day came when she mourned the loss of her dog. Finding she had no one place to call home, she continued to wander alone until the good Lord would take her home.

Crossing the ravine to Iver's farm, Gusta knew she could easily slip to her death, but threat of death had never stopped her. The day invisible hands had pushed her into the bush, she had given herself the freedom to come and go as she pleased, unafraid. She laughed at the funny names people called her. They didn't understand that the gods had touched her, allowing her to wander and stay close to those things seen and unseen. Her soul was in tune with the beat of nature. No wonder she preferred to speak to trees and animals, for they were the only ones who listened and assisted her across the canyon in the worst of conditions. Gusta was neither a slow, nor a fast walker, but somewhere in-between. Her gait was a simple step, back and forth like a clock's pendulum. This odd way of walking side to side allowed her to travel long distances without needing to rest. Later, some would surmise it was her ghostly nature and quiet step that had kept her from slipping to her death on the broken path, while others would say she put a spell on the wind, which blew her to safety. She never commented one way or the other, finding the stories recounting her journey much more interesting than her own. The fact remained, she crossed impossible paths and never once broke her stride nor did she stop to turn around when an avalanche rumbled down behind her.

Unharmed, she reached Iver's farm and leaned up against the house, brushed the snow off the window and pressed her face against it. Gusta had the odd habit of peering through windows before going into any house. She liked being on the outside looking in, forever the voyeur. She could see Anna in a great deal of pain, kneeling on the kitchen floor, trying to reach something on the table. By the time Gusta opened and closed the door behind her, Anna had crumbled to the floor and was surprised, but happy to see Gusta smiling down on her, gently touching her forehead. Never had Gusta looked so good! With somewhat of a struggle, she was able to get Anna back into bed. Relieved to have someone in the farmhouse with her, Anna began to calm down as she listened to Gusta's silly chanting sounds coming from the kitchen while she prepared a warm broth. That she could cook came as a surprise to Anna who had never seen her in the kitchen doing anything other than eating. Gusta was thankful Iver had piled the logs so high the house would be warm for hours. She guessed it might be a while before the baby would show up and sometime before her nephew would be back with the midwife. Just in case no one showed up, she would get everything ready.

Iver and Jenny moved quickly, taking advantage of every second of reasonable weather and calm waters. They rowed effectively by technique as much as by sheer force, which was crucial now as they handled only one oar each. Iver had to admit Jenny was doing quite well and much better than he had expected.

"Jenny, you handle the oar well."

Jenny turned toward him and smiled. "An attentive student and an excellent teacher make a good result. Don't you think so?"

Her smile made his heart jump, warming up his body, softening his muscles except for one that was getting harder, making him ashamed of his reaction.

"Certainly. Lars has obviously taught you to pull at count one, resting at two, three and reposition the oars at four. What else has he taught you?" He felt she had been leaning more and more toward Lars, so if any of them could win her, it would be his brother.

The tone in his voice indicated jealousy, but why? She hadn't done anything other than be a friend, and after all, she wasn't dating any of them. "He told me not to trust anyone who doesn't speak their mind." She looked at him one more time and smiled.

Iver didn't comment and began to pull his oar so hard that the boat changed course and headed directly to shore. After slowing down and blaming Jenny for not keeping up, they adjusted the course and pointing at the tongue of land Uksneset, continued rowing in silence. The only sounds were squeaks from the oars and slapping waves against the bow. A couple of curious seagulls followed, gliding back and forth above the boat's wake. Like a dark snail on a wood path surrounded by a dense forest, the boat moved steady through the narrow fjord. It was tempting to row alongside the west shoreline, but the danger of avalanches forced them to keep a middle course.

For years, Iver had rowed these waters and knew every ledge, ravine and boulder on either side.

Even as the snow had begun to accumulate all the way down to the waterline, he could still recognize the landmarks. He glanced briefly at the Bluehorn Mountains and saw a stream of snow pushed by the wind across its summits, then falling down to a rock fall like a giant bridal veil. When they reached a point between Litlevika, the little bay, and the Skrenakk Mountain, the weather worsened. The first gust of wind hit them with full force, striking their faces with icy snow, making it almost impossible to see and within seconds, the shoreline was no longer visible. The sudden change in the wind, which had been characteristic for the Sunnylvsfjord for as long as people could remember, had once again come true. It was like the wind and snow squalls dropped right out of the sky without any warning and were transforming the fjord into a roaring hell.

Waves slammed into the boat and splashed over the rim. The two in the boat would soon realize what a hell the fjord could become in an instant, reminding them that when it comes to weather, there is indeed not much difference between the sea and mountains. In nice weather, both places could be like heaven; in bad weather, like hell.

Well aware of the change in wind direction, Iver shouted, "Let's get to shore as fast as we can now. It can get nasty where the fjord branches out; the currents there are very unpredictable."

The locals called that area the water graveyard where many boats had disappeared. To avoid the area, they couldn't proceed as planned and began to row toward Litlevika in hopes of finding shelter. Then, out of nowhere, a large wave took them by surprise and both Iver and Jenny lost their grip on the oars and fell backwards. Jenny managed to retrieve hers, but Iver, who was more concerned about the water filling up the boat, let his oar go as he began scooping out water.

"Iver, grab your oar!" Jenny tried to rescue it but was thrown off balance, hitting her head against the boat's rim, cutting her forehead. She saw blood on her skirt, but she couldn't feel any pain. The cold salt-water must have anaesthetized the wound. Not concerned about herself she yelled, "Iver, you lost the oar!"

Iver dropped the bucket immediately and fumbled around until he pulled out a spare that Jenny could use to keep the boat steady while he was scooping out water the best he could, but as soon as she tried to put it in place, another wave hit them and swept the second oar away. Jenny scrambled and pulled out a six-foot gaff, a rod with a hook the end. After several attempts to catch the oar, she gave up as it had drifted too far off. It seemed like their fate had fallen into the hands of Rasmus, a sailor's name for a roaring sea.

Jenny felt the same fear creeping over her as she had felt the time she got stuck on the mountain ledge - a feeling of helplessness of being at the mercy of the power of nature. "Oh my God, Iver, I am scared! I think we will go down!"

Iver stuck his head out from the bottom, "Not we, Jenny girl!"

Jenny shouted, "Look out!"
A huge wave with a foaming ridge lifted the boat up, holding it for a second before dropping it. With pounding force, the heavy timber boat collided with the next wave which filled it instantly with ice cold water.

With only one oar, it was useless to try to keep boat steady, so Jenny bent down on her knees and joined Iver in scooping water as wave after wave tossed the boat like a cork, causing Jenny's body to be thrown into the arms of Iver. He lost his bucket and instinctively held his arms around her for a second before releasing her and grabbing the bucket again. The boat was now getting dangerously close to an abrupt section of the mountainside.

At Holseth, Marta moved between the windows, checking the weather then going back to her cooking. Neither gave her solace. She prayed to every dead relative she could think of for assistance, and then begged the mercy of all the old Viking gods she could remember. Those she couldn't, she made up. She wanted to be with her daughter, to comfort her, but was unsuccessful at persuading Andreas to let her cross the ravine before the snow had stabilized.

A window separated her from the drama she couldn't see on the fjord; she laid her warm hand on the cold glass and watched as it formed a milky imprint that slowly disappeared. She did this many times as if she was trying to make the imprint stick. Then she blew at the window, making her breath fog the glass, forming patterns that quickly vanished. She wondered if the imprint of her hand and the designs of her breath on the window were like the warmth from her heart and her love for her children. One last time she breathed on the glass and sent her love. "God speed," she whispered and returned to the kitchen where she soon caught herself humming an old favorite hymn of her mother's. In times of struggle, it was always her mother she thought of. She picked up a broom to clean the kitchen floor when Andreas appeared at the doorway.

"This is the third time you have swept the floor today."

Marta looked at her father a long time as if she didn't recognize him, then she looked at the broom. "Have I? I don't remember." She put the broom away and walked back to the window and stared out. As she looked aimlessly into the snow, a memory of the family that had perished on the fjord came to her. They were going from the village of Stordal to Stranden to participate in an engagement party for their son when a sudden storm caught them by surprise and capsized their boat. They became an easy prey, drifting helplessly in the ice cold water. People from a nearby shoreline farm reported later they had heard screams for help, but in the strong wind and poor visibility, there wasn't much they could do. After the weather calmed down, they searched the area but found no traces of the boat or the people on board. Several days later, the corpse of a woman was found drifting by the boathouse at a farm several miles from where the fatal journey ended. The body was identified as one of the eight and the mother of the three children who drowned. She had drifted back to her husband's birthplace, where she had arrived as a would-be bride, twenty-five years earlier.

Marta went back to the kitchen and began preparing for dinner, even though it was not time for it yet; going idle only made her think about sad stories.

When she got the dinner ready, she called Andreas and Kari and was beside herself not to find Gusta in the loft. "Father, where is your sister?"

"Leave her be; she may be out in the barn with the animals. She'll come when she's hungry."

At the table, no one but Kari had an appetite for this noon dinner. Marta moved the food around on her plate, not tasting any of it, trying to come up with a plan to get to Anna. She looked across the table at Andreas. "Father, tell us the story about Mother and the lambs."

Andreas looked hard at his daughter, knowing what she must be going through but he didn't feel like talking.

"Father, please tell us about Mother."

By the tone in his daughter's voice, Andreas knew he'd better start talking. He could tell she was almost in tears and he hated it when she cried. And she cried ugly. He laid his bread down on his plate and began the story about how he and his wife had met one summer long ago in the mountains. She had come to help out on a dairy farm and he wanted to impress her but she never seemed to notice him.

Kari spoke up. "The lambs, Grandfather, get to the part about the lambs."

"In good time, now let's see, we were picnicking one Sunday near the waterfall called the Three Sisters..." He had told this story so many times and today, for his daughter's sake, he would make it last a long time.

On the fjord, waves pounded against the bedrock with explosive force, transforming the previously silent water into a brown foaming witch's pot of tree roots, moss and debris. Like a giant magnet, the bedrock pulled the boat into the pot and repetitively slammed it against the rock. In a frenzied and desperate attempt to maintain control, Iver grabbed the only oar, stood up and straddled across two thwarts, held the oar like a spear and pointed at the mountain wall, not aware of a huge wave moving very quickly toward them.

Jenny noticed the wave and screamed at him. "Are you crazy Iver? Sit down!" She moved forward to pull him back, but was too late. The wave hit them with such a force it threw the boat against the mountain causing Iver to lose his balance and plunge into the water. It happened so fast he hardly knew what was going on before the ice cold water begun to soak through his frieze clothes. The sudden change in temperature made breathing into a pulsating struggle for oxygen.

Jenny screamed and leaned over the side to look after him and managed just to see a glimpse of him struggling to keep his head clear of the water before she lost her balance and fell back into the boat.

The forceful impact with the mountain wall had cracked the boat and as it began taking in water, Jenny managed to hold onto a tree limb embedded in the mountain. With only seconds to react before the boat would slip away, she motioned to Iver to take her hand. He reached out, but couldn't get a firm grasp around her hand before she was forced to jump from the boat's stern as it sunk under her. She slipped and fell into the water, but she was lucky. A tree branch was sticking out within her reach and she managed to pull herself to safety. Dripping wet and shivering from the cold, she could only helplessly watch the waves bounce Iver up and down against the mountainside like a piece of driftwood. The low tide exposed a two-meter tall layer of slick seaweed and algae on the bedrock, making it almost impossible to get a firm grip, and every time he seemed to have a grasp, the next wave pulled him away again. The powerful return waves and undercurrent began to drag him away from shore. Sometimes his head was under water, sometimes above gasping for air. The frigid water had begun to affect his limbs and was slowing down his movements.

Jenny climbed down to a boulder pointing into fjord and knew she had to get hold of Iver before he suffered the effects of hypothermia. "Iver, swim to the boulder!" she screamed. "Iver swim to that boulder, damn you, go on!"

Iver saw Jenny to his left but he could barely keep afloat. Through some miracle, he began to tread water, heading in the direction of a wire. Luckily his hand found the cross wire under the water's surface. It was a wire used to anchor a buoy away from shoreline. While pulling himself to shore, he lost his grip several times from the slick seaweed entangled in the wire and every time he dropped into the water, it became harder and harder to pull himself up again.

Jenny screamed, "Iver, wrap your feet around the wire and pull yourself to the rock!" After several failed attempts, she realized Iver wasn't able to lift even his foot. With the great risk of sliding into the fjord, Jenny lay down on the boulder, crawled forward and reached out for him. "Grab my hand."

Iver managed to lunge forward so their hands met.

Jenny prayed she wouldn't lose her foothold. "Iver! Move slowly. I need to swing you to the side of the boulder. I can't pull you up; it's too slick. I need to swing you sideways."

Their eyes met and Iver nodded to Jenny and smiled.

"You can do this, Iver! Just hang on."

They started slowly moving back and forth until Jenny felt he was ready. Iver said, "Let me go."

Jenny questioned his approach, but when he said, "Let me go!" again, she opened her hand and Iver dropped down to a ledge, close to the waterline. He screamed out as his right foot hit the edge of a rock and he looked up at Jenny, his face anguished in pain. "I think I have broken my damn leg! You need to go and get help."

"Where, where do I go?"

Iver pointed toward a three-to-four-hundred foot elevated pass. "On the other side of that pass!"

Jenny hesitated, "but you can't stay there."

"Don't worry ! Just go, Jenny. Hurry up!"

As Jenny began climbing up the slope, she realized it was not like the spring day when she had climbed an even steeper part of the mountain. Now the cold had already sucked most of the energy out of her, even before she started. But there was no time to speculate whether she could make it or not; it was just to move on one step at the time. She lost her footing several times, fell over rocks and slid, creating small rockslides and for every time she fell, it became harder and harder to get up again. She could hardly move her fingers and toes, which felt like someone was sticking needles under the nails. Her hair looked like it had been braided with ice; her skirt was so frozen and heavy that it was impossible to pull it up to make it easier to walk. Instead, it was tugging at her waist and sweeping behind her, slowing her down. Her teeth chattered and her entire body shivered from the staggering cold. As she reached a plateau partly sheltered from the horrendous wind about half way up toward the pass, she felt dizzy and a strong taste of blood. She spat into the snow, wondering if she was bleeding in her mouth; then her knees buckled and she fell face down. She managed to turn around and wipe the snow off her face and found herself staring into the sky.

Sometime later, she became alert again - confused, but warm. Her eyelids became heavy and again she drifted off. Dreaming, she saw the fuzzy image of their maid and her mother back in Kristiania. They both smiled and beckoned her to join them at the fireplace. How beautiful they looked! Their eyes reflected the amber lights from the fire. Then Andreas showed up by the door. It appeared that he had been there before; her mother seemed to know him, but he was looking worried and his gruff voice had the resonance of a warning bell. "If your bones are chilled and you want to lie down, you're doomed if you stay." Facing death, the human body has many times shown amazing abilities to pull out its last resources, but sometimes the soul may trick the body into believing that everything is comfortable and all right when it is actually dying.

Armed with a dust cloth and her wooden spoon, Marta moved restlessly about, scraping frost from the windows. She wanted to see the path and had taken great pains to keep the window clean. Every time she scraped and paced in front of him, Andreas would grit his teeth. There were no more meals to prepare, no dust or speck of dirt left in the house. The house was as clean and sparkling as the fresh layer upon layer of snow that had descended upon the land.

"I feel so helpless sitting here, just waiting."

She took her dust rag and wiped the windowsill before walking back into the living room where she bent down to pet Iver's dog. He had bravely stayed on the top step as his master had ordered until the snow forced him inside. He had now positioned himself at the front door, refusing food and water, awaiting Iver's return. It was obvious both mother and dog were having difficulty waiting; she told him Iver would be back soon and he licked her hand. As she walked away from the doorway, a picture fell to the floor and when she went to retrieve it, she cried out. It was a picture of Iver and Lars as children and there was a crack in the glass across Iver's face. That was how Andreas found her - on the floor, crying, holding onto the picture of the boys.

"Marta, what is it?"

Marta held up the picture. "It is Iver. Something's happened at the fjord." She had turned ghostly pale. There was no consoling Marta; the best anyone could do was to be quiet and wait.

In the snow, Jenny was feeling warm and comfortable and fought not to fall asleep. She knew she had to stay awake, but was not aware of the real danger she was in. Feeling warm in these conditions was a sure sign of hypothermia. Suddenly she found herself walking on the path to Anna's house where she saw Olaf on the top steps crying. "Why are you crying?" she asked. The little boy pointed at the door and Jenny walked into the house calling out, "Anna, where are you?" She opened her bedroom door and walked in. It was dark and cold. As she approached the bed, she found Anna covered in blood with her dead baby at her side.

Jenny's eyes shot wide open, it was only a dream, only a dream! *Anna is not dead. Anna will not die. And Iver, he needs help!* She moved with a great deal of pain and forced herself to get into a crawling position, rocking back and forth as every part of her body felt like thousands of pins were being shoved into her skin. Finally she stood up and propped herself against a tree until she could stand on her own. "I remember why I'm here. I will not forget why I am here. Anna is not dead and nothing will stop me from bringing the midwife to her." She staggered up the hill in a desperate attempt to find help.

Iver had managed to pull himself up to a safe spot, preventing the tide from sweeping him off the ledge. He was not going to be tortured like the victims of the ancient warriors by being tied to a rock during low tide and letting the high tide slowly drown him. If he was going to die, he wanted to go down with dignity, at least fight the merciless nature to the bitter end. He stood up and tried to stand on his foot in the hope it had gotten better, but the unbearable pain made him retract it as if he had stepped on hot embers. Walk or not, he would have to move his body somehow to generate heat from the inside; otherwise, a cunning death would get him. He began flexing his arms and soon, like a wounded animal, he limped and crawled alongside the shoreline.

His mind had left his body and like a headless chicken, he continued moving on when a fawn suddenly jumped out from behind a bush, bolted beside him, stopped to look back before disappearing into the trees. Startled, Iver looked back to where it had vanished and that's when he noticed something that looked like a shed. A jolt of hope flowed through him, giving him a little more strength to move through the thicket toward his vision. He was not able to judge whether it was real or not and knew that maybe the extreme stress to his brain had created a hallucination for what it wanted to see. He just continued, crawling through the thicket until he lay outside the door.

Then he remembered the shed; it belonged to a farmer who used it when he was fishing in the fjord. Iver stood up and pounded his body against the door until it gave in. Once inside, he accidentally knocked an oil lamp off the wall, shattering the glass globe. The shed was actually a one-room cottage made of thin boards mounted lengthwise. Glitches between the boards clearly indicated it was only used during the summer. It had a small wood stove, one bed, a chair, a small table and an old chest of drawers. He began to rummage around in the hope of finding matches. After emptying the chest, he came up with a package of the matchsticks he was looking for and managed to light the oil lamp. While warming his hands, he noticed a fly come to life from the lamp's base; the warmth must have fooled her into believing it was spring. He thought about his grandfather telling him about the insects and saw an old man and a child, both on hands and knees, observing the smallest of God's creatures.

Before them, ants searched for food, spiders attended their webs or the bees...the bees...what was it about the bees? He could hear his grandfather's voice, "Honeybees, Iver. Did you know honeybees hibernate during the winter by coming together as a colony? See this hive - those bees are still alive. They form into a ball, causing the center to reach above eighty degrees Fahrenheit and keeping the heat by eating honey and flexing their muscles. As soon as the bees on the outside are cold, they switch places with those closest to the circle and so it goes in an endless circle until spring. Warmth and food keeps the bees from dying. Nature, my boy, has all the answers." Iver rummaged around some more in the hope of finding something to eat, and to his surprise, he found a box of crystallized brown sugar, just what he needed to get little bit warm inside. But the oil lamp didn't give off enough heat to warm his body, so he realized he must start a larger fire.

He began collecting pieces of wood and was soon sitting before a roaring fire, leaning up against the shed with an old sheepskin covering his body and his clothes strung out on branches to dry. Lost in thought, he didn't notice that the intense heat from the fire was melting the snow on the roof, right above his head, and exposing the easy ignitable dry wood bark used as part of the roof covering. Now the wind was blowing embers over the roof and it would just be a matter of time before it would ignite.

Exhausted, Jenny stood outside the first farm she ran into and had no idea of how she got there. She used the last part of her energy and knocked several times before letting herself in. It wasn't long before the farmer came into the house and found her asleep on the floor by the stove. As she was getting dressed in warm clothes and eating a bowl of hot soup, she told the farmer about Iver and the midwife she needed to find. The farmer told her to relax and get her strength back. "Your part of the journey is over. The stick is in my hands now," he said and assured her he would send help to Iver and to find the midwife for Anna. What Jenny didn't know was that the midwife had been sent out on another call, so the farmer came up with the idea of asking an old retired midwife living a few miles away, and within the hour, he headed to the valley in search of Olianna.

The shed was full ablaze, but it was the smell of burning wool that got Iver's attention. Quickly he retrieved his clothes and then he remained as close to the fire as he could without getting burned, frequently turning around. Slowly the sensations in his toes and fingers came back, first as a sticking pain, then as a warm and comfortable feeling. He sat and watched the shed burning down, hoping the smoke towering above the pines would help them find him.

It was dark by the time the farmer arrived at the door of a gray-haired, strong-boned woman in her late seventies with a kind, weathered face. Olianna lived in a cozy house kept in repair by the families she had attended over the years. Her brother had moved in with her ten years ago, after his wife had died. The two elderly siblings lived a contented and quiet life together. After a brief explanation from the farmer about Iver Holseth and his sister Anna's condition, Olianna stuck her head outside to get a sense of the weather. She came back in and stood in front of her brother and the farmer. "I will have to go over the mountain." She knew when a mountain farmer called for a doctor or midwife, it was seldom a false alarm.

"Mountain? Can you make it in this weather?" her brother asked

"I have to make it."

Making the journey to Holseth in a blizzard wasn't an easy task. It was difficult enough in good weather.

"This snowstorm is the worst I've ever seen; don't you think it will be impossible to climb over the mountain?"

She shrugged her shoulders. "Impossible or not, I have no other choice." In her bedroom, she pulled out her worn black leather box secured by metal bands and checked its contents before putting it in her large satchel. She went into the kitchen and added bread, cheese, some cookies and a small tin of brown sugar to her bag. Olianna understood all formations of snow and the pulse of the mountain. As a young woman, she had been an avid mountaineer, capable as any man. Her brother had preferred books while she followed after her father doing many of the chores expected of men. So it wasn't surprising she felt she could take on the mountain to get to Holseth even in the worst of storms. She was born to bring babies into this world and God helps them in good weather and bad. "God will be with me. You may doubt me, but don't doubt the power of God"

Her brother nodded; he knew the strength of his sister's mind. "By the way, which path are you taking?"

"East, up the north peak of the Bluehorn Mountains."

Her brother shook his head. "It's a while since you have been up there."

"A few years."

"A few? I bet you haven't walked those slopes in thirty years! It's way too steep for a seventy-eight year old crone. Holseth is directly east of us. After walking a few hundred yards up through the thicket, you need to turn south in a V formation to cross the ridge at the basin of the two Mountains."

A neighboring farmer had a hunch something was going on and had just stepped into the kitchen where Olianna's brother had the map spread out on the table. He quickly brought the neighbor into the situation as he pointed at a button he had placed on the table between to candleholders. "Right here at about twenty-five hundred feet elevation is a large boulder. It looks like a troll with a dwarf birch growing on its head, and here is where you turn. If you keep close to the brook, you can't miss it. It's about a half an hour past the cheese farm. It's an altitude incline of fifteen hundred feet in a distance of less than a mile."

"I need to get to the Duklidals Tarn on the other side of the ridge."

"You'll get there by following this route and you'll know if you are on the right course by a cave on the other side of the ridge."

Olianna looked doubtfully at her brother.

"Olianna, I know the area like my own pocket. Just behind the ridge and at the beginning of a sharp incline on the northern peak is a cave. From there, you turn a bit to the east and go directly down to the tarn. There's a lone pine tree by the south side of the tarn. You keep to its right to find the hidden path."

She realized that her brother knew the area quite well and put on her coat, ready to go.

"What if I miss it in this storm?"

"You can't miss it because it is crucial. Do not proceed until you have found the tree; trying to get down to Holseth on any other path would be dangerous. A steel cross has been nailed to its trunk."

Fully outfitted, she thanked him for his help but never said goodbye. She would see him again.

Before she shut the door, he yelled out,

"Don't forget your safe passage is to follow the V and find the silver cross!"

From the storage shed she took out her old, worn country birch skis, glad their leather straps were still intact. Her weathered face barely noticed the sting from the cold and biting snow as she pulled the hood and mask over her head.

Her brother watched her from the window, thinking about the absurd scene before him - his hefty sister, dressed like a bear in skis, heading out in the dark with a snowstorm beating down on her! He was proud of his dear sister and had never met anyone in his life with such a sense of duty. After waving her goodbye and blessing her trip, he returned into the kitchen and placed a kettle of soup on the stove.

After walking for an hour through the snow, bundled in her long gray coat, a black scarf tied over her head with a heavy woolen hood and another scarf wrapped around her mouth, Olianna reached the cheese farm just above the timberline. She found the key and once inside, slipped on her trousers and dropped her skirt into her backpack. She always wore pants when she walked the mountains; usually she would change behind a tree or shed before arriving at a house so no one knew her secret. *For heaven's sakes,* she'd say, *I'd be a fool to try and cross the mountain with a skirt whipping about my body*! It was strictly against local customs for a woman to be seen in pants and she quoted the old phrase, *"Den kvinde som ifører seg mandens klede skal ikke arve Guds rige."* "The woman who puts on a man's clothes shall not inherit the goods of God." Long ago when she began delivering babies, Olianna had made a pact with God - as long as no one saw her in pants, God would look the other way.

She left the cheese farm and entered the mouth of the Fjørstad Valley, moving to the troll boulder. Even with her advancing age, Olianna considered herself a brave-hearted woman and seldom thought about her own physical condition or limitations. She often forgot her age, except when the weather changed and her joints swelled, or upon passing a mirror, catching a glimpse of an old woman peering back at her. Then she'd laugh at not recognizing her own reflection. Vanity had never been her sin; stubborn and opinionated yes... never vain.

As a former mountain climber, she knew nature had its elements of surprise and those unexpected events were the key in either saving one's life or taking it. Frequently resting, taking only a few moments to stand on solid ground and lean against her ski poles, she constantly checked the path ahead. The heavy clouds made it a moonless night but the white snow gave her light enough to see. Reflection always came to Olianna while walking. After all these years living near Stranden, helping with the birth of countless babies, she had many faces in her head. Her brother memorized lines from books; his sister memorized faces, all of them, the young, the old and especially the new ones. She could tell if a newborn baby would be a good child or a bad one just by its look; *it's in the eyes*, she'd say. She never minded the faces of the women and the children who died. They most of all touched her heart for their faces spoke to her of rest and God and the path we all take at the end of our lives. She remembered helping Marta Holseth with all her babies. It might ease Marta's soul to welcome a grandchild, especially now with her son-in-law gone. She liked Marta and remembered her face belonged to a good woman with a dear heart. *My*, she thought, *I think I'm feeling lonely. I wish the moon would come out. Could use a friendly face to talk to, even if it's just the moon's.*

She made a quick turn on the path and cried out, "Mr. Troll, how good to see you." Just as her brother had described, the dwarf birch stood on top of the troll-looking rock. She moved her hand along its side. "You are the oddest shaped rock I've ever seen." After taking off her skis, she crawled in through the troll's mouth, smelling goats as she slid into the underground chamber. When her eyes had adjusted to the dark, she noticed the rock slate at the cave's opening was covered by pea-size pebbles of manure. She brushed the slate and sat down. She had reached the bottom of the V.

After a short rest, she prepared to take on the steep, one-mile slope up to an elevation of thirty-six hundred feet, about a three-mile walk. She walked three hundred feet in one direction, turned and walked three hundred in the opposite direction. She would continue in this upward zigzag fashion until she reached the ridge. Several times she had to stop and catch her breath and after the sky cleared, it helped her to spot the next landmark, a boulder barely visible above the snow halfway up the slope. Upward she plodded, stride by stride, then she leaned up against a boulder to catch her breath, and then up again, moving into the slope, the wind and snow pushing against her body. She used the wind to her advantage; it helped to keep her on the right course. She leaned forward to lessen the wind's impact and shifted her point of gravity, making it easier to walk uphill, and trudged through the snow. With a solid grip on her poles, she took one step at a time, looking forward to the moment when she could take her wet clothes off and be warmed by a fire.

Sometime later, the wind intensified and she could hardly stand upright. It blew through her clothes, forcing a pricking chill into her bones. Drifts formed quickly about her and she needed desperately to find the cave. With her head tucked into her chin, she tried to not lose sight of her direction. She thought about returning to the Troll. Going back was always an option on any journey but she soon realized the blizzard had wiped out her tracks, so she proceeded forward, hoping God hadn't forgotten her. A fierce wind gust took hold of her, pushing her headfirst into a snow bank. While struggling to get up, she felt rocks under the surface and knew she had arrived somewhere along the ridge between the two Bluehorn peaks, halfway up the second leg of the V. Unable to stand up, she took off her skis, tied the leather straps to her poles and began to crawl across the ridge, dragging the skis behind her, hoping to come across a shelter. Boulders had broken loose from the mountain throughout the years and lay scattered about. The wind swept the snow; one wrong move could be fatal.

The wind started to ease up enough for her to see a cave. She crawled up the hill and pushed her way into its opening and dropped to the ground. After brushing herself clean of snow and lighting a candle, she saw that the cave had room enough to hide a large family. Traces of animal waste were scattered around and when she moved to a corner, she saw wolf tracks. Quickly she moved back to the opening just in case she wasn't alone. Nothing stirred from within and since wolves normally kept away from humans, she decided to stay. She warmed her hands before she pulled off her boots and began massaging her toes, some of which she hadn't felt for the past hour. In case of frostbite, she rubbed them gently.

Within the hour, the weather eased up and Olianna, warm and fed, poked her head outside the cave, delighted to see stars. The snow had subsided. After putting her boots back on, she draped her pack over her shoulders, crawled out of the cave and strapped on her skies. Thanks to the stars and moon, she saw the contour of the Duklidals Tarn buried under a thick layer of snow-capped ice. Only a discerning eye or the locals would know it wasn't just a white meadow, but a lake underneath the snow.

She steered straight at it instead of zigzagging down the slope, but miscalculated the slope's steep angle and soon raced out of control. The snow drifted and she straddled wider and wider. She leaned over to one side, lifted her poles in the air and sat down, emitting a huge cloud of snow behind her, and came to a complete stop. She took her time getting the snow off her clothes and went to look for the pine tree with the silver cross. After circling around the tarn twice, she was disappointed there was no sign of a tree. Then the wind picked up, reducing visibility to only a few feet. Soon she lost her direction and ended up at the edge of a cliff where she dropped to her knees. "The cursed wind," she yelled.

She knew Holseth was only six hundred feet below the cliff and she needed to find the cross. The ground gave way underneath her and before she could catch her breath, she dropped in mid-air, waving her poles in a desperate attempt to connect to solid ground. Cursing the gods, her screaming must have aroused them, for instead of being flushed off the ledge by the avalanche, she landed in a snowdrift, buried to her shoulders. Quickly she freed her arms, spit and wiped the snow out of her eyes. *Great! A fine mess I'm in!* To her right, she saw the canyon and to her left, a path that seemed to lead back to the cliff. Now she needed to free herself. The snow had forced its way up between her sweater and coat and pressed against her chest, making it difficult to breathe. She moved her body back and forth trying to get more room; instead, she sunk deeper into the pit. She prayed, "Holy Lord, if this is the time to take me home, so let it be, but then you will have to take care of the baby yourself." She was tired and closed her eyes; then like in a dream, a golden light broke through an opening in the clouds, giving the snow a soft glow. It became stronger, and then it began rotating first slowly, then faster and faster, slowing down again before abruptly stopping. She could almost touch it. She was no longer struggling and easily climbed out of the snow and walked effortlessly toward Holseth. She was feeling young and light on her feet and not an old woman forced to walk slowly by the sheer weight of her life. One by one, people she had known walked next to her. Ahead of her was Syver, her childhood friend, still young and strong as ever. He had died years ago from a fall into a ravine. She hurried to catch up and hugged him so hard he laughed. As they walked on the path, he remained quiet while she jabbered on and on about how good it was to see him and how much he had been missed and how her life had turned out. He smiled down on her and pointed ahead to a pass free of snow explaining this was where she needed to go. She looked out at the pass and wondered why she needed to go there; she wanted to go with the rest of them. He touched her shoulder and softly told her to wake up. *Wake up! You can't go with us now Olianna, it isn't your time.* He kissed her on the forehead and she opened her eyes.

If she didn't get up and move, she would be dead within the hour. Slowly she stretched her arms, managed to get hold of one pole and then, as she reached for the other, she found herself eye-to-eye with a wolf. Two almond-shaped amber eyes moved back and forth in the darkness. Trapped in the pit and without taking her eyes off him, she slowly picked up the pole. *What more could happen to me? Freezing to death would have been better than being attacked by a pack of wolves!* She looked around for his mate; they never strayed too far apart, but she didn't see one. He must be either very young or very old. *Very old,* she thought, *much like me.* The clouds parted and the moonlight made it possible for her to see his hunger. His pacing began to frighten her and as courage returned to her, she found she had the strength to move her legs and soon managed to free herself from the snow. If he planned to make a meal out of her, she wasn't going to give it to him without a fight!

Olianna knocked both poles together and thrust them at him yelling, "Go! Get away from me you mangy wolf! Be gone with you. I'll have none of this. I've come a long way and you won't stop me. I may look to be an old woman, easy prey to fall upon. But I'll have your tail above my mantel if you don't let me be."

She yelled, threatened, wailed and pleaded but the wolf never once broke stride, continuing to pace. She pushed her poles into the ground spitting snow in the wolf's direction, frustrated at not being frightening enough.

The wolf, undaunted by her antics, began his own lament; he yelped, groaned and growled and then let out a long howl. Olianna waved both arms in the air, let out a screech and then became quiet. Instead of the wolf running back into the woods, he sat down. Both had become tired of talking. All of this had brought warmth back into her limbs and again she wondered what would happen next. *The mountain and bad weather have not gotten the best of me and why now, when I'm so close to Holseth, did this old tattered wolf show up?* "I'm old, I'm tired and I'm not very tasty. So if it's a good meal you're after, you might as well move on," she grumbled, waiting for the wolf to make the next move, realizing her mountaineering friend might have been wrong; she might be climbing with them sooner than expected. The animal began to dig feverishly in the snow. "You don't have to dig a hole for me. I have just come out of one," she yelled

He stopped, stepped back to look at the old woman, then went back to the hole and resumed digging. While keeping an eye on him, she slowly backed away. He stopped his digging and as she moved, so did he. When she stopped, so did the wolf. It became a game. She watched him, he watched her and she wondered when he would strike. As soon as she stopped moving, he resumed digging. She had a knife in her pack but didn't want to take her eyes off him until the timing was right. She quickly eyed her position, realizing the only direction she could go was towards him and with some trepidation she started to walk.

"I'm getting off this ledge to a safe path down to Holseth and you must let me pass and since you can't make up your mind to eat me or dig a hole, I'm coming through." He didn't move an inch; instead he sat down in the snow, allowing her to pass. She closed her eyes and braced herself for his attack when she remembered the tales of the Norse god Odin, "...When not in Valhalla, Odin would assume the form of a wolf, lurking around for prey..." When she looked back, the wolf had vanished. "No, it couldn't be you! You are not Odin. He only comes when someone is about to die a violent death!"

She was startled by the sound of feet dropping hard into the snow directly in front of her. The wolf clenched a rodent in its jaw. At first she shuddered when he, with one powerful bite, crushed the animal, then she wondered how he had managed to pass her on the ledge. Had he climbed a straight wall up to the cliff to get around her? He ate quickly. Was he indeed Odin? *He is leading me, but why?* She saw two possible paths, wondering which one lead to Holseth.

What happened next, she could never explain, even if she lived for another hundred years. She obediently followed the wolf. When they reached a depression in the mountain, she recognized it as part of the pass, the same pass Syver had pointed at in her dream. The wolf jumped up on top of a boulder, looking out over Holseth. Olianna was surprised at the scene below. The moon lit the small pasture and a flickering light could be seen coming from the windows of the farmhouse. Tears flooded her face and before she could speak, the wolf had gone. She moved down the path, feeling like a young girl, blessing both the wolf and Odin. On the front step of Holseth, she set her skis up against the house, knocked on the door, then let herself in. She found Gusta in the bedroom, standing over Anna, with everything neatly in place for a delivery.

Gusta turned to her wide-eyed and smiled while Anna moaned.

"Oh my," said Olianna, "it looks like we don't have much time."

The story would be a testament to Olianna's life. All the villagers would be talking about the incredible journey of the retired midwife, who alone, journeyed out in the worst snowstorm along the dangerous path across the Bluehorn Mountains to help with the birthing of Anna's baby. Olianna would remind them when they would tell this story in her presence...that she was never alone. Another hero was the young woman from Kristiania, who had continued her courageous achievement, escaped the embrace of death and stunned everybody by saving the life of Iver Holseth.

The Vengeance

"Everyone finds his superior once
in a lifetime." Norwegian Proverb

Anna had a healthy boy whom she would name Jon, and Jenny escaped from the strenuous trek without any major injuries. Iver, on the other hand, came down with a severe fever in addition to his sprained ankle, and if it hadn't been for the shed he set ablaze, they might not have been able to find him in time. Both he and Jenny were invited to stay with the farmer in Uksvik Bay for as long as they wanted and Jenny had decided not to leave until Iver was well.

When the weather calmed down and Olianna felt comfortable that Anna and the baby were all right, she left Holseth and offered her assistance of nursing Iver. Olianna knew much more than bringing babies into the world and now she stood on a stool held by Jenny, pulling cobwebs from the corners of the room. "This web will help him get some relief into the night," she said, rolled the webs into fine balls and forced them into Iver's mouth. Two hours later, he was no longer thrashing about and slept peacefully throughout the night.

Days passed and now everyone feared they might lose Iver. Olianna and Jenny took turns by his bed during the long days and nights, anticipating his awakening. His body had beaten the infection but he showed no signs of waking up. Olianna told Jenny not to worry; she believed he was fighting his demons and would open his eyes where there was nothing more to fight. She also talked to her about Anna and the baby and told her old mountain stories, while Jenny sat quietly, not sure of what to say, staying safely within her own thoughts. As she watched Iver, she almost felt she knew what he might be thinking by the twist of his shoulders or the drop of his legs; everything about him was now familiar to her. *How he ignites my feelings!* she thought. *I'm moved to anger and frustration whenever I am near him and yet when we were told he was ill, I wanted nothing more than to be at his side. I pray I have the power to remain aloof and keep my feelings to myself.*

Jenny brought hot pea soup into Iver's room and found him sitting up. He was shielding his face from the light, fumbled with the bedding.

She almost dropped the bowl. "You're awake!"

"Where am I?"

"In Uksvik Bay."

Out the window, he could see snow falling softly, unthreatening. *Why so calm?* he wondered. *When had the storm stopped?* "Where are my clothes? I want to get out of this bed." He looked hard at Jenny. "How long have I been here?"

He heard her voice speaking words that didn't register. "Anna, how is Anna and the baby?"

Upon hearing Iver's voice, Olianna bustled into the room. "Anna is fine, and you have a strapping nephew, strong and handsome like all the Holseth men born before him. I do say he takes after his great-grandfather Andreas, cries constantly, another born storyteller." She reached out for his bedding that had partly slipped off him and fallen to the floor and looked at the farmer who was standing at the doorway. "Why don't you help this young man put on a pair of pants since he obviously has some life in him!"

She took Jenny by the hand and led her into the kitchen. *Oh dear,* she thought. The way those two looked at one another, her suspicions were confirmed; there was indeed potential for great heartache between them. Her own feelings were stirred as she remembered her own passion when she was young.

Jenny quickly excused herself and went outside where she leaned against the front door and held her hand out to catch the falling snow. She pulled open the bodice of her dress, rubbed the snow over her chest. No one had ever excited her so, not even Robert. As the snow melted between her breasts, the cold water trickled down her stomach to meet the heat between her legs. When she returned, Olianna caught her eye, saw the wet stain on her dress and smiled. She couldn't fool Olianna who understood the tension between a man and a woman. It was obvious by Jenny's gasp when she had spied all of Iver that this was the first time she had seen him unclothed. It would be interesting how this might play itself out between these two! Jenny looked anxiously at Olianna.

"Don't worry, he'll be fine...it just takes time. We need to let him talk and help sort it all out."

Jenny nodded. "I have a tendency to make him angry. I'm, I'm just wondering if we should get Marta and I'll return to Holseth."

"Come on, Jenny, you saved his life! He can't possible be angry at you now, and if he is, I dare say it will be good for him, get his blood moving."

It was a different Iver who later in the afternoon started asking Jenny about how she managed to get over the pass and find help. Although his face looked a little more weathered and pale, the anger lines around his eyes had disappeared, the tone in his voice had changed and the ambience was more peaceful. Still Jenny noticed that it was hard for him to say *thank you for saving my life*, as if it was something he was obligated to say.

"You saved yourself, Iver. I just helped you out of the water. You are strong and now you need to get home. Olaf and your dog are waiting for you."

"And you Jenny, do you want to go with us after everything I've said and done to you?"

The directness of his question took her back. "I, I, well of course, why wouldn't I? I'll stay until it's safe to go back to Kristiania," she stammered.

"That's not what I asked you. I asked if you..."

The front door slammed shut and the farmer came into the bedroom. "It's Olianna, please Jenny hurry! She's fallen. She's as big as a barrel but if the two of us work it, we should be able to help her into the house."

He looked at Iver. "Incredible isn't it? She journeys across a mountain pass like St. Joan of Arc and makes it without a scratch, but she can't walk to our little chicken coop by the house without falling down and hurting herself!"

Iver was disappointed with the interruption and wondered how Jenny might have answered his next question - if she would promise to never leave Holseth without him.

Two weeks after Iver and Jenny returned to Holseth, freezing temperatures and more snow forced the family into isolation again. Marta had brought Anna and the baby from Iver's home to live with her, but Gusta surprised everyone by staying with Iver. Marta tried to thank her for helping Anna but she would hear nothing of it and asked to be left alone.

"She's a funny duck," remarked Andreas. "I believe there is a glint of light in her eyes and she enjoys the attention - just won't give us the pleasure of it."

Iver and Olaf were not excited with the prospect of living with their dreary old Aunt in the dead of winter, until they found her one morning in the kitchen performing miracles. She told them to hush and never say a word to the family about it, especially to Marta, who believed she was the best cook at Holseth. "It doesn't do me any good to prove I can cook. I've better things to do." She swung her spoon at them, "And don't you two think I'm going to stay around here to take care of you! I'm off in the spring and if you say one word to anyone about my cooking, I'll call you both liars and make lumpy porridge for every meal."

One late evening Marta found Anna pacing in the kitchen, talking to herself, looking at an envelope of money on the table next to an heirloom candle stick. The second she saw the candle, Marta knew something serious was going on in her daughter's head. She quietly sat down at the table and gently touched the carving of the man in robes holding his arms outstretched to the heavens with a candle above his head. The wax began to drip down the side. "Why?" was all she asked Anna.

"I needed the strength to make a wish."

Marta swallowed hard, "And the wish, does it

have something to do with this money?"

"I had such high hopes for me and Jon but now I can't bring my child up on a farm by myself. I have a plan and I hope you will help me."

They talked long into the early morning hours. The money would help Anna apply to the university to become a nurse and the baby would stay with Marta for the first term until Anna could secure a proper living arrangement. A resigned and tired Anna went to feed the baby while her mother watched the last of the candle wax drip to the table. She touched the hot wax. How was it possible that within just a month, everyone at Holseth had been set down on a different path? She felt lonely. She picked up the candle and took careful pains to clean it and set it back on the glass shelf in the front room. This wooden candleholder had been in the family for years. It was foretold it could never be sold or given away except to a member of the family, for it brought luck if kept in a place of honor - and ill luck if lost. She thought about Jenny and how she would be returning to Kristiania as soon as spring arrived. Now her quarrelsome suitor was back in England, doing the Queen's bidding and the rumors of Jenny's affair by now having faded, her parents were ready to receive her with open arms. She would miss this beautiful young woman. Marta looked hard at the candleholder and then quickly pulled it down off the shelf, set it back on the kitchen table and with passion, struck a match and made a wish.

One morning when the winter weather had let up, opening the passage down to the boathouse, Andreas walked into the kitchen, threw his old worn pouch stuffed with a few mementos and clothes on the table and said, "I've decided it is time now."

"Time for what?" asked Marta

"Time to die"

"Die? What are you talking about?"

"My funeral plans are in this envelope and my casket has already been dropped off at the boathouse. Iver helped me hang it from the rafters."

"He what? What casket? What are you talking about Father?"

"My casket! Why do I feel I'm talking to a magpie? Stop chattering and listen to me. I've decided my time has come to head down."

"Down where? If I understand you right, you are dying, have planned your funeral and are going to hell - is that correct?"

"Well I don't like to think of it as hell, but yes I don't expect I've been good enough to go to heaven, unless your dear departed mother has talked them into it," he paused, "and that's not likely. She was always too quiet."

"Father, this isn't something to joke about."

"I'm dead serious."

Marta moved away from him and tied an apron around her waist. "Could we please leave out the dead?"

"Why leave them out? I plan to join them soon."

"What prompted all of this? Have you been to the doctor? Has he told you your days are numbered, or is something wrong in your head?"

"No, I have not been to any confound-it-doctor. I know my body and it's saying goodbye. When I was younger, all my limbs were soft and flexible except one, but now all are hard and stiff except one. What more do you need to know?"

"Nothing. I don't need to know any more. Well goodbye then." Marta emptied a bowl of bread dough on the table and began to knead.

Andreas thought he would get more of a fight from her. "Marta, let me tell you my plans."

"Your plans, your plans!" she shouted. "You buy a casket and don't even tell me about it! You purchased a shroud which I can see sticking outside your pouch and I bet you've set aside your funeral beer too. I'm surprised you're not wearing your good suit to make it easier on us!"

"I didn't think of that. Do you think I sh..."

Marta took a handful of bread dough and threw it at him. "You come down this morning and say you are going to die as if you were telling me you are planning a trip to the village and I'm supposed to just sit here and listen?"

That's better, thought Andreas. This was the Marta he could understand.

"Let me tell you something, Father. You and I have been through a lot over the years - the death of your wife, my mother and my husband. You're not dying until I say you can and that's final!"

"It's my heart, Marta. I don't think I will live to see the spring. If I died tomorrow, you couldn't get my body down the path. Better I stay in the boathouse until my time comes."

"What nonsense is this?"

"I don't want to be like your great-grandfather, who died in the dead of winter and we had to place his coffin in the snow. You remember, he lay frozen until spring when we could finally get him to the village for a proper burial. I swore years ago if I still lived on this mountain, that would never happen to me. I think he's the only one who has died up here. I've provisions enough, except for food. If you could spare me a little, I'd be most grateful. Iver should be here today; he promised to help me down the path."

"You may be wrong."

"I may be, and if I am, I will be back to let the goats out for the summer."

"You, you're impossible! Go then, go! I'll let you pine away in the boathouse for a few weeks and when you grow tired of telling your stories to the walls, you'll be back. I'm sure of it but you're not going today or tomorrow. Three days from now is soon enough and it gives me time to turn a bit of bread and fish cakes for your meals. I'll send you with enough to get through a few weeks of bad weather and on good days, I'll come down. Agreed?"

"Agreed, and now that's settled, if it wouldn't be too much trouble, do you think you could make a tin of your sugar cookies, in case I get a hankering for something sweet?"

Marta rolled her eyes. "Only you would think of cookies at a time like this! Yes, I'll fill your tin...but you must promise me that as soon as the weather lets up, and if you're still alive, you will visit the doctor in Stranden. Otherwise, no cookies."

"It's a promise." Andreas tried hard not to laugh at his daughter's request. A dead man doesn't need a doctor.

Three days later, Iver arrived to assist Andreas

to the boathouse and asked his mother if she knew when Jenny planned to leave. Jenny, on her way out of her room, stopped when she heard Iver mentioned her name. Marta explained she would be leaving as soon as traveling would be safe, closer to spring. Jenny strained to hear Iver's comment, but he said nothing, probably glad she would be leaving. She had spent little time thinking about her own situation, caught up in the life on the farm and the Holseth family's drama.

She walked into the kitchen and found Andreas pacing, anxious to get moving. "How will we know if you need help?" Marta asked.

"I'll raise my brown long johns on a pole."

"Better your newly-bought white shroud than your long johns, don't you think?"

"That won't work if there's snow on the roof; you won't see it."

"Brown will do nothing against the brown roof if the snow melts."

Iver wondered what next these two could argue about. Kari, believing she could help, ran to her bedroom returning with an old, worn colorful dress. "Here Grandfather, take this. I've outgrown it and we will be able to see it against the snow or the brown roof."

"Thank you. This will work fine." Andreas kissed her cheek and glared at his daughter. "Are you satisfied now?" he asked, holding the dress up over his head and waving it back and forth. "May I go now?"

Marta kissed him on the cheek and walked back into the kitchen as he left the house. She looked at Kari, who had started to cry. "He'll be back."

Within a few minutes, Andreas came back into the house. "Marta, I forgot the tin."

Kari laughed and handed the tin of cookies over to her grandfather. "See, I told you he'd be back and as soon as that tin is empty, we'll see him walking up the path to visit."

Andreas felt their eyes on him as he and Iver walked across the pasture and when the men reached the path to begin their descent to the boathouse, he finally gave into his stubbornness and turned to take one last look at his mountain home. He couldn't fight the tears and after wiping his eyes, he turned to Iver, took a deep breath, shook his head and said, "When a man lives too long he turns into a woman."

He walked slowly and when his foot came down on a cluster of flat rocks, the sound and feel were gentle reminders of his childhood. The rocks were like old friends still in place where he had stepped a thousand times throughout his life. He stopped a moment and rubbed his hands against the rock. *So much of this mountain is a part of me and my ancestors.* He looked around. *Three hundred years is a long time for blood and bone to endure this mountain, to call this home. I've grown old missing the touch, the feel of my wife, her body pushed into mine. When she died, this mountain remained so much a part of me. I see now how it gently wooed me all these years.*

The boathouse looked the same as he left it. The old jackets and moth-eaten sweaters hung on the wall where they used to, under the ceiling dangled the seine and in the corners, the same bulge of broken furniture and fishing gear. The only thing that was different was the casket Iver had brought in. Every farm was expected to have a casket ready for the one they thought would be the first to die. Now, Andreas wanted to see if it was big enough; hopefully there would still be some time to change it if it was too small. He opened the casket and measured it thoroughly with his eyes before stepping into it, lay down and stretched out his legs. "Damn it! I told him it was way too narrow! I can't even move my arms in here." As he wriggled his body, trying to get comfortable, the casket moved a little, causing the top to suddenly snap down with a wham. A second later it flew open again and Andreas bounced back up like a puppet, looking astonished toward the ceiling. "My holy Lord! I didn't know you were in such a hurry. I haven't even taken off my shoes yet!"

As the days went on, Andreas performed three main tasks: sleeping, eating and keeping the fire going. Several times a tug on his blanket or his shirtsleeve would wake him to the embers dying. At first this gentle reminder frightened him but as the days wore on, he became accustomed to it. Memory after memory came to visit. Never alone, he would chuckle with a friend and with just a turn of the head, a sneeze, some movement, that person would show up and disappear, soon to be replaced with another. Try as he might, he could never keep anyone with him for too long. He became tired of the disappearing images and after more or less sleeping over two weeks, boredom came and he picked up a knife and a block of wood and started carving. At first the wood between his fingers turned into simple shapes of animals, barely recognizable. But the better he felt, the more the shapes took form and one morning, as he followed the intricate lines of an eagle's wings with the blade of his knife, he wanted to see the look on his great-grandson's face when he gave it to him. Andreas had never been a patient man. When he didn't die as planned, he carefully wrapped the carved animals in his clothes and decided to join his daughter for dinner. As he stepped out of the boathouse, ready to get back up to the farm, he noticed a large ship heading his way. He had never seen an ocean liner that early in the season; tourists usually didn't come in through the fjord before the beginning of June, but as the ship got closer, he saw it was a cargo ship.

"Turn your ship and sail straight back. There's thunder over Norway," boomed an old English sailor to the crew. Just the sound of his voice made the younger men cringe. The English crew had difficulty concentrating on their work as the British ocean liner, the Northland, sailed from the Norwegian Sea in through the Sunnylvsfjord. The towering mazes of mountains made the ship appear no bigger than a jolly boat and the men the size of sand. The haunting scenery and wild roaring spring waterfalls unsettled the crew, while the old timers began their whisperings. Odd a ship this size sailed into the backwoods of Norway before setting sail across the Atlantic for America. Odd such a large ship was empty of passengers and cargo except for its owner, Robert Blackstone, his Chinese companion, Mr. Chen, and a few necessary crewmembers. Dramatic stories of sea serpents and water spirits were passed on deck and as the ship moved into a foggy mist, imaginations heightened. The stories were so bold and vivid of the underground people and the Nisses that the sailors began watching their backside and by the time the last tale was told, everyone wished for warmer seas, believing this to be an ill-fated trip. Some sailors invoked protection by crossing a blessing over their chests and touching their rosaries to their lips, while others rubbed tokens of luck stuffed deep within their pockets.

To wile away the hours, Mr. Chen stood on deck tying knots while studying the mountain terrain. His skillful fingers tugged and pulled rope against rope, forming knot upon knot until he could produce a knot with his eyes shut. Mesmerized, the sailors often watched his hands moving with such speed that a knot would appear out of thin air. With the fisherman's knot, he could join two ropes and finish it off in a single bowline faster than any sailor on board and the Captain, in jest, had offered him a job. Now, whenever Blackstone came into view of Mr. Chen, he noticed the hangman's knot swaying in his hands.

Mr. Chen had been summoned to meet Blackstone on deck, but all agreed to steer clear of the dark master, believing it was bad luck to cross his path. Blackstone stopped right behind him. "This Fjord leads to no major city and the cold sea water is nothing but a Viking graveyard. I'll never return to these waters."

Mr. Chen turned around and followed Robert.

"Can you climb these mountains Chen?"

Respectfully Mr. Chen nodded.

"Good, that is all I wanted to know. It won't be much longer. Get your gear ready."

Mr. Chen nodded a second time and headed to the lower deck. The Chinese man's quiet demeanor and fastidiousness irritated the hell out of Robert. Mr. Chen was a cutthroat negotiator and though they worked at the same side of the table, Blackstone was never at ease in the company of a man whose personal life mirrored his own. Mr. Chen lived alone in a handsome brownstone on the edge of Southampton, near his own people, with only a maid and cook attending. By all appearances, he lived a solitary life with one great passion, climbing. His ability to scale a mountain had today become a business matter.

While he waited for Mr. Chen to return, Robert Blackstone grew anxious about seeing Jenny after all these months. Between supplying ships for Queen Victoria's war in Africa and the worst winter storm of the century, he had seen to the building of his new home across the ocean. The day had finally come and as soon as the Northland returned to international waters, the Captain would pronounce them man and wife. By the time they stood near the river's edge of the Potomac Bay in Virginia, she would be carrying his child. Her fool of a father would look for her in England and when he finally caught wind of her whereabouts, it would be too late. Robert had written a vicious letter full of lies, knowing it would keep Jenny on the mountain until he returned.

It was when Andreas saw the British Union Jack hoisted on the flagpole he knew what was up and regretted that he couldn't run the path fast enough to pull the ladder and block the way.

The ship slowed down, but hadn't even come to a complete stop before a jolly boat hit the water. A rope ladder was thrown over the side and soon three men rushed down and jumped into the jolly. Andreas watched the men begin to row toward shore. As they got within shouting-range, he cupped his hands over his mouth and shouted, "Mr. Blackstone, what brings you here when you are not welcome?" He didn't get any answer and a moment later, the boat reached the dock and the men jumped out. Standing before him were the dark Mr. Blackstone, an agile Chinese man and the largest sailor he had ever seen in his life.

Robert looked around, making sure they were alone, nodded at Chen to follow him and asked the old man, "Where is Jenny Mohr?"

"In the village. You're wasting your time."

"Is that a fact?" laughed Robert. "The villagers said I'd find her here."

"It's too late, Mr. Blackstone, the ladder is up; you might as well go back to your boat."

Robert ordered the sailor to keep Andreas quiet and when Mr. Chen dropped his climbing equipment on the ground, Andreas knew the ladder didn't matter to them; whether it was up or down, they could scale any part of the mountain. With bolts and rope, climbing that vertical portion of the path wouldn't be a problem. Andreas could only watch the men taking off up the path, increasing the distance back to him with every step.

As soon as Marta saw the men, she sensed what was going on and sent Kari away to get Iver. Then she patiently waited until they came within talking range. "Why do you come so far when you have been told countless times to stay away, Mr. Blackstone?"

"This is a friendly visit. I just want to talk to her and then I'll leave," he told Marta as Jenny walked out of the barn and hurried away from him. He caught up to her. "Will you stand still long enough so I can at least explain myself?"

Jenny spun around and dropped the buckets she was carrying on the ground. "What do you want to explain Robert? How you threatened my father, your past, your lies? Go ahead if it pleases you but nothing will change my mind. I return home in a few weeks - not to you or any other man."

My, she is beautiful, even in rags. Blackstone looked at the surroundings. "Why are you living here?" He couldn't believe how many months she had lived on this deserted mountain with peasantry. Had she gone mad? "Come with me, Jenny. I can give you every thing."

"You said you would explain yourself; don't beg me to go with you."

"Last spring, when I held you in my arms, you told me I was everything you ever wanted. What happened to turn you against me?"

"Your past, your lies. I did love you. I don't now."

With force, he pulled her to him and held her tight. His kiss was soft and tender, then hard. She wrenched herself out of his arms and yelled, "I love someone else!"

He couldn't believe his ears. "You what? Who do you love?" He looked closely at her. "Not the farmer - the idiot farmer! They've bewitched you. As soon as you leave here, your senses will return."

"When I leave Robert, it won't be to be with you!" Jenny retrieved the buckets and saw Gusta outside the house.

Mr. Chen had been entertained, watching the entire scene, wondering how they would ever get the red-headed woman with lightening eyes down the path without a fight. It looked like Robert had met his match.

Gusta was not so entertained. Like a soldier about to strike, she had suddenly appeared with her broom, waiting for Robert to make his next move.

In anger, Robert followed Jenny and pulled her back. "I've come for you and I'm not leaving without you."

Jenny pulled the comb out of her hair and threw it in front of him. "You can take this; I don't want anything reminding me of you!" He picked up the comb and dropped it into his pocket, then picked up Jenny and yelled for Mr. Chen. Then all hell broke loose. Gusta hit him on the head with the broom, catching him off guard, causing him to release Jenny. After regaining his balance, he turned around and jerked the broom out of her hands. By the time he had forced Gusta to back away, Jenny had already disappeared. He cursed the old woman and barked at Mr. Chen, "Do something. Find her!"

Jenny rushed up the slope, kicked and tore loose rocks and slate to slow down her followers. She headed toward The Ledge again, following the same path Iver used when he ushered her down last spring, making sure she stayed clear of the area where she had almost got herself killed.

When Robert realized Jenny had outmaneuvered him, he first became furious, but clamed down when he thought about the time he, as a young boy, had chased his neighbor's cat up in a tree. It reminded him about the vulnerability of a stuck prey. He chuckled inside, knowing his persistence had always paid off; he just needed to let time aid him. He clutched his hand around his pistol holster to assure himself the pistol was still there. If he couldn't get her, he certainly wasn't going to let any one else have her either.

Iver found Gusta holding a broken broom and both she and Marta were looking upset. It didn't take him long to get an overview of the situation and with the dog in lead, he headed up through a ravine, cursing Jenny for going up to the unstable area again, suspecting she would be heading to The Ledge. *Just like children,* he thought, *always wanting to play in the most dangerous places.* He took a side trail to get around Jenny's followers who seemed unable to find the easiest path. Most mountains in the area had paths trudged by animals throughout time and when you know where animals go, you also find those paths. For a non-native, finding those paths could be very difficult.

As Iver reached The Ledge, he realized he was right; just in front of him sat Jenny on a boulder, looking down after her followers. When she became aware of Iver, she instinctively pulled back like a frighten possum.

"Hey calm down! I am your savior, not your enemy."

"Just leave me alone. I don't need to be saved." Iver nodded toward the end of the ledge.

"What about the men chasing you?"

"I don't care. Just leave me alone."

Iver flung out his arms. "Ok. Fine. Do what ever you want. Go with them. I am not going to stay in your way." *She hadn't caused anything other than problems wherever she went anyway, so better she leaves and I can go on with my life. How stupid I was to believe that she cared for me after what happened on the fjord! Every normal human would do whatever they could to save a person. She would, of course, do the same thing to others, including the nurse at the farmer's house afterward. She didn't care any more for me than any other nurse in a hospital; smiles and compassion were just part of their job.* Suddenly his thoughts were interrupted by Robert's voice.

"I'll take care of her now."

Iver spun around and looked right into the barrel of a pistol, wondering how Robert had got there so fast. He must have found the same path as himself after all.

The dog leaped immediately in front of him and started barking.

Robert waved his pistol and kicked the dog. "Make the damn animal quiet or I'll blow its brain out."

After Iver had silenced the dog, Robert looked at Jenny. "Chen! Tie her up!" Chen hesitated. "Tie her up damn it or I'll kill all of you!"

Chen didn't see any point of arguing with an unstable and unpredictable person waving with a loaded gun; he knew that his time would come. He just needed to be patient and to be ready to take advantage of any mistakes Robert would make. He felt certain he would make a mistake or become inattentive long enough for Chen to strike. Any person who is outside his familiar territory would before or later make a mistake. He ushered Jenny away from the edge and began to tie her hands around a tree trunk while looking at her with a comforting look in his eyes.

Suddenly the dog started barking again from the top of a boulder nearby.

“Who else is coming?” growled Robert

“No one. Must be a rabbit.”

Neither of them saw the wolf that the dog had spotted.

Iver backed away from the edge of the cliff; he could feel which slates were unsafe and straddled to safer ground where he noticed Mr. Chen was doing something with ropes. He had no plans to warn Robert that the ground he walked on was unsafe.

Robert growled at him, “How dare you take advantage of my woman! You’re not even a gentleman.”

Iver stepped slowly backwards, looking Robert in the eyes. He knew the eyes of an animal would reveal its next move a fraction of a second before the action and to him, Robert was no more than an animal. When he noticed Robert was about to step on an unsafe rock, he yelled at him to divert his attention from where he was walking.

“Why don't you just shoot me right away? Or maybe you don't have the guts?”

Robert laughed. “Guts, shooting an oaf like you doesn’t require guts! Prolonging the moment of death of the doomed just enhances my satisfaction.” He nodded at Jenny. “Take a good look. It's the last time you see her.”

Jenny tugged at the rope, trying to get loose and scrambled for words to say, anything that could change the situation. She noticed Iver appeared to be very calm in spite of Robert pointing a gun at him, and she wondered if his knowledge of the area could help him now. She screamed out, “Robert, I'll go with you if you spare him. I promise you. If you kill him, you will never get me down from here alive! It’s your choice, Robert”

"Why would I want to spare your lover since I am going to get you anyway?" Robert asked without taking his eyes away from Iver.

"You will get me, no matter what. The question is, alive or dead, what do you prefer?"

Iver continued stepping slowly backwards, patiently waiting for Robert to step on a rock that could bring him down or an opportunity to jerk his feet off the ground. He yelled, "Hey mister! Look behind you."

"Don't try that dumb trick on me, Mountain Oaf."

Suddenly, a shot was fired from Robert's pistol, as he waved his hands in the air just before disappearing off the plateau. Iver wondered, *What happened? Did the bastard miss?* Then he saw the loose slate. He leaned over the edge just in time to see that Robert had landed on a narrow ledge, five yards down. He was apparently unharmed, looking after his pistol which was tumbling down the ravine.

Robert screamed, "Give me a rope!" Mr. Chen had noticed Iver's caution with the ledge and had positioned himself where the ground appeared to be safe. "I'll be right back." He released Jenny ordering both of them to get back to the farm.

Iver took Jenny's hand and walked off the ledge. He didn't see any point of arguing with the Chinese who obviously had some unresolved issues with Robert. He would take Jenny to a safe place at his own farm - a place Robert would never find her. Could this be the break for both of them? A common threat puts people together; just holding her hand sent waves of warmth through Iver's body and he didn't even dare to think about what kind of feeling holding the rest of her body would ignite. Soon the steep and difficult terrain required both his mental and physical attention.

Jenny was relieved to get out of Robert's way and in spite of the difficult path back down to Holseth, she had never felt so safe before since she had arrived at the mountain. It was a feeling that nothing could ever happen to her as long as she was holding onto Iver's strong and firm hand. This was a different feeling than the one she had when Lars had held her the day Robert wanted to abduct her during the Midsummer feast. Several times she lost her foothold on the loose gravel, but even before hitting the ground, Iver pulled her up. She tried unsuccessfully to meet his eyes in the short moment he looked at her.

A moment later, Chen lowered two ropes with hangman's knots. "Put one around your chest and the other around your thigh."

Robert wondered why he wanted him to put it around his thigh. "My thigh? For what?"

"Just extra security."

Robert didn't see this as an appropriate time to question Chen so he did as he was told and shouted, "I'm ready. Pull me up."

Chen waved his hands. "Walk to the end of the ledge!"

"End of the ledge?"

"The rocks above you are too sharp and may cut the rope. You need to climb in a slightly diagonal direction."

Robert checked the knots and began to climb as Chen had instructed him. Halfway up, Mr. Chen leaned over the edge. "Mr. Blackstone."

Robert clutched on to a cleft, "What?"

"I had a sister once; she disappeared from a ship - a slave ship under your command. Her name was Leih Chen. I have waited many years and have come a long way to find you. Why would I otherwise want to work for you? Today I bless my sister and avenge her death."

Chen obviously knew about his past and Robert remembered the young girl whom his slave broker in Calcutta had paid him a handsome amount of money to get rid of. He looked up at Chen. "Just get me up. I can explain! It was an accident. I had nothing to do with it. I swear on my mother's grave. I'll promise you more money than you have ever seen."

"Your promise is worthless to me."

"Damn you Chen!"

"Damn - you are the one who is damned!" With that, Chen threw a head-size rock over the cliff. It was attached to the rope Robert had around his chest A second later, a sharp whiff from the air, a squeak from a tree trunk, a wham, and before Robert knew it, he hung upside down like a Bat.

Robert screamed out when the ropes tightened around his chest and thigh. Threatening to tear his body apart, the cords of rope cut through his skin. Soon his leg would become numb from the weight of the rock, preventing him from getting up. He tasted blood, and with every breath, a jolt of pain shot through his chest; the sudden jerk from the rope must have cracked several ribs. Dangling upside down from the cliff, he saw the image of a young Chinese girl, petting a wolf on the edge of the ravine. Her long dark hair blew in the breeze as she stroked the animal's fur. Then the image began to fade and was replaced by one of a young woman, rushing down a ladder onboard a ship to get something from the deck. As in a dream, Robert tries to shout at her to get back, but she doesn't hear him. He then sees himself leaping across the deck, poking his way through a throng of slaves while firing his pistol in the air. Almost within her reach, the woman looks up at him, wondering what's going on. Then a rope gets caught around her feet and yanks her off the deck. Her body hits the railing like a rag doll and she is dragged overboard and disappears in the water.

Further down the slope, Jenny stopped and looked at Iver. "What sound was that?"

Iver had heard that sound before, but this time he felt different about it. A kind of peacefulness, knowing that he didn't have to face the Englishman anymore, came over him and he turned toward Jenny and said, "Nothing to worry about. Seems like the sound of someone about to lose a battle to the mountains." He then grabbed her hand again and continued down the slope.

Mr. Chen walked back from the edge and sat down by a tree trunk. He would sit and wait as long as he needed before getting back down to the ship. He would take Robert's crew back to England before sailing home to China to take his place as the head of the Chen family. As soon as he returned, he would remove his oldest sister from the family, publicly humiliate her and have her tried for her crimes against her youngest sister, Leih. He would bestow his lifetime protection and care to the family of Lui Ming in their Grandfather's memory, having kept his secret about Leih until he had grown into manhood.

Andreas was inching up the path and stopped abruptly when he saw Mr. Chen rushing toward him. He held out his cane to stop him.

Mr. Chen stopped and looked at Andreas; his face showed no sign of that of a murderer.

"Where is Mr. Blackstone?" Andreas asked.

At first Mr. Chen ignored his question and then he said, "Mr. Blackstone took another route down."

The Message

"Odin's sacred raven had two attendant
birds, Hugin and Munin, who flew over
the world during the day and returned
at night to report what they had seen."
The Encyclopedia of Superstitions

Jenny gazed over the scenery. It had been a year since she had arrived at Holseth and now she was free to go home, but free to go to what? Robert was gone, but not in the way she wished. No matter how bad he had been in the past, he hadn't been treating her so badly that he deserved to die. Actually, he hadn't treated her badly at all; it was all about a past, a past when she didn't know him. Now he was dead and she felt partly responsible for it. If she had ignored her parents and stayed with him, he would be alive now and God knows, maybe he would have turned out to be that gentleman and lover as she had known him. His past might never have surfaced again. Maybe it would have, maybe not; she would never know and neither would anyone else. He took all his past with him down the mountain.

She watched the soft rays of light streak through the clouds, slowly floating above the mountains as the sun shared its energy across the sky. The sun's rays stroked the season's last layer of soft snow and the bright morning light outlined the rugged mountains as they proudly protected the fjord that traversed through this magnificent Norwegian scenery. On the Bluehorn Mountain, between snow and timberline, streams trickled down the bare mountainside before disappearing into a sleepy forest. Soon they reappeared as one massive river, roaring over an abrupt cliff, tumbling through air, colliding with the fjord and exploding in clouds of white mist spurting out from the mountainside. On both sides of the waterfall, the mist became airborne by an uplifting draft and fell softy onto the growth of ferns and bushes climbing the mountainside. The sight and sound of such water against rock has a stirring effect on one's soul. Emotions are forced to the surface which would otherwise lie dormant. Surprisingly, this force of nature, rock, mountain, water, sun, all coming together in sound and splendor, might incite one man to propose and another to kill.

Jenny Mohr and Iver Holseth might never really face their desires, like blood surging through their veins nurturing sensations and setting into motion feelings so strong that a spring day like this could pass unnoticed. The newly-sprouted flowers and tender young dwarf birches illuminated by the sun, or the sounds of mating birds, could not interrupt their thoughts either. In spite of their emotional absent-mindedness, nature would behave as usual, a beautiful backdrop to their unfolding drama.

Jenny went back to the house; she had a letter to be mailed and knew Iver was going to the village. She had hardly gotten inside when she noticed Iver's dog rushing out from a grove of trees with Iver and Olaf trailing behind. Iver planned to finish the woodpile for his mother and then, just past noon, he and his brother would begin the long journey to Trondhjem. He disappeared into the barn as his dog stopped, lifted his back leg, scratched behind his ear, shook his body and headed to the house to greet Kari who was pouring milk into a saucer for a handful of hungry kittens.

Iver reappeared with an axe in one hand and Olaf by his side. "I'm off to find Grandma," said the boy as he skipped to the house.

As the axe fell on the first log, splitting it in sections, Iver burst out, "And I'm off to find a way to keep her."

A moment later, the front door opened and Jenny stepped out with a letter in one hand and a bucket in the other. A princess standing on her throne could not have looked lovelier as the gentle breeze blew hair about her face, stroking her cheeks. The mountain air had been good for her. Her bright eyes shone as she surveyed the morning scene; she took a deep breath and walked down the steps to begin her day. Looking like a peasant's wife, her mother and aunt would never, ever recognize her. She walked to the barn with a bucket, catching the attention of a raven from the spire of a pine tree. The bird lifted its wings and glided to a post where it settled to watch her tip the bucket of leftovers into the pig trough. She turned back while the raven swept down, landing a secure distance behind the pig's feast where it began a bouncing dance back and forth until it could snare a morsel and return to the post. Jenny pulled the letter out from her pocket and headed toward Iver. It would be interesting to see his reaction, she thought, and wondered if he would ever get the hint that she was planning her departure. It probably wouldn't make any difference if he did or not; she doubted that he would show any kind of emotion.

As she walked up to him, he appeared not to notice her until her shadow crossed the stump and he finally looked up. *Such beauty.* His body became stiff.

"Iver, would you please post a letter for me? Marta told me you're going to the village and will be away for several days - is that not true?" She held out the letter.

I knew it! She is leaving, Iver thought. *Well, probably the best for both to get her as far away as possible. What a man doesn't see doesn't hurt him.* He wondered if his mother had told Jenny the reason he was leaving for Trondhjem; if not, Lars had most likely told her. He would speak both his own and anyone else's mind.

He planted the axe in the tree stump, wiped off his brow, snatched the letter and stuffed it in his breast pocket. He tried to say something, but found his throat dry and all he could do was nod.

"Thank you, Iver." Jenny waited, hoping he would say something, or even ask about the letter; instead he turned away. She started walking to the house and had a sinking feeling she would never see him again. Halfway back, she stopped, turned around and looked long and hard at him, before heading back to the house.

Iver picked up the axe and with all of his might, brought it down, shattering the wood and splintered the stump. Never had he felt so lost!

An hour later he came into the house, certain the letter had something to do with Jenny leaving Holseth and he wondered if he should just let her go without asking any questions. He had always been a practical man, a man of safe dreams within the boundaries of his mountain life. After his wife Christine had died, he had vowed never to love again, only to marry a strong, plain-speaking woman, a farmhand. He told himself a year ago when he met Jenny to keep a safe distance. Now he was traveling to Trondhjem to sell dreams, for what? A woman whose anger he could incite by just walking into a room? He could only hope her anger was backed by a passion, much like his own.

After the noon dinner, Iver left Holseth in silence without a word to Jenny. He would meet his brother in the village and together they would travel to Trondhjem to sell his inventions.

A week after the two brothers had left, Jenny was packed and ready to journey home to Kristiania. Marta would help her down to the boathouse and take her to the village. Once at the village, she would stay overnight with Suzanne and then travel by steamboat the following afternoon. Everything was set and no one tried to persuade her to stay; they understood how homesick she must be and excited to get back to her family. She took a final look at Holseth. *How different everything seems now that I'm leaving; it's impossible to find words.* Saying goodbye to everyone was harder than she had expected and with that done, she and Andreas were left alone while Marta struggled down the path with part of her luggage.

"You never know how life unfolds, Jenny; sometimes it doesn't turn out like you think. Look at me. I didn't expect to be here this spring." He gave her a quick hug and walked away.

"Goodbye Andreas and thank you. I'll miss your stories terribly." The old man turned back and waved.

Dressed for travel, Gusta had kept her distance from the family until all the good-byes were over. Then she made her move, ran out of the house, pushed past Andreas and disappeared down the path.

As Marta started to push the boat away from the dock, a rattling noise from the bushes caught her attention and before she knew it, Gusta had jumped into the boat almost tipping them into the fjord. Marta held her tongue and shrugged her shoulders at Jenny.

Gusta never explained herself, just sat with her knees around her pack, looking straight ahead. Jenny watched her from the back with as much curiosity as the first day she had met her. She had barely spoken to her all these months. Jenny had discovered she interacted with the mountain differently then anyone on the farm. She had the most incredible habit of going so close to something it took on a totally different look. She would pick up an insect and bring it up to her face where the two would eye one another until one of them became bored and flew away. If one cared enough to look closer at Gusta, they would realize her language was one of visual wonder. Gusta knew how to bring even the smallest creature into focus.

No one spoke during the two hours' journey to the village, and as they arrived, Marta noticed they had built a new wharf after the tidal wave. The village was like a forest renewing itself after a fire, building back its presence on the land. As soon as she helped Gusta out of the boat, she scurried off without a word and didn't stop until she reached the telegraph station where she pushed her nose into the plate glass window and startled a young man who had been quietly reading his papers. After sending the telegram to Iver telling him Jenny was leaving and that she had made plans to keep her in the village one more week for him to come back, Gusta declined the young man's offer to wait inside for a response; instead she walked out. She never understood why people would want to be in a building for very long.

Three hours later, Iver responded and confirmed he would return the following week and Gusta began to check the timetable for the steamboat. Counting the days, she headed to the home of the grocer's sister.

Since the tidal wave, the grocer had been running his store from his home. He now worked and lived with the one person who drove him mad, his sister. He peered out over his newspaper as Gusta appeared at the door, looking in like a duck out of water. It was obvious she had been outside for sometime in Stranden's first of many spring showers.

"What do you want?" he asked, hoping she wouldn't stay long.

"Your sister."

He knocked on the railing with his cane. "Sister, you have a visitor."

His sister bounded down the steps and joined Gusta outside.

"Follow me!" demanded Gusta.

As the curious man he was, the grocer had to get up several times to watch the women standing under a tree, wondering what they were up to. He couldn't hear a word, just noticed his sister nodded several times while Gusta whispered into her ear.

Jenny's friend Suzanne wanted to know what it would take to make Jenny live in the village. Although they hadn't had a chance to meet very often, the woman from Kristiania had made a great impact on her. "You could stay with me. It's a little bit more civilized here than Holseth," she said.

Jenny laughed. "In Stranden? What would I do here?"

"Why not marry? There are a few eligible bachelors - the minister's cousin, the Larsen twins and..."

"Stop it, Susanne. I'm not marrying anyone...the minister's son, how dreadful! What made you think of him? And look at you, why haven't you remarried?"

"You're right; there isn't anyone in this town I would consider except one."

"And who is that, pray tell?"

"As long as you don't laugh at me. He is only a few years younger than I, but every time I see him, I think what it might be like to be close to him."

"So who is it?" asked Jenny, remembering what a horrid man Susanne had originally been married to.

"Never mind; let's talk about something else."

"Susanne tell me who! I'm dying to know. I'll tickle you until you tell me," said Jenny, laughing. Both women rolled on the bed until Susanne finally said, "Alright, stop it, stop it, enough, I'll tell." She lifted her head and looked at Jenny. "It's Iver, the man you have been living with this past year."

Jenny stopped laughing, sat up and became very still.

"What's wrong? Did I say something?"

"No, no it's just that... it's nothing."

"Nothing, it's Iver isn't it?"

"I thought so but now I'm not sure."

"Jenny, you can tell me. Why are you leaving us like this, so sudden?"

"I have to go back. I miss my family."

Susanne nodded. "I understand." But she wasn't quite satisfied with the answer and had a feeling there was more to it.

Hours later after Jenny went to bed, Susanne sat up wondering what she could do to make her stay. And Iver, what about him? How could he possibly not care for her? Why had she found this out so late with Jenny leaving the next day?

The morning of her departure, Jenny paced in Susanne's front room, moving to the clock and then to the window. "Where are they?"

Susanne looked resigned at her. "It's not like him to be late."

Suddenly a knock at the front door caught their attention and the next moment a young boy looked at them. He handed Susanne a note from her brother and ran off.

Susanne read the note and looked at Jenny. "He's had an accident with his carriage. It says he will be here as soon as he can."

Then Jenny heard a whistle. "The steamboat seems to have arrived. How much time do I have before it departs?"

"Depends on how many people and supplies it will be dropping off and picking up. I would guess several hours, but don't worry, if my brother doesn't come soon, we will find someone else to help us."

But the grocer didn't arrive and an upset Jenny saw a hand carriage by the barn and the next moment the girls were heading toward the wharf, holding one handle each. It took them longer than they expected and by the time they reached the wharf, the steamboat had already left. "It must have been the departing whistle we heard," gasped Susanne.

"I can't believe this! When is the next boat?"

"Next Tuesday."

"What do you mean, next Tuesday?"

"The boat comes again a week from today."

"What other boats are going?"

"Dear, there aren't any others."

"Are you telling me the steamer doesn't come back until next week and that's the only one that can get me to Aalesund?"

Susanne nodded, "Afraid so."

Jenny jerked the handle of the carriage up from the ground and muttered, "I need to find someone who can row me; I am not going back to Holseth."

"Please calm down. You can stay with me for the week, but if you must go, I have a friend who might take you."

It didn't take long to find her friend and get him to agree to take Jenny to Aalesund the very next day. He explained to Jenny that his boat was not a steamer and they might have to find lodging along the shore. A steamboat out the fjord to Aalesund would have taken a few hours, but a rowboat could be dangerous, taking one or two days, depending on the weather.

When she and Susanne left the warehouse, Jenny barely recognized Gusta with a group of woman. She waved at her and Gusta nodded. *Odd*, Jenny thought; she had never seen Gusta so neighborly with the villagers.

Later that day, Susanne's brother stopped by and told them what had happened to his carriage. He was on his way when Gusta appeared out of nowhere to tell him something, startling the horse in such a way it had taken off on the side of the road where the carriage hit a huge pothole and broke the wheel.

The next day, Susanne's friend walked briskly past a group of women who had showed up at the wharf to see how their plot would unfold. His boat was gone! "Damn! I'll beat the crap out of whoever did this," he said.

A moment later, Jenny discovered her luggage had been removed from the warehouse. "What shall I do?" she asked. "I can't seem to get out of this village!"

Susanne shook her head. "Something is going on here; you are coming home with me and next week we will make sure you get on the steamboat." When they returned to the Susanne's house, Jenny's bags were neatly arranged on the top step.

Susanne's friend pounded on the door of the grocer. He saw several of the villagers around the kitchen table. As the grocer let him in, he nodded at the men and said, "Do you know what has happened to me?"

The men chorused, "Your boat is missing."

"How would you know? I just found out! haven't told a soul yet."

His jaw dropped. "Who took it?"

"Calm down," said the grocer.

"No one here took your boat."

"How do you know?" he growled.

"Because all of the boats have been stolen," he laughed. "All the boats in the entire village disappeared last night and there isn't as much as a float at the wharf."

"Boats don't just disappear; they got to go somewhere, don't they?"

One of the men at the table spoke up, "That's what we've been trying to figure out. So far, all we've come up with is the King of Nidaros sent his men to storm our village."

"That King has been dead for centuries."

"Don't you think we know that...it doesn't make sense to any of us either! The question we are trying to answer is why anyone would steal the boats. History tells us that's how the Vikings disabled a village - by removing all the boats before letting lose the horses and taking the women. And so far, the women are still here."

"My head is spinning. I need to sit down," he said and joined the men at the table.

"The horses are gone too."

The following day, search parties went out only to return to the village empty handed and as the days went by, the men began looking for any reason why their boats were missing. Someone suggested that the Resident Ghost of Holseth, Gusta, might have something to do with it. The day before the steamboat arrived, the boats were discovered and the horses returned. The men felt foolish when they realized the boats had never the left the village; in fact, they were hidden in obvious places under hay bales, in-between church sheds, in the barns, dressed up like flower pots, hay bins and pig troughs. They turned to the women only to hear tales of pranksters called Nisses. These small, four-fingered creatures, who dressed in gray clothing and wore red caps, lived in the barns and stables. Men rarely saw them and it was good they didn't. Several women claimed that they had seen the Nisses racing about the night the boats and horses returned to the village. Whether the men believed in them or not, they kept the minister busy all week, blessing their boats to keep the Nisses away.

The arrival of the Trondhjem Steamboat stirred the villagers and had become a great social event. Everyone gathered at the wharf or in front of the warehouse, watching passengers and cargo disembark. Susanne nudged Jenny, "Do you notice anything odd today with the women standing over there?"

"Odd with the women? I don't think so. What are they doing?"

"Watching you."

A crewmember came to take Jenny's bags.

"Goodbye dear. Write, please write," begged Susanne. Both women hugged and started crying. As Jenny walked to the gangway, she saw Gusta and waved one last time at the odd but endearing aunt of Holseth, standing in the middle of at least twenty silent women. After boarding, Jenny leaned over the railing and blew a kiss to Susanne. On the wharf, the grocer's sister walked briskly up to Gusta. "Where is Iver?" Gusta shrugged her shoulders

"Did he miss the boat?"

"Hush, hush," said one woman. Everyone quieted; they could hear seagulls sweeping over their heads, waves lapping against the wharf, men's voices shouting orders, the stir of families with children running about. The women looked up at the steamboat in pure disappointment; they had attempted to alter the course of fate and lost. All they could do was watch the young woman from Kristiania sail for home while the son of Holseth missed his...a shout...and then a whispering chorus, "There he is! There he is!" As they watched the scene about to unfold, their romantic natures surfaced and they all smiled.

Jenny watched Susanne and the women, wondering why she had caused such a stir, when she saw the group pointing to the opposite side of the deck. She turned to find a man dressed in a handsome suit approaching her. It wasn't until he was up to her that she recognized Iver.

"Jenny, I was off to Trondhjem in search of gold and come home to find you leaving me without saying a word, running away. Was I that bad to you? Do you hate me that much?"

Jenny blushed, "Here I am in flesh and blood. You can say goodbye to me now."

Iver looked at her, then turned and walked to the gangway.

Jenny was spinning. "Where are you going? How dare you talk to me about running away! You left me at Holseth without a word. You are the same inconsiderate..."

Iver stepped back and put his hands on her shoulders. "Dear lady, I guess I have been, and am, inconsiderate." He looked at her a long time without saying anything. He wanted to say that he loved her and wanted to be with her all the way to the sunset of his life, but he couldn't get it out. Never before had he wanted anybody so much! Nobody had stirred his emotions like this, but now as she would be gone, he could go on with his life without being reminded about something he thought he couldn't have. "Have a nice journey back to Kristiania. Maybe we'll meet again one day." He turned around and walked down the gangway.

As the Steamboat backed out from the wharf, the women looked stunned at each other, not knowing why the final part of their plot didn't work. Why didn't they see what they had been hoping for - the man from Holseth and the woman from Kristiania embracing each other and walking off the ship together? Why wouldn't there be a happy ending, as they knew it? The young woman from Kristiania had not only stirred the bachelors' emotions, she had touched hearts in a way no one had ever done before. How could it be that a woman who was judged as only a rich man's brat could shed so much light into so many hearts? After having met Jenny, nobody was ever the same.

Gusta left the group and headed for a mountain trail. The path smelled of spring, her favorite time of the year to wander in the mountains. She headed in the direction of her late husband's grave; it had been months since she had last paid him a visit and it was about time to see him again. She would tell him about her nephew and the beautiful woman from Kristiania. He would not be surprised to hear the ending. They both knew happy endings were the hardest to come by, but maybe he had the answer for why her plot didn't work. Gusta had always found comfort talking to her deceased husband, even forty years after he left her. Knowing that they would meet again gave her inspiration to carry on.

Days passed and one day Iver woke up, beleaguered by sadness. He had never felt so empty and had a strange feeling something extraordinary was going to happen. Hopefully, it was not going to be another natural disaster! Certainly, the region had had enough tragedies, so he wondered if it had something to do with Jenny. Part of him was glad she was gone and another part wished she was still around. Whatever is was, he hoped she would have a safe journey home. After finishing with the barn's morning ritual, he postponed some other chores and headed to his favorite lookout place. Although taking care of the animals was usually the best remedy for sadness and dark thoughts, this morning he had a deep desire to get away and to be alone, but what he didn't know was that he would not be alone very long and was about to have the most odd and bizarre conversation he had ever had.

The sun wasn't up yet but the glow behind the eastern mountain ridge signaled it could break through any time. He sat down on a boulder, covered by a layer of soft moss and looked aimlessly across the fjord. Why had Jenny come into his life, stirred his emotions and then just left? Why the play, the game, the enticement? He wiped off a tear as if he wanted to hide it from the trees, to not let them know he wasn't the strong man he ought to be. Never had he felt so low, so useless, so weak. "A weak man is not worth much," his grandfather used to say. "Crying is for women and children." How would he be able to run his farm now, after his sister had decided to move to the village? How could he do the daily work without anybody in the house cooking, cleaning and keep an eye on Olaf? The long hours would be even longer, but he dreaded the thought of moving back to his mother and grandfather. So maybe Jorun would be the answer; he knew it would be just a matter of a snap with his fingers and she would be ready. She had obviously been waiting for him, as she had said, but how long would that last? God knows what had gone on in people's minds about him and Jenny. The more he thought about it, the more he felt certain Jorun had most likely been bombarded with lies about them; so he better move quickly before she was be standing in front of the altar with one of the two men he knew had a crush on her. As his mind was far away, he heard the crack of a twig. He turned around and saw Gusta approaching him, wondering what she was up to. She usually stayed inside her loft room and hardly went outside during the day. "What are you doing here Gusta so early in the morning? Isn't it time for the night owl to go to bed?"

Gusta smiled and sat down beside him. "I am here to tell you."

"What are you going to tell me?"

"Many things. They sent me to tell you."

"Who sent you?"

"The ones that have passed way; the ones that stay on the other side."

Iver had always paid special attention when shy people or people who normally didn't talk much suddenly open their mouths, and hearing Gusta talking was an incident in itself. No matter what she was talking about, he would certainly be listening. He looked at her in anticipation of what was coming next.

"Life is hard to understand. Sometimes I was sad too, when Jenny left. I hoped she would stay, but now I understand."

"What do you understand Gusta?"

"Jenny came to save you."

"What? Save me? Save me from drowning in the fjord?"

"No, save you from your self, from the dark side of you."

Iver turned toward her, "I don't understand."

"You have been your own enemy by keeping your feelings inside. When you do that, spirit can't reach you and gets frustrated." She waved a finger in front of his nose and whispered, "You don't want to get your spirit in a bad mood, do you?"

Iver frowned.

"Remember, you are not a body with a soul, but a soul with a body. Our spirit or soul wants to talk to us and give us good advice." Gusta flung out her arms. "Many people don't recognize spirit; they walk the path of life with eye blinders on, like horses. It makes them vulnerable to stepping off the trail or missing great opportunities." Unmovable, like a totem, Gusta looked out over the fjord just as the sun broke through and sent its rays illuminating her long gray hair flickering in the breeze like a curtain. "They even get afraid of dying; I think they will be surprised when they come to the spirit world realizing they are not dead at all, just having another coat on." She paused and turned toward Iver. "You can't have what you want by keeping your desire for yourself and being angry. Jenny came to help you open up your heart, but you didn't listen, so spirit caused you to fall into the fjord to get your attention."

Gusta's speech baffled Iver and the pause between each sentence and the distinctive deep breaths made him wonder if she indeed could be communicating with the other side as his grandfather always believed she did. Anyway, whenever Gusta showed up, strange things always seemed to happen and nothing would ever surprise him.

"Your feeling of love toward Jenny was your soul's whisper you heard, but you ignored it. Instead, you became mean and angry and listened to the voices from your head that told you to keep a lid on your emotions. You don't want to keep a tight lid on a pot of boiling water for very long do you? You and Jenny could be together, but now you have turned her away. The dark part of you, your ego, told you what to do; it was your ego that made you angry. The ego has been controlling you for a long time."

"What you mean by ego."

"The ego is like a child inside of us that shall protect the body."

"Protect the body from what?"

"From getting hurt."

"So the ego is good to have then? Nobody wants to get hurt, so it seems like it's a good little child then, protecting us." Iver tried as best as he could to communicate on her terms, even though he didn't quite understand what she was talking about.

"As long as it does only the physical protection, but the ego wants to control the whole body, the mind and heart too. And the more it gets, the more it wants until it has chased spirit back to the spirit world; when the ego takes over the mind, you can't think clearly. Life on earth will be much easier when spirit takes the control away from the ego and lets the ego do what it does best, protect the physical body."

"What do we do then to give room for spirit?"

"That's the easy part. You do nothing. Just be aware of spirit's existence."

Gusta stood up and walked a few steps away before turning around and facing Iver again. "When you truly understand that you are a soul with a body and not a body with a soul, you will have more peace inside and your mind will be clear and focused. You will not be concerned about what other people think of you and not be afraid to reach out to people and speak your mind. The ego can not dominate you and the fearful thoughts it sends will glance off like water on the goose."

"Does the ego always send thoughts about fear, distress and concern to us?"

"Most of the time, but it's also the ego that cheers us up when someone recognize us; the ego would do whatever it can to make us feel good about ourselves. It would even persuade us to lie about our accomplishments."

"Isn't that what life is all about, having joy and feeling good about ourselves?"

"Yes, but not only when someone praises and admires you. The source to make us feel good about ourselves must come from the inside, from the peace of spirit, not from the outside. When it comes from the inside, joy lasts; when it comes from the outside, joy doesn't last. When men drink beer, they are only happy as long as there is beer left in the cask." Gusta was quiet for a long time and then continued. "You just need to learn when to take advice from the ego and when to ignore it."

Finally, there is something tangible to ask about, Iver thought. "Gusta, how do we tell one apart from the other?"

"You must distinguish between rational fear and irrational fear. It's simple; you don't have to make it difficult. Your fear of getting close to Jenny was irrational; your fear in the ice cold water was rational. I don't know why that is so difficult to understand. The ego feeds on fearful thoughts about what can go wrong in the future by using failure in the past as reference. It doesn't know that mistakes in the past were meant for our soul to grow."

Confusion mounted in Iver's head and even though he found the subject interesting, he wondered if maybe it was best for everybody that Gusta had been silent all these years. He couldn't imagine what people in the village would think if she had been talking to them like this. They could easy turn it around to make everybody at Holseth into witches and wizards.

"I don't understand, Gusta - if my ego wants me too feel good about myself and then prevented me from reaching out to Jenny. It doesn't make sense."

"The ego is afraid of everything it can't see or has not experienced. It's afraid of the unknown; your ego could not foresee you and Jenny coming together, and instead it wanted to prevent you from the possibility of getting hurt. The ego is always in a state of fear, whereas spirit knows that there is nothing to fear other than the fear itself, and spirit is always in a state of love. Only spirit could foresee that you and Jenny were meant to be together."

"Jenny and I were meant to be together?"

"Yes, I thought you knew!" Gusta's face lit up with a smirk. "In the spirit world before you were born, your soul and her soul agreed to meet in this lifetime. Jenny is your soul mate."

In spite of the subject's weirdness, Iver needed to admit that a lot of what Gusta was saying had some logic and truth in it. His feeling and actions toward Jenny was somewhat like how Gusta described it. "Soul mate, what do you mean by soul mate?"

"We have many soul mates in the spirit world, some as friends or family members, but we have only one true soul mate. Some call it our twin soul; it would be like the other half of our self. This twin soul is what most people are searching for on earth, either consciously or unconsciously."

"How do we find our twin soul then?" Iver asked her.

"We need to let spirit guide us by paying attention to our emotions. Spirit talks to us through our feelings and emotions, whereas the ego talks to us through our thoughts. When we meet our twin soul, we will feel a very strong sense of love, peace and compassion, and after a very short time, it feels like we have known each other for a long time."

"Can't that happen with other people we meet? I mean that we have strong feelings?"

"Yes we can, but the feelings when we meet our twin soul are so unique and special, we just know deep inside. We would not hesitate to give our life away for our twin soul if we had too."

"Is our twin soul always at the opposite sex?"

"Not always, depending on the agreement made in the spirit world. Remember, you can be a man in one life and a woman in the next." Gusta looked at him and waved her finger in front of his face again. "When we are searching for our twin soul, we must distinguish between love and lust. Love needs to come before lust, because the spirit governs the love, whereas the ego governs the lust." Gusta was quiet for a long time; then she looked at Iver. "Jenny came for another reason too; she needed to experience how it feels like to save somebody, to be cold and scared and to live by simple means. She needed to feel her physical senses the same way as you needed to feel your emotions."

Gusta was obviously fired up by Iver's close attention and took him on an adventure into a world he never knew existed. She told him that everything on earth happens for a reason and she began talking about a startling life on the other side consisting of a vast number of souls of different levels - from the new and fresh ones to the more advanced levels, the ones that had hundreds of lifetimes on earth. She said we all belong to a soul group of different levels and that a low level soul, a beginner soul, many times would incarnate to become a king or a dictator with very much earthly power, whereas an advanced soul, with spiritual power many times, would incarnate to become a poor farmer, a person with disabilities or someone with the purpose of serving others, like Jesus and Buddha.

She continued telling him about the preparation and process of incarnation, how souls get together with the elders to discuss what they are to accomplish in the upcoming life, where to live, which parents to have, which people to meet and so on, even how and when they were going to return to the spirit world. She said that just before incarnation, when the soul was ready to go, it went to a place where it would wait for the final departure. Here it would meet other earthbound souls, souls that were returning from earth, or others that were just hanging around to chat and say goodbye.

After doing his best to digest it, Iver looked at her and shook his head. "You make it all sound so easy Gusta, just like you were going to Kristiania with a folder of guidelines of who to meet and what to do, or chatting with people on the wharf when the steamer arrives."

Gusta lit up. "That's it Iver! I knew you would understand. It's that simple; people make it difficult because they don't understand."

If it is difficult because we don't understand, Iver thought, *then it's the understanding that is difficult, but certainly she must have put some of her weird stuff out of order. Obviously our parents choose us and not the other way around. Perhaps she doesn't know how a child is conceived.* He began to ask her about accidents and disasters; he could not understand there was a reason for all that misery.

She told him that sorrow and grief was not easy to understand on earth; it has to be seen from spirit. When a mother leaves a small child behind, the child's soul had already agreed to experience how it is to lose a mother and the mother had already finished up with what she came to learn in that specific lifetime. Besides that, to experience grief and sorrow causes our soul to grow more rapidly. The tougher the task, the better the lesson. That holds for the soul as well as for us while we are on earth and when the whole purpose with life is to learn lessons and grow our soul, then we might expect that in some lifetimes, we will stumble across some very difficult times. She said the reason some are wealthy and strong while others struggle through sickness, poverty and disability was that their soul had chosen that specific life experience. She said we should honor the poor and disadvantaged and the ones who are taking care of them, and look at them with respect for they have taken on greater tasks and larger burdens than many others.

"In the wake of the wave, when many people died, it had nothing to do with punishment from God as some people believe," she said and pointed out that it is always difficult to understand when many people leave the earth at the same time. "A disaster creates many lessons for many people and when things settle down again, everything will be new and fresh. When a forest burns, it gives space for new trees to grow. When an old house is taken by an avalanche, a new one will be built somewhere. Sometimes it is necessary to shake up old things to give room for the new, and during that process, everybody involved directly or indirectly gets an opportunity to fulfill their life's purpose."

Iver's head spun. He looked over the fjord and scanned the snow-covered mountains and the multitude of crevasses reaching all the way down to the waterline. He needed to digest and find calmness from Gusta's intensity and watching nature made him feel tranquil. It seemed like no matter how many times he had been looking at the same mountains and the same fjord, he always found something he hadn't seen before. Watching the scenery was like admiring a painting; you would always find new, exciting details.

A raven suddenly swooped down, settled on a treetop close by, then began to wail while turning his head back and forth. Gusta looked at the bird respectfully. "The raven is a messenger from spirit and we should pay attention." She watched the bird intensively until it lifted its wings, glided off and disappeared. "I think he wanted to remind us about freedom, true freedom and to listen to our soul. First then, are we truly free? A freedom no money or material things can buy; a freedom you can only get from the inside when you let your spirit govern the ego to conquer the fear. Our soul is like the raven; it sees everything from above."

Iver couldn't refrain from asking her about the future. The first thing he remembered about Gusta as a young boy was that people said she could see into the future. "What about the future Gusta? What do you see?"

Gusta smiled. "It seems like everybody wants to know about the future. I don't know why, since we have only the moment. What I see is that great changes are coming, more changes then the world has been through since creation. You shall not worry about the future. It will take care of itself." And with that, she took off as gently as she came.

After Gusta left, Iver went back to his house, thinking about all the things she had been talking about, but it was especially one phrase that stuck "...could see you and Jenny together as husband and wife." What if something in what she was talking about was true? What if she really talked to the other side? Was it Christine she saw or was it just her imagination and what about all this ego and spirit talk? It all seemed both logical and illogical at the same time. He was confused, more confused than any time before, and thought he would be better off pushing that dream aside. It was time to feed the animals and start a new day, but it would not be a regular day; neither would the coming days be the same. Nothing would ever be the same again. The time with Gusta had had a profound impact on Iver. Although he didn't believe in everything she talked about, it was like something had changed inside, something that made him think and ask himself the same questions he used to ask before, at a time when he was open to listen to the word about the unseen and untouchable.

When Anna came into the kitchen, she looked at Iver. "Have you been crying?"

Iver tried to avoid her eyes, but Anna had inherited her mother's ability to see a man's hurting heart. "What's happened?"

"Gusta."

"What about Gusta?"

"She began speaking to me."

"Gusta spoke to you?"

"Yes, she spoke flawlessly. I have never heard her like that. We had the oddest conversation you can ever imagine."

"What did you two talk about?"

"About the unseen and untouchable, soul mates and.. .and Jenny."

"What about Jenny?"

"She said Jenny might have stayed if I had said what I felt for her and not been so angry."

"She would have Iver. I know that."

Iver moved toward Anna, embraced her and began sobbing. "I cared for Jenny so much. Sometimes I couldn't tell my right foot from the left. I don't know why - why has it been so difficult for me to talk about my feelings? The anger just came out of me every time I saw her. I wanted to be with her and away from her at the same time." He sniffled. "I can't take this any longer; it's so hard."

Anna wiped the tears off his cheek. "Come on, Iver, speak out. There's no man around to see you cry; as you know, Olaf is with your mother."

Iver took a deep breath and exhaled slowly. "The first time I knew I was in love with her was the day on the ledge. I remember Grandfather and I were down in the boathouse, when I heard somebody in that area. I knew it was Jenny. I ran so fast like I'd never done before and hardly paused before I saw her sitting on that boulder," he sniffled again, "and what did I do? I shouted at her and was angry just because of some seeds she was planting."

Anna patted him on his back. "It's ok, It's ok."

"At the Midsummer feast, I would do whatever to save her from that man, and then there was the wedding where I desperately wanted to dance with her, but didn't have the courage, not even after several mugs of beer. After the tidal wave, I was so proud of her I had no words for it, and when I saw her in that ballroom gown at Christmas, I thought I was losing myself." Iver sniffled, wiped a tear off his cheek and tried to smile. "I had to douse myself in ice water!"

"What dress ? I don't remember a dress."

"She didn't wear it; she only tried it on and I happened to pass by her window."

"Why didn't she want to wear it?"

"I guess she didn't want to stick out. She wanted to be like one of us and not make us look like poor peasants.

That was when I realized her inside was as beautiful as her outside."

"I really hoped that you and Jenny could be together, but you know, she might never been able to stay long here. She belongs to a city, but now you have a friend in Kristiania. Maybe you can go and visit her one day. So why don't you write to her?"

"Write, what do I say?"

"Tell her what you have just told me."

Iver nodded and gave her another hug. "I love you, Anna. You have always been a wonderful sister."

The cry of a baby made Anna turn toward the bedroom door. "The little one seems to be awake so I better go and feed him."

Back in Kristiania, Jenny couldn't stop wondering whether Iver cared for her or not; could there possibly be any warmth behind his cold surface as his sister had suggested? Now, a month after leaving the mountain farm, she tried to push him away from her mind the best she could, but images of the strong and handsome man, the beloved son of Holseth, with Viking blood flowing through his veins, came back to her more often than she cared for. She couldn't hide from herself that he had aroused her more than he would ever know. It wasn't until the moment she met Svein again that the memory of Iver begun to fade away; maybe there was some truth that the best remedy for a hurting spirit was to light up an old flame. But she soon found out that the old flame would not ignite for her the way she hoped for; Svein was already married.

When Jenny later told her mother she had run into Svein, her mother was at first concerned and instantly pulled out a clipping from a newspaper that pictured Svein as a newly-graduated honors medical student. Obviously, she must have changed her attitude about him and forgotten that he came from a long line of lumberjacks, but when Jenny told her he was already married, she could see the disappointment in her daughter's eyes.

A week later, Jenny received a letter from Iver. She rushed to her room, slipped down on the bed and with shaking hands, opened it and began to read.

Dear Jenny!

How could I ever believe that I would meet a person who would stir my emotions the way you did, emotions I never thought I had. Emotions so strong that my body trembled when I was near you and my heart cried out when we were apart; feelings so powerful that I couldn't tell one part of my body from another, like if all the cells were liquid and flowing thorough me like the streams down the mountain. You made me realize that I couldn't negotiate with my feelings by pretending I didn't have them.

But now, I at least understand why I was so angry at you. Although I had an odd way to show how much you meant to me and how much I was in love with you. It wasn't you I was angry at - it was myself, my own feelings. I was afraid of where those feelings would take me, afraid of getting hurt, of not being good enough, not measuring up, afraid of losing you, so maybe it was best for both of us that it ended the way it did, wasn't it?

You gave me a gift Jenny that can't be measured in money, goods or glitter, the gift of myself. When you left, I felt you took my heart with you; now I realize that you actually came to give me back the heart I had already lost. For years I have been fighting an invisible enemy, a fight I didn't know I could never win. Now, as you have helped me to finally surrender, I have found the peace my spirit has been longing for, realizing that losing a battle wasn't that bad after all.

Lars has gotten work with the University in Trondhjem to develop his invention; the professors were all impressed and predicted a bright future for him. Anna and her baby boy have moved to the village and the bachelors are already lining up to propose. My grandfather is still alive and I expect that as the fall comes along, he will prepare for his death in the boathouse again and go though the same squabble with my mother as he did last winter. Kari has been very helpful taking care of Olaf while I am working the farm; they are like brothers and sisters. And Gusta, she wanders around like she had always done, talking to the trees, spirits, ghosts and her dead husband.

Now after you have left, I have been wondering many times what would have happened if both of us had taken the chance to let our feelings guide us. Would it be another heartache or would we live out our hearts' deepest desire and experience the true unconditional love between a man and a woman? Are we indeed soul mates that never really understood that we were looking for each other or are we just another couple that just happened to meet?

Although we never kissed or touched each other, I felt our spirits somehow communicated across the cold wall between us, like if we both had one half of a combined heart. But asking what ifs is useless, isn't it? The past is gone, the future is not promised. We have only the now. I belong here, to the mountains and the fjord. The rocks, the trees, the ledges and ravines - they are all a part of me. I guess I could not assimilate to a life in Kristiania any more than you could assimilate to a life on the mountain. I want to thank you, Jenny, for giving me the greatest gift of all, uniting myself by lighting up the path to my soul and spirit.

Your friend, Iver.

Emotions rumbled through Jenny like thunder as she staggered to her feet and dragged herself across the room, slipped down on the windowsill and stared out the window the way she always did when her mind was going haywire. Why now? Why couldn't he have said something when she was there? Not even a slightest hint that he cared for her! She thought about what her friend recently told her about men and their difficulties of expressing feelings; she could understand that, but all the hostility and anger! Was it really true that unexpressed emotions could make a man angry?

She soon found herself in a battle between her heart and mind. Her heart cried out for him, getting its support from the letter, but her mind could only see an angry face. She thought about all the warning signs she had gotten the last year when she even thought about getting closer to that man. Nature speaks to us through the wind and trees she had heard, but then there was this deep inner voice that stirred up every thing and never seemed to let go of the man on the mountain ledge. She became more and more confused the more she thought about him and the next couple of weeks she spent most of the time inside her room, reading, trying to get away from the two battling forces inside of her, but no matter how exciting her books became, she found herself re-reading the pages more and more.

One morning, she went out early and took a walk around their massive estate. As she reached the large oak tree she used to climb when she was a little girl, memories from her childhood came rushing back. She sat down and leaned up against the tree trunk, wishing she could become a child again; how easy life would be! No complicated decisions to make, no worries and no regrets. She wondered what it was with children that made their lives apparently so fun and easy. Was it because they were living in the moment, living there and then with no past or no future, only the now? A little girl could sit forever peeling apart a flower just to see what its core looked like. *Children are explorers* she thought, they wanted to see how things were made of and to experience as much as they could, while adults were getting more and more the attitude of been there and done that. *Will we all get more jaded as we grow older ?* Jenny wondered. While she sat there philosophizing, a cat strolled up to her and began to strike her legs. She lifted it up and held it in her lap; their eyes met a short moment before the cat relaxed and began to purr. Then he suddenly jumped down on the ground and began chasing a squirrel. Jenny watched the two animals as they razed around before the squirrel disappeared up in a tree, leaving a confused cat wondering where it went. Then the cat noticed a bird busy nibbling from the ground, unaware that someone was watching closely every move. The cat sunk down in the grass and lay unmovable. Then he slowly began to crawl toward the unsuspecting bird. As he was about to strike, the bird lifted its wings and flew graciously away and landed softly on a tree limb nearby, while the cat pottered away. *Losing two chases in a row couldn't be easy,* Jenny thought as she walked over and grabbed the cat and held it close to her chest; the furry animal seemed to not care. After all, it was just a game.

Watching the scene with the animals made Jenny think back when they, as children, would sit and fantasize about what kind of animals they would like to be. Her best friend would always like to be a white swan, gliding graciously around the pond, whereas a boy in the neighborhood wanted to be the dragon, eating the swan. Jenny would like to be a small bird that could fly away when she wanted to.

She was back in time for breakfast and during a conversation with her mother, she knew what it was with the animals that had enticed her. She wanted to be free and play again, to be herself and not to be concerned about how to behave all the time, realizing that there was something more than Iver that had enticed her on the mountain.

After hearing what her daughter was up to, Marion was outraged. "I don't understand, Jenny, how you can let all this go. The whole Mohr estate for your so-called 'love' in the mountains! You could stay here and never ever have to worry about anything. A man to love you can find in Kristiania; by the way, I know about a handsome man you should meet...."

"I am not interested," interrupted Jenny. "I don't want to meet anybody and about love, you can't possible know what love is, Mother. How could you, as long as you always have put wealth, power and family reputation first?"

"What about freedom?" Marion glanced out the window. "What you see here can keep you free for the rest of your life."

"Free from what, Mother?"

Marion turned around to face her daughter. "Free from ever having to worry about making ends meet; isn't that freedom?"

"That's not freedom. All the wealth in the world can not make you free; the more goods you have, the more attached you become, which inhibits freedom. Real freedom is something that comes from the inside and can never be taken away from you."

Marion looked stunned at her daughter; she had never heard her talking like that and wondered if someone on the mountain had put a spell on her.

The next couple of days were tense. Jenny hardly spoke to her parents and even though they both wanted the best for their daughter, this had obviously taken both of them with surprise. Her father suggested that they take her to a psychologist, something her mother refused promptly. "You can't be serious,

Christian! What do you think people would say if we bring Jenny to a psychologist?"

At Holseth, Gusta was back at her husband's grave when she saw the slow-moving dot down on the fjord. She didn't need to ask him what it was or who it was - she knew. She then let the breeze lift the hair away from her face, closed her eyes, took a deep breath and mumbled, "It seems like the heir from Kristiania now understands that she doesn't need wings to be free."

About the Author

Bjørn Dimmen is the author of *The Life I Was Born to Live* and native to the area in Western Norway he writes about. Early on he became smitten with his ancestors legends and curious as to why they would settle in such hostile and unapproachable locations. After moving to the US the idea of writing a story about them was initiated in co-operation with an American friend; however, the manuscript was never published until now.

Several years later after he had moved back to Norway, he released *The Life I Was Born To Live*, through a self-publishing company. With the positive experience of this publishing process and his inherited never giving up attitude; the manuscript was "dusted", given a substantial re writing, a new name and life.

Bjørn works offshore and spends most of his spare time in North East Thailand.